BY REBECCA STOTT

FICTION

Dark Earth

The Coral Thief

Ghostwalk

NONFICTION

In the Days of Rain

Darwin's Ghost

Darwin and the Barnacle

DARK EARTH

DARK EARTH

A Novel

REBECCA STOTT

RANDOM HOUSE | NEW YORK

Copyright © 2022 by Rebecca Stott

Published in the United States by Random House, an imprint and division of Penguin Random House LLC, New York.

RANDOM HOUSE and the HOUSE colophon are registered trademarks of Penguin Random House LLC.

Originally published in the United Kingdom by Fourth Estate, a division of HarperCollins UK, London.

Library of Congress Cataloging-in-Publication Data
Names: Stott, Rebecca, author.
Title: Dark earth : a novel / Rebecca Stott.
Description: First Edition. | New York : Random House, 2022
Identifiers: LCCN 2022010968 (print) | LCCN 2022010969 (ebook) |
ISBN 9780812989113 (hardcover) | ISBN 9780812989120 (ebook)
Subjects: LCGFT: Novels.
Classification: LCC PR6119.T69 D37 2022 (print) |
LCC PR6119.T69 (ebook) | DDC 823/.92—dc23
LC record available at https://lccn.loc.gov/2022010968

Printed in Canada on acid-free paper

randomhousebooks.com

2 4 6 8 9 7 5 3 1

First Edition

Book design by Susan Turner

For Elsie and Winnie Rhodes

[P]erhaps at midnight, when all boundaries are lost, the country reverts to its ancient shape, as the Romans saw it, lying cloudy, when they landed, and the hills had no names and rivers wound they knew not where.

—Virginia Woolf, *Mrs. Dalloway*

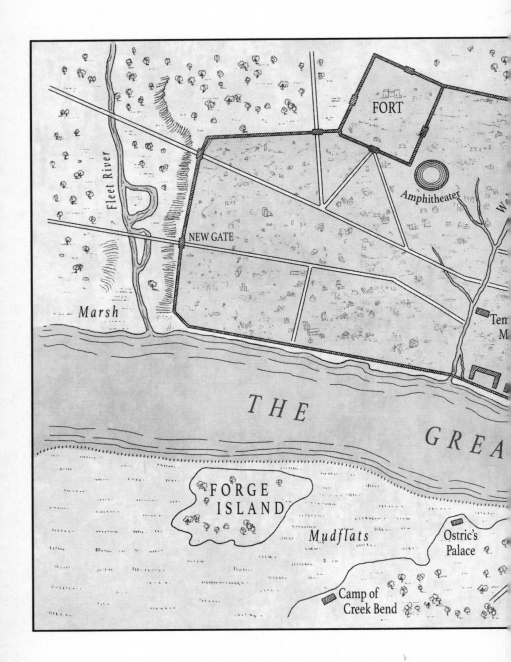

FORT

Amphitheater

Fleet River

NEW GATE

Marsh

Tem
M

THE

GREA

FORGE
ISLAND

Mudflats

Ostric's
Palace

Camp of
Creek Bend

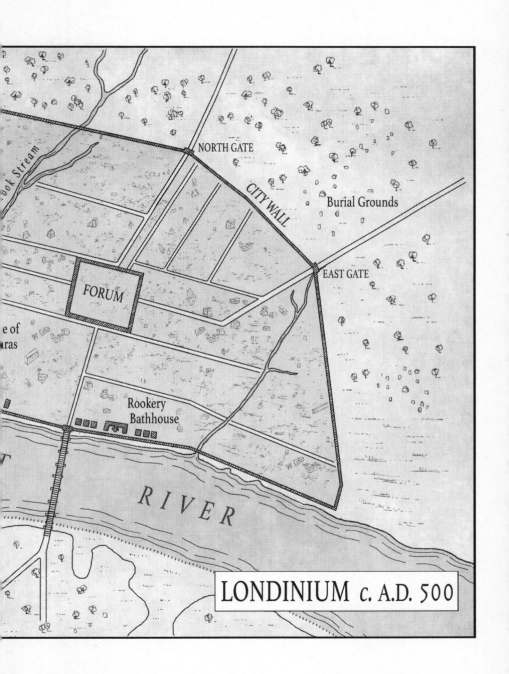

LONDINIUM c. A.D. 500

AUTHOR'S NOTE

Around A.D. 410, after nearly four hundred years of occupation, the Romans withdrew their remaining imperial staff and armies from Britain. For a further four hundred years, the ruins of the mile-wide city of Londinium lay abandoned. Neither the native Britons nor the steady stream of migrants who came to live among them had any use for the carved stone and towering walls, symbols of a fallen colonial power.

Sometime between A.D. 450 and 550, however, a Saxon woman must have walked across the fallen roof tiles of a derelict Roman bathhouse on the north bank of the Thames, because she dropped her brooch there. Archaeologists discovered it while excavating the site in 1968 after the demolition of the London Coal Exchange. Now the brooch sits in a small frame on an otherwise empty white wall in the Museum of London.

ONE

✝

1

An island in the Thames, c. A.D. 500

Isla and Blue are sitting on the mound watching the river creep up on the wrecks and over the black stubs of the old jetties out on the mudflats, waiting for Father to finish his work in the forge. Along the far riverbank, the Ghost City, the great line of its long-abandoned river wall, its crumbling gates and towers, is making its upside-down face in the river again.

"Something's coming, sister," Blue says. "Look."

Isla looks. The wind has picked up. It scatters the birds wading on the mudflats. It catches at the creepers that grow along the Ghost City wall. It lifts and rustles them like feathers.

"Could be rain," Isla says. "The wind's turned."

It's late spring. There has been no rain for weeks. No clouds, just the baking, glaring forge fire of the sun. At first, after the long winter, the sisters had welcomed the sun coming in so hot. Dull roots had stirred. Flowers came early: first the primroses and bluebells in the wood, then the tiny spears of the cuckoo pint and the blackthorn blossom in the hedgerows. The bean seedlings had pushed up through the soil in their garden, fingers unfurling into sails.

Now the reeds whisper like old bones. The sisters swim in the river when they can steal away from the field or from Father's forge. Around them the sun beats down on the mudflats. Meat turns. Flies gather.

Every evening the sisters climb the mound to watch for the sails of Seax boats coming upriver from the sea, the sails of the great wandering tribes, from the Old Country and the Drowned Lands of their ancestors, all heading west to find new land to farm. Some months there are no boats at all. Other months there are four or five, sailing alone or in clusters. Blue gauges a notch into the doorpost for each new sail she sees.

"The river is a firetongued sword tonight," Blue says. She is making a necklace from the cowslips and the violets she's picked, lost in that half-dreaming mood that takes her sometimes.

Isla looks. Blue is right. Between their island and the walls of the Ghost City on the far riverbank, the river runs between the mudflats in puckered silvers and golds, blues and reds, just like the swords that Father makes.

"What did the Sun Kings know?" Isla says, gazing over the river to the ruins beyond. "What happened to make them all go and leave their city like that? Was it the Great Sickness, do you think? Or worse?"

"What's worse than the Great Sickness?" Blue says, holding the necklace up to the setting sun, humming a tune Mother used to sing in the Old Times.

Blue sometimes talks in riddles. She asks questions Isla can't answer. Sometimes Isla tries. Usually, she doesn't.

"Did they mean to come back?" Isla says. "Did something happen to them to stop them from coming back?"

Isla has been thinking about these questions for always and forever. The whole Ghost City is a riddle to her.

"Perhaps the marsh spirits chased them away," Blue says, pulling down the skin beneath her eyes and baring her teeth, "or perhaps the Strix turned them all into crows."

But Isla knows her sister doesn't know any more about where or why the Sun Kings went than she does.

"We don't know," she says. "No one knows. We'll never know."

And then, with a sigh, Blue puts down her flowers and says, her eyes wide:

"Mother said there were gardens inside and pools of hot water and temples as big as ten mead halls and fountains full of coins and men who fought with bears and giants and—"

"Stop your nonsense," Isla says, but she isn't really listening. She is thinking that Father is late finishing his work, and that the food will spoil. She is wondering whether he has finally finished twisting the iron rods as she asked him to, so that she can start working on the blade tomorrow. Most nights he is out through the forge door long before they can see the first stars. He'll be putting his tools away, she tells herself. He's just taking his time.

"Mother told me," Blue says again, her eyes closed, drawing shapes in the air with her long fingers. "She did. She said. She knew."

Blue makes Isla wild sometimes with the things she says.

"You're making it up," Isla tells her. "Mother didn't say any such thing. Anyway, how would she know? The Sun Kings left a hundred winters ago. The Ghost City is empty. There's nothing living in there now except kites and crows. It's all just mud and broken stone."

"And ghosts," Blue says, "and the Strix."

Isla gives up. Blue's face is flushed. She's been sitting in the sun too long. Father says Blue is touched. Isla sometimes wonders if there is something wrong with her sister that often she seems to know what Isla is going to say before she says it, or she sees things others can't see. Fanciful, Mother used to say. Your sister's just fanciful, Isla. You mustn't mind her.

"You've listened to too many of Old Sive's stories," Isla says. She can't help herself. She is cross and hot and tired and the old darkness is gathering down inside her. It's making her want to run again.

Wrak, the crow that Blue has raised from a chick, calls out to her sister from the thatch of the forge, then lands on her shoulder in a flurry of black feathers. *Wrak. Wrak.* Though she would never say it to her sister, Isla wishes Wrak would fly off to join his kin, the crows roosting in the Ghost City. He is dirty, full of fleas and ticks. Always looking for scraps. Stealing food. Up to no good. The way he looks at Isla sometimes, his head cocked to one side, his eyes shiny black like charcoal, that tuft of white feathers under his beak. It makes her skin crawl. But Wrak doesn't go. He stays.

"Hush, we're your kin now," Blue says to him when she sees him gazing up at the birds flying overhead. "Hush, hush. Ya. We're your kin." She cradles his dirty oily feathers in her long fingers as if he is a child.

Blue has secrets. At low tide on the night of each new moon, she takes the path down through the wood to the promontory on the south side of the island, where she keeps her fish traps. She tells Father she's checking the traps, but Isla knows she's gone to speak to the mud woman. When the tide falls down there, the woman's bones make a five-pointed star in the mud, her ankles and wrists fastened to four stakes with rusted iron cuffs, her bones white, the remains of her ribs the upturned hull of a boat. Curlews wade between her thighs.

Isla went only once. She won't go again. She doesn't want to look at that open jaw a second time, the black holes of the woman's eye sockets.

Blue says that when the moon is full, the mud woman whispers.

"She's dead," Isla says. "Bones can't whisper. They drowned that poor woman hundreds of years ago. Stop making things up."

"Sometimes on the new moon," Blue says, "she roars and swears to kill the men who pegged her. She pulls at her straps."

"Enough. Enough of all that. Stop it. Just say nothing."

"But sometimes," Blue says, "she just calls for her mother."

When Isla had once asked Father about the bones, he'd said the elders of the mud woman's tribe must have staked her out to teach the rest of her people to hold their tongues and do what they were told. He said they'd made a scapegoat of her. They'd done that back in the Old Country too, he said.

"Poor creature," he'd said.

"What's a scapegoat?" Isla had asked.

"You put all the bad luck in the village into one goat and then you drive it away," he said. "Or you kill it."

"Are we scapegoats?" Blue said.

"Not yet," Father had answered. "Not if I can help it."

The lights on the river have started to bleed in the dusk. Isla can't see one thing from another out there. When she sits down next to her sister again, Blue drapes her necklace of flowers between the pair of brooches that Isla wears in the crook of each of her shoulders. When she's got the flowers where she wants them, Blue puts her fingers on Isla's eyelids and closes her own. She seems to be praying. She kisses each of her sister's eyelids in turn, and then each of her brooches. Isla can't tell if she is playing some new game or just being Blue.

All at once the crows scatter up and over the Ghost City, pouring up like the ashes from a great fire into the night sky, across the first evening stars, across the sliver of the new moon, roiling this way and that, making a great scattery and flinty noise with their beaks, and then roiling together all over again.

Isla starts to run. Across the yard, round the goat pen, and then she is pushing hard against the door of the forge. Inside, the room is dark. The fire has shrunk back to embers. Shadows from the guttering candle dance on the walls. And there is Father's body on the floor, all crumpled, his hammer still clenched in his hand, his face twisted on one side, his mouth open like he's trying to say something. And when she looks up, Blue is standing there in the doorway, quiet as anything.

2

Father is dead. They have waited, watched for a breath. No breath came. They have straightened him out and hauled his body into the woodshed, covered it in the old wolfskin rug and closed the door.

By now it is dark, deep dark, only the thinnest of red lines over the scratchy black forest to the west where the sun has gone, and the stars are making their bright studwork. The first owls are out hunting, the wolves calling to each other in the woods on the other side of the creek. It is just like any other night. Except it isn't. It will never be like any other night, Isla thinks. It will never be like any ordinary night ever again. The Great Smith is dead. The Great Smith is dead. Father is dead.

She drags wood to make a fire right there in the yard,

between the hut and the forge and the woodshed, and makes them up a bed of willow branches and reeds next to it.

"We're going to sleep outside?" Blue asks, her eyes wide. "Can we?"

"It's too hot for inside," Isla says. "Who's going to stop us? He isn't. He can't."

They pray to Freja, god of crossing places and kin. They ask her to watch over Father, to keep the bad spirits out of the woodshed.

"Where are we going to put him?" Blue whispers as they lie on their bellies under the rugs, watching the flames.

"Why are you whispering? He can't hear us."

"Maybe he can. You don't know. He could be listening right now."

"Stop that talk. He'll go next to Nonor of course," Isla says. "Under the great oak at the top of the burial ground, right next to her."

When they had lived in the Seax camp at the bend of the creek, their cousins had buried their grandmother up on the hill, alongside their other Seax kin in the burial ground. The men had built a shrine over her, made of hazel and ash wood, woven with willow. Isla and Blue and the women had hung it with wild roses.

"They'll have to dig a very big hole," Blue says. And then they are quiet. Isla thinks about how big that hole is going to have to be and how long it will take for the worms to come. Soon enough Blue is asleep, but Isla is lying awake staring at the stars, worrying. She is going around inside the same riddle and not finding a way out.

Where are they going to put him?

Father lies in the woodshed in the heat under the wolf-skin rug. When the sun is up, Isla will burn pans of dried sage in there and gather nettles and push them through the gaps at the bottom of the walls to keep out the bad spirits and the flies, just as Nonor had shown her back at the camp. She must make sure not to leave any gaps. But the sage and the nettles won't hold the flies out for more than a day or two. No spells or herbs will do that. Father's body will not last long in the heat. It is going to turn like bad meat. It will go maggoty.

They must get him over to the camp burial ground and get their cousins to bury him, up next to Nonor. They'll have to do it quickly, before the maggots get to him.

But they have no boat.

And even if they had a boat, and they could get his body onto it, and if they didn't run aground on the mudflats or get swept away in the fast currents out there, then their cousins probably wouldn't let them land on their shingle beach any-way, not after all this time and after what happened. They might even throw rocks at them like they did the day the lepers had tried to beach their boat.

And then what will they do?

Isla counts the winters that have passed since the night of the Great Fire. It has been five winters since the night raiders attacked the camp, torched the huts and dragged off Mother and the other women. Five winters since the camp elders banished the Great Smith and his daughters to the mud island in the Great River.

Days after the night raid, with all the cross-beams and fallen thatch still smoldering, the camp elders ruled that the

Great Smith was to blame for bringing the bad spirits that brought the night raiders who torched the camp. They said he had the evil eye. How else could he make those fire-tongues, raise those ghostly patterns from the blades, they said, unless he could conjure the fire to do his bidding? Isla, her ear pressed to the crack in the wall of the Mead Hall, her heart breaking for Mother, heard her cousins saying that they should have turned Father out long before.

"The Great Smith might be Seax kin," she heard Old Sive, the Charcoal Burner, say, "but he has the devil's work in him. There are some things you don't risk—not even for kin."

When she heard this, Isla clenched her fists so hard that she buried her fingernails into the palms of her hands and left red marks there.

But it wasn't just Father who had turned their kin against them. Mother belonged to the Ikeni people and Isla had been born with one green eye and one brown eye. When things started to go wrong in the camp—the barley blighted, people dying from the Great Sickness, the long hard frost— the Old Ones started to whisper stories about her family and, winter in and winter out, their whisperings got louder.

Ikeni, the boys chanted, when they thought Father couldn't hear. Ikeni. IK-EY-NEE, IK-EY-NEE. Your mother is Ikeni. Isla tried hurling stones at them. But it only made them louder. Better to stand still, she had whispered to Blue when the boys cornered them behind the Mead Hall. Better to look down and wait for it to stop. But Blue wouldn't be told. She stood there, staring the boys down with that look of hers, her teeth clenched, her hands fisted, growling like a wolf, until they stopped their taunts and sloped away.

Mother. Tall and brown and willowy Mother. Mother with the dimple in her chin. Mother with the brimming eyes. Her ancestors, she said, had come from a village somewhere far to the north of the Ghost City, on an estuary looking out to sea. The Ikeni ruled this land once, she said. After the Sun Kings came, an Ikeni queen had marched on the Sun King cities, razed them to the ground. When the Sun Kings had finished burying their dead, they made sure that the Ikeni people could never rise on them again.

The Ikeni were scattered now. Their hearths broken. Their roofs burned.

Isla can remember the feel of Mother's hair against her fingers, even if she can't quite remember what her smile looked like. If she closes her eyes for long enough, she can see Mother's sad, proud face, see the way her eyes gleamed when she watched the sun set or showed them the hoarfrost. When she found Mother's dark hairs on a comb dropped on the floor of the scorched barn two days after the Fire, Isla wound them around an old bobbin. She keeps that bobbin in her box of special things now, alongside the monkey god amulet she found in the midden, and the crystal hanging ball that Nonor left her. The box is hidden above the cross-beam in the hut, lodged into a notch in the wood.

"You are the mother now," Nonor whispered to Isla after the night raid, nodding toward Blue, who was curled up asleep in the roots of a tree, her hair knotted and scattered with fallen leaves. "You are the mother now."

Isla is. She will be. She promised. She is the mother now.

+ + +

Of course, it isn't the camp elders who decide what is what and who gets to live where and who is banished. Not anymore. Lord Osric, the Seax Lord of the South Lands, decides everything now. Their forge island and all the camps along the river's edge are part of Lord Osric's kingdom. He rules as far as Isla can see from the mound on a summer's day and a long way beyond. Osric's father had ruled before him. His grandfather ruled a great kingdom back in the Old Country. People say Osric is half god, half man, that he can trace his kinline back through Hengist and Horsa, the first Seax warrior brothers, right back to the great god Thunor himself. Osric, they say, sees and knows everything.

So after the Fire when the elders of Isla's camp asked Lord Osric for his judgment on Father, it was Lord Osric who ruled that the Great Smith and his daughters were to go and live on the mud island in the river. It was Lord Osric's soldiers who brought them here and built their hut and the forge, who cut down the trees to make a clearing so that she and Blue could have goats and chickens and a kitchen garden. It was his men who dug the well and ordered their cousins to send out meat and grain and charcoal from the camp for them every full moon. Lord Osric also sent them gifts: chickens, bolts of fine wool, cakes, goblets, braces of hares from his huntsmen. He promised the Great Smith and his daughters protection in return for the Great Smith's firetongued swords. He kept them safe.

Blue had lived through twelve winters when they first came to the island and Isla fifteen. Now, if Isla is counting right, Blue has seventeen winters and she has twenty.

But now that the Great Smith is dead, Isla thinks,

struggling to remember what she knows about the Kin Law, feeling hope rising at last, surely Lord Osric must grant his daughters Kin Protection? When a woman has no husband or father to protect her, she must claim protection from the lord himself. She and Blue will go to Osric's palace and petition him in the proper way. When he grants them Kin Protection, they will wear his colors, pin on the brooches carrying the three-pointed star and the boar's head of Osric's shield. Then, wherever they go inside Osric's kingdom, people will have to give them food and shelter. They will be safe. If they go back to the camp at the creek bend their cousins will have to take them back, even if they don't want to, give them a hut and a little land to farm. They'll be able to walk to the little grave on the hill where they buried Nonor and lay flowers. No more being stuck out on the island, keeping Father's secrets, doing his bidding. They will go home. Blue will get married. Have children. There'll be food and dancing on winter nights. Laughing in the Mead Hall. And people to help them mend the roof.

But they have no boat. How are they going to get to Lord Osric's palace? How will they ask him for Kin Protection?

And then Isla is right back inside the same riddle again and rattling the doors for a way out. She eases herself out from under Blue's sleeping limbs and walks up to the mound to see the river.

With the tide so low and the mudflats glistening in the pale moonlight, patches of ooze drifting sulfur yellow, white and frothy, across the tide pools, Isla can imagine striking out over the mud from their island across the creek where the little river fans out into the Great River, around the scattering of mud islands, in a line east straight across to their old camp where Nonor is buried up on the hill. But they can't walk across the mudflats. That mud is treacherous, girl, Nonor had said, cuffing Isla around the head when she caught her setting out across it toward the old Sun King wreck all those years ago. Never let it fool you. That mud will swallow you up, girl.

With no boat, Isla thinks, they won't be able to get their cousins to come in time to bury Father properly, and there'll be no way to get to Osric to claim Kin Protection either. There is no way out of the riddle the gods have made for them.

3

W e're going home," Isla whispers when Blue wakes crying next to the burned-out fire in the early hours of that morning. The first birds are already singing. "It's going to come right," she says. "You'll see. We're going home, Blue. Our cousins will have a big feast and kill a cow, and there'll be dancing. Remember dancing?"

"But Father said we can't go home," Blue says. "Not ever. It's not safe."

Nothing is safe.

"I've been thinking," Isla says. "Lord Osric has to give us Kin Protection now. That's written in the Kin Law. He'll make our cousins take us back. Things are different now that Father is dead. You'll see."

But she can't be sure that they will be.

"Remember how it used to be before the Fire?" she says. "Tell me again."

Isla stokes the embers to give them warmth against the chill and puts her arms around her sister.

"Close your eyes," she says. "It's winter. It's cold. You're wrapped in the old rug and you're playing with the wooden doll Father carved for you. Remember? The wind is whistling round our hut and in through the slats. The geese are honking. You can smell the smoke from the fire over in the Mead Hall and the meat cooking in the pot for the feast. It's good. Can you smell it?"

"But it wasn't always good, was it?" Blue says. "Sometimes there was shouting and blood. The babies died. Sometimes we had to hide in the woods."

Isla wants to remember herself back inside the Mead Hall, the hearth fire, the taste of Nonor's stew, the sight of Mother squatting on the floor peeling vegetables among the other women, all of them laughing. She can blot out the rest. If only Blue would stop talking about the other things.

"We're holding Mother's hands and walking across the yard," she says. "We're walking around the pens where the pigs and chickens and goats are tethered—remember the pens?—past the kitchen garden, and right in through the open door of the Mead Hall. Can you see it? Inside, everyone is talking at once. It's warm and smoky. Father is singing on the top table. Mother lifts you onto her lap and pulls her cloak around you. You try to sit up to listen to the song, but already you're falling asleep. You can't help it."

"And then the men came," Blue says, and she shudders

in Isla's arms. "The ones with the torches and the painted faces. The ones that took Mother."

"They did. Yes," Isla says. She is too tired to argue and she is afraid she might cry. She mustn't cry in front of Blue.

"And we ran into the wood. And when all the shouting and the fires had burned out and we came back out of the wood, Father went off looking for Mother, but he never found her."

"I'm supposed to know what to do," Isla says, as tears come in great gulping sobs. "But I don't. I don't know."

Nonor would know what to do. She'd tell her. Now Isla, don't you take on, she'd say. All will be well.

And then Blue kisses her sister and whispers: "Don't cry, Isla. There's a boat hidden in the reeds. I'll show you."

Isla turns to look at her sister. Blue's face is white in the dawn. She has the heavy-lidded, blank stare she gets on her sometimes. "Sweet gods, why didn't you say before?" Isla says. "Where in the reeds? What boat?"

"Hidden. Father made it. It's only small."

"Don't make things up, Blue. Not now."

"I've seen it. It's beautiful."

"Can you take me to it? Do you remember where it is?" Blue nods.

"If there really is a boat," Isla says, "then we can row across to the camp as soon as the tide's up. We'll get our cousins to row a bigger boat across for Father's body. If there is a boat, Blue, we can go home."

"Oh, but the boat's not for us," Blue says, her voice stern. "It's for Father. We have to send him off with the fire from the forge, like they did with the Great Smiths in the Old Country. Father said."

"Why do you say these things? Are you sick? Boat burning is against the Kin Law now. You know that. Only the
kings are allowed to have boat burnings."

"It's against the Kin Law for women to make firetongued
swords, too, but you make them."

"That's not fair. Father made me. You know he made
me."

There are more and more laws to obey every year, Isla
thinks. There are the Seax Kin Laws from the Old Country.
Then there are Osric's Kin Laws. Sometimes they aren't
the same. Then there are the new laws that Osric's tithe
collectors had announced to their cousins in the Mead
Hall when they came to collect the tithes, or now when
they came out to the island to check on Father. You weren't
supposed to ask any questions about the new laws. You had
to be careful.

"If we don't send Father off in the old way," Blue says,
"he'll be stuck here with us on the island. Think of that, Isla.
Think of what he might do."

"Stop it. Don't talk like that. Just don't."

Father had been angry alive. Angry-dead, angry-roaming
and angry-vengeful doesn't bear thinking about.

"Father said," Blue goes on, "that if we don't send him to
Thunor in the fire, in the old way, in the right way for a
Great Smith, Thunor will send storms and fires across the
land. There'll be no end to it."

"Did Father really say that?"

"He did."

As the silence stretches wide like the river between
them, Blue sits up and lifts her arms toward the sky. A

skein of geese flies right overhead, white and heavy, as if Blue has released them herself into the reddening sky.

4

The boat is exactly where Blue has said it will be: deep in the reeds on the west side of the island, covered in an oilskin and hidden under a pile of alder branches. It is beautiful. Blue is right. Though it is no bigger than a coracle, Father has dovetailed the joints and tarred the hull inside and out to make a watertight seal.

Once they've heaved it right side up, dragged it out onto the shingle beach, pulled off the ivy roots and washed the hull down with river water, they stand back to admire it. Father has carved the prow with animals and a double-tailed merman. The sight of it catches at Isla.

"How did he do that?" she says. "How did he carve all those beasts with his hands so stiff and gnarly? And why did he tell you about it, but not me?"

Blue shrugs. The whole world is a mystery to her. It would be better, Isla thinks sometimes, to be more like Blue.

As the sun passes its midpoint and starts to dip slowly toward the west, they pile wood up inside the boat, making a flat surface along the top with smaller logs, pushing twigs and dry leaves and brush in between. When Blue goes to fetch straw, moss and leaves for the top of the pile, Isla fills a bucket with river water and takes the path through the wood to the woodshed to prepare Father, bracing herself to open the door. It is already late afternoon. She still has so much to do.

Thin streams of blood have run from Father's ears, from his nostrils and from the corners of his lopsided mouth. A fly sits on the ridge of his upper lip, rubbing its hind legs together. Isla bats it away. Cursing is better than crying. She isn't going to let the flies have him, she tells Freja, god of sisters and kindness and fire. She won't let them lay their nasty eggs on him. Taking a deep breath, she throws open the hatch. The fire will burn Father free from the flies and the maggots and the smell and the rot. It will burn him free from all earthly things. He will fly clear. He will be light and clean as air, as ash, light as the wind. Soon she and Blue will watch him fly in the fire.

"Take us with you," she says.

He doesn't answer.

"Not long now," she tells him, wiping his face with the fresh water from the bucket. "We found the boat. We built the pyre. We did what you asked." She tears a strip of cloth and ties it around the top of his head and beneath his jaw to keep his mouth in place. "Are you ready?"

She thinks she hears him whisper back.

Are you ready? Are you ready? Are you ready?

"I'll take Blue back to the camp," she says, pouring water over Father's feet where his muddied toenails are curled and blackened. "I'll see her married. You always said no one will marry me with my eyes the way they are, and, truth is, I'll be glad to look after the children, mend things, grind the corn, make the bread. We'll be safe. You don't need to worry about us."

She isn't sure that Father is worried, but it feels better to pretend that he is, and to remember that he had been once.

Father had been kind. Before the elders banished them to the island. Before his Dark Notions settled on him. Before Mother got taken by the night raiders. Before she disappeared into the wood and never came back. He had been kind before the Fire and the raid. It was only after the Fire that he started to speak as if one bad thing followed another as sure as the moon followed the sun, as if the gods had already decided everything, carved it all in stone.

But Nonor always said that the Fates don't carve, they weave. Isla does her best to make sure her sister always remembers that. The Fates take the threads that we make from the things we do, Nonor would say, the choices we make, big ones and small ones, all of them, and they weave them in and out, through and under, all the time. They never stop their weave. But they can only use the threads we give them.

"Every choice we make in this life, Isla," Nonor said, "changes the pattern in that cloth. Sometimes only a little. Sometimes the little things we do can change everything."

Once Isla has washed the mud and the soot from Father's limbs, and the mess from his face, and has tied his jaw into shape, she rubs his hands, face and beard with the scented oil that Blue has kept from the bottle she found in the Sun King cemetery, under the hawthorn bush. The smell is still heady—hedgerow roses, wet soil and wild jasmine. Father's hands are the color of the leather of his apron, cross-hatched just like her own with the scars, nicks and burns of the forge. His swollen joints make his fingers curl like ram's horns.

Isla finds his best tunic in the chest. She ties the leather apron and his toolbelt back around his waist.

Father is himself again. He is the Great Smith again.

"Banished?" she remembers him roaring after they came to live on the island. He had brought his hammer down on the anvil so hard that the word came to sound to Isla like iron itself. "Banished? How dare they banish the Great Smith? The gods will venge me. You'll see. The Great Thunor will venge me with his fire and his mayhem. They will be sorry."

Isla and Blue push the handcart along the path through the marsh to the beach, with Father's body strapped down with ropes. It lurches about so much that they have to keep stopping to rearrange his arms and legs, all down the path that leads through the long reeds that hiss and shiver in the wind.

At last, they have heaved and hauled him onto the boat pyre just as the first small waves from the rising tide begin to lift and nudge the boat from side to side. Laid out like that, all straightened out in the golden, falling light of the evening, he looks like an oak felled across the marsh.

Isla wants to do something, say something, but she doesn't know what. "We need the wiccan," she says. "We need Nonor. We aren't supposed to do this by ourselves.

What if we do it in the wrong way? What if we say the wrong things?"

"First we have to offer him to Thunor," Blue says.

"But only the wiccans can do that."

But Blue starts straight in before Isla can stop her, calling directly on Thunor, god of thunder and of smiths and of metal and mayhem, to tell Father's story: "The rains fell heavy in the Old Country," she begins.

"You can't," Isla says, trying to clap her hand over Blue's mouth. "We can't. Nonor said. You'll upset the gods. Only the wiccans can send off the dead."

"One of these days a wiccan is going to claim that daughter of yours," Isla remembers hearing Nonor saying to Father once, nodding toward Blue, who had been staring off into the woods again. "See that child looking over into the other world like that? A wiccan came for my cousin back in the Old Country. She wasn't much older than Blue. The whole village feasted for days afterward. It was a blessing to be prayed for. An honor above all honors. But it's not like that here, not in this country. Not anymore. You wouldn't wish a wiccan child on any family, not here."

Isla had sworn that day that she'd make sure the wiccans never came for Blue. She'd heard the stories of what happened to wiccans sometimes now when they told people things they didn't want to hear. She'd seen their bodies hanging from the trees where the old Sun King roads crossed.

Blue pushes her sister's hand away. "We have to," she says.

Blue goes on. There is no stopping her:

"The Great Rhine swelled," she says, her voice rising and

falling. "The water swallowed up the Seax land in the Great
Rage. For ten long winters the river swallowed it up. The
crops spoiled. The house posts rotted. Children drowned.
The Great Sickness spread. Then the Great Smith and the
Great Smith Mother packed their sea trunk. They took a
place in one of the boats sailing up the Great Rhine to the
sea to join their cousins who had gone on ahead to the new
lands. Their boat was four weeks at sea. The storms near on
killed them all."

"The Great Smith Mother sat through those storms,"
Isla says, stuttering, when Blue nudges her to take her turn,
trying to remember the stories Father and Nonor told at the
winter hearth fires. "The Great Smith Mother sat with the
bear skins pulled up over her at the back of that great boat,"
she continues, "waves crashing over them, the men groaning over the oars, Nonor reading the stars to make sure the
hull was pointed in the right direction, praying . . ."

"Or howling," Blue says, laughing. The flames from the
setting sun are catching in her eyes. "Nonor howled as if the
gods were deaf and she had to shout to make them hear."

"The Great Smith sang to the Great Smith Mother
when she was afraid," Isla adds. She is smiling. She can't
help herself.

Nothing matters anymore. Nothing matters but this.
Just this.

"And they ate fried fish as big as oak trees."

"And whales with wings leaped across the boat from one
side right across to the other."

When Isla reminds Thunor that Father is the only Great
Smith in the whole of the South Lands, how much he has

suffered, and how great his skill is, she forgets her fear, the catch in her throat. She is sure for a moment that the birds have gathered to watch them, too. Three otters swim in, along the edge of the river. Their dark heads turn toward them, nostrils flaring, and then disappear.

Blue takes out the objects that she's chosen for Father to take with him to the Next World. She places them about his body, moving around the boat pyre in a kind of slow dance.

She has chosen:

Father's short sword.

"You'll need your knife to eat with," she says, tucking it into his hand, closing his gnarled fingers around it and pressing her lips to them.

Father's spear.

"You might have to fight," she says, laying the polished spear in the crook of Father's shoulder. "It is a long way to the Next World."

Father's clamp and his hammer.

She slips these into his belt: "You'll need your hands free for your spear," she says.

Finally, she tucks his tweezers inside the purse on his belt.

"For your beard," she says. "And your eyebrows. You always forget your eyebrows."

When Blue gives the signal, and Isla leans forward to kiss Father's hands, her tears run across his oiled skin. Blue places thrift flowers and marsh marigolds on his closed eyelids. In the very last of the twilight, Blue begins a prayer song to Freja, her voice sweet in the evening. As the river water rises up the sides of the boat and the first flames from the forge coals lick around the kindling, the two sisters nudge the boat out into the current. A single swan rises off the river, wings beating the air, flying in great circles, calling for its mate.

The fire boat is the only thing visible out there in the dark heart of the river that night, a glow through the curtain of fog. The smell of burning skin and burning hair drifts on the night wind. How, Isla wonders, as they watch from the mound, how could anyone not recognize that smell?

"They'll be asleep," Blue says, as if she has heard her sister's thoughts. "No one will see or smell anything. And if they do, they'll think they've dreamed it."

At dawn, the sisters walk to the promontory to watch the geese and cormorants crisscrossing the mudflats. The fog has burned off in the morning sun. The glow on the horizon has gone. The river has swallowed the boat, the fire, the bones, all of Father's tools, as if none of it had ever been more than a dream.

5

When Isla wakes a few hours later, Blue is leaning over her, white-faced in the morning light, dressed in her shift, her hair wild. Isla hears the geese barking down on the shingle beach, sees the sun streaming in through the window. It is late. Her bones ache. Her eyes are swollen. She remembers with a shudder: Father is dead. Father is gone. They burned his body in a boat and it is against the Kin Law and they are in trouble. She should never have gone to sleep. She should have kept vigil—with the Fates throwing so many threads at them all at once like that. How could she have been so lax?

"There's a boat on the beach," Blue says now. "There are two men coming up the path. Osric's men."

"Which ones?" Isla is pulling on her tunic and reaching for her knife. Her hands are shaking.

"I only saw Caius," Blue says. "Then I ran."

"Caius? Oh, but that's good. We'll ask him to help us. He'll help us, Blue. I'm sure of it. He was always kind to Father."

Caius is one of Osric's private bodyguards. Father said that his ancestors came from the high Afric deserts, that they had been rounded up by the Sun Kings to fight in their armies. Most men like Caius, men who came from long lines of Sun King soldiering families, worked for the Seax overlords now, Father said. It was Caius's job to guard the Great Smith's island and to get hold of scrap for Father for the forge. Father trusted him.

"That man is the only damned soldier in Osric's palace," Father said, "the only man south of the Ghost City who understands the difference between good iron and bad iron. The rest of them are fools."

If Caius came out to the island alone, he brought gifts. Sometimes he stayed to help fix the roof and the fish traps. Once Blue had taken him down to the woods to help her collect honey from the bee skeps. Some nights, if Caius had to wait for the tide to turn, Father lit a fire up on the mound under the stars. Then Father let Isla and Blue lie on the wolf skins listening to Caius's ancestor stories, about the horses of the high desert, of the great cities hidden in the sand. When he and Father talked about iron and Caius told Father about the new iron bars that were coming in from over the sea or how he'd heard that an iron mine had been opened up again in Frisia, Isla always felt like she'd burst with all the questions she wanted to ask him, but Father wouldn't let her. No one was supposed to know that she worked in the forge, that she made all the firetongued swords now, that she could tell the difference between an iron bloom and a lump of bog iron with her eyes closed. One of the Seax lords to the north had hamstrung a smith once for letting his daughter into his forge, Father told her. His soldiers had taken a sword to slice across the tendons on the back of the smith's thighs to cripple him. And although Isla had wondered what they might have done to the smith's daughter, she hadn't dared to ask.

Isla and Blue peer through the window, making sure to keep out of sight behind the old sacking. Caius appears first, carrying a brace of hares on a stick on his shoulder. He waits at the gate on the far side of the yard, the morning sun glancing off his old Sun King breastplate. A few moments later, a short fat man appears behind him, picking seed heads off his dark green cloak and mopping his forehead with his shirt cuff, all cross and sweaty.

"Who is it?" Isla says. "Can you see yet?"

"Oh, Isla, it's the Exactor, the one they call Thorsten."

"The Exactor? Dear gods." Isla can hardly breathe. "Someone must have seen the boat."

Thorsten is Osric's chief tithe collector. The very worst of Osric's men, Father called him. A man of appetites, Father added once, darkly, and when Isla pressed him, he said that Thorsten took his own dues in his own way. If the harvest was poor and there wasn't enough grain or cloth or meat to hand over to Osric's soldiers, then Thorsten would say there were other ways a man might pay. And, of course, Isla knew what that meant for the daughters of those men, even if Blue didn't understand. That was why Father always made them hide in the cellar or in the wood. He wasn't going to take any chances.

If Osric has sent the Exactor to the island, then they are in trouble. Big trouble. Someone from one of the riverside camps must have seen the burning boat and told Osric.

"We've got time to get down to the reed beds and hide," she says, trying to catch her breath, trying to stay calm. "If we climb through the back window and follow the deer paths, we can get to the Sun King hulk on the mudflat and wait for them to go. They'll never find us there."

"But we'll leave tracks," Blue says. "They'll follow us."

"How many weapons do they have? Can we fight?"

"And then what?"

After what happened to Mother, Father made sure to teach them how to handle swords, but Blue is right, even if they could fight Caius then get away and hide in the reeds, more Seax soldiers will come. Without a boat, they'll easily be found. And even if they get hold of a boat, once those soldiers have found the Great Smith and his daughters missing, Osric will raise the hue and cry and there'll be horses and soldiers and dogs thundering through all the riverside camps looking for them.

"We're going to have to talk our way out of this," Isla says, straightening out Blue's tunic. "You understand?" Blue nods. They've done it before. They've done it with Father often enough. They are good at talking their way out of things. They can do it again, if only Blue doesn't blurt. Isla can never be sure that Blue won't blurt.

"Let me do the talking," Isla says. "Just keep your head down. Don't speak. Do you hear me? Nothing. Not a word. Act stupid."

Blue presses her finger to her lips and smiles in a stupid kind of way. It makes Isla laugh to see it, even with death at the gate. She can hear the men's voices now.

Isla and Blue listen for the sound of the goats bleating and the chickens squawking as the two men cross the yard.

One breath.

Two breaths.

Three breaths.

Then the rap on the door.

Thorsten had not expected to see a woman open the door of the Great Smith's hut. He's forgotten they live there too. Isla can see that. He has not expected to see a woman with eyes like hers, one green, one brown. He gasps and takes a step back. Then he crosses himself like the Christian priests do. It has been so long since Isla has seen anyone other than Father or Blue—or sometimes Caius or Old Sive—that she's forgotten what happens when she looks straight at people in bright sunlight. It is easy to forget out there on the island. She smiles. Behind Thorsten, Caius smiles back, looking straight at her, his eyes on hers in a kind of question. His face is gentle.

Blue comes to stand beside her, slipping her arm around Isla's waist, laying her head against her shoulder.

"You are most welcome here," Blue says.

"It is a great honor indeed," Thorsten says with an irritated bow, but Isla knows he doesn't mean what he is saying any more than she does. He is shifting from one foot to the other, doing his best to avoid Isla's eyes.

"The honor is ours," she says, trying to remember the way she'd heard the above-boards visitors speak when they came to see Father.

They are all in disarray, standing there by the open door to the hut, the sun white-bright, a peregrine calling to its mate high overhead, the wind shaking the white willows silver and blowing dust clouds about the yard.

"We come on the Lord Osric's business to see the Great Smith," Caius says. "We bring him gifts."

"Will you come inside out of the sun, sir?" Isla says, making sure to keep her eyes down and her forge-scarred hands out of sight.

Why didn't they run? She is cursing herself now. Why didn't they run as soon as Blue raised the alarm? They could have been far away by now, deep in the reeds, following the deer tracks to keep on dry ground, or hiding in the hold of the old Sun King wreck out on the mudflats. Why did she listen to Blue? Even if the two men had followed their tracks down to the reeds, they wouldn't have made it out to the wreck. Blue and Isla know how to follow the deer tracks across the marsh, but the men don't. They would have been down into the mud in no time, swallowed up.

But they hadn't run. They had stayed. Now they'll have to use their wits.

Thorsten blinks in the dark of the hut, taking in the made-neat beds, the hearth fire, the pot hanging over it, the swept floor, the table with the bunches of cut herbs and bowl full of eggs. Isla watches him turn his eyes on her sister: Blue arranging the bowls and the long stools, turning toward him, smiling. She's plaited her hair in the Seax way and twisted some flowers into it, but she's also hitched Nonor's glass ball onto her belt alongside the blackbird skull she wears there on a thread. It is a good touch.

"We don't have bread today sadly, sir," Isla says, her blood rising as she watches Thorsten's eyes linger on her sister.

"The barley is finished," Blue says. "But there's fresh eggs and oatcakes and we have honey mead, made from our own honey. Please sit."

The mead. Isla has forgotten the mead. Last winter, the batch of mead that Blue had brewed went awry. Or that's what Blue said. Father tasted it. Then he helped himself to more. After he swallowed that first cup, he smiled in a lop-sided way, his eyes fogged. Blue smiled back and kissed the top of his head and stroked his hair, and he let her, so mild and tame that it made Isla think that the brew hadn't gone awry at all. She might have guessed it was henbane seed that Blue had mixed in there, but when she asked, Blue just shrugged her shoulders and smiled.

Or perhaps it was the rye. Isla had heard Nonor talk

about how rye could turn. How you had to be careful how you stored it. A whole camp back in the Old Country had gone to sleep for months, she said, and when people had finally woken up they had talked of seeing their own limbs burning and cows that bloomed roses from their horns, girls flying on the backs of crows, rivers flowing backward, bones of the ancestors walking abroad. Rye can do that, she said. Wet rye, stored in the wrong way, can do that.

Blue had gone out to her still and brought back more of the mead, put it on the high shelf. Father sloped off into the woods with a flagon and brought it back empty the next day, his face and clothes all creased from sleeping in the reed beds out under the stars. It would take him another whole day sometimes to sleep it off. While Father slept, Blue and Isla did what they wanted. They swam in the creek, or lay up on the mound watching the clouds drift across the sky or climbed the old oak to try to catch a glimpse of the boats and their cousins over in the camp.

And now there are two whole flagons of that mead left.

"You must be thirsty," Blue says. Isla tries glaring at her, but Blue turns her back.

Blue isn't supposed to be saying anything. She is supposed to be playing stupid. She promised. She isn't sticking to what they agreed.

Thorsten nods and takes a seat on the stool near the open window. He's fanning himself with a wooden plate that he's taken from the table.

"Where is your father?" he says. "We don't have much time."

"He went out to the fish traps, sir," Blue says, filling

Thorsten's cup to the brim, and then pouring a cup from a different jug for Caius. Isla feels herself wince. They hadn't agreed on how the story would go. There wasn't time. They are as good as done for now.

"One lie is perhaps as good as any other," Mother said once. "If you need to lie, girls, if there's no other way to save yourselves, make sure it's a good one." Nonor said that lying was always bad, but now Isla thinks it must depend a little on how much trouble you're in. Now one lie will have to keep on following the last. And Isla is going to have to keep up, pick up her sister's threads and spin alongside her.

"He went out yesterday," she says. "He must have decided to make camp near the weirs," she says. "He won't be much longer. He'll be hungry by now. You must wait for him. He'll want to show you the sword himself."

The sword. Thorsten hasn't come all the way out to the island to question them about a boat burning at all. Of course he hasn't. He has come to collect the sword. She and Blue have been so busy that they've forgotten the sword. It is still out in the forge, unfinished, the fifth of the great firetongued swords that Osric has ordered from his Great Smith; each one, Isla has heard Caius say, more dazzling than the last. Isla had blushed with pride when she heard him say that.

"And what of the sword?" Thorsten says now, dropping his voice. He is so close Isla can smell the rot of his breath, see the string of spit stretching between his teeth. She glances over to Blue, but her sister is leaning over the pot, eyes down. Caius looks puzzled. He is trying to catch her eye, but Isla won't let him.

"Your father promised to send word with Old Sive the Charcoal Burner," Thorsten says. "We have heard nothing."

"He's been busy," she says quickly.

"We don't want any trouble here. We don't want any trouble with the Great Smith or his family."

Thorsten looks at Blue then, just a flicker of a glance, but he makes sure that Isla sees him do it. When he turns back toward Isla again, he raises his eyebrows. She does not miss his meaning. If it weren't for Caius standing there at the door, she'd take the poker from the hearth and bring it down on Thorsten's head, there and then, for that threat he's just made. She'd crack that shiny, vein-mottled skull of his open like an egg. She'd watch his insides spill out over the mud floor.

Trouble. Thorsten doesn't want any trouble. She'll give him trouble.

But she holds her tongue. Father might always have been angry, she thinks now, he might have railed against his exile, but he had always held his tongue, always done what Osric ordered him to do. When any of Osric's men came out to the island, she and Blue had watched Father bow and scrape and smile, his lips tight, his hands clenched behind his back. She always thought Father a coward for doing that. He'd be furious in the forge, swearing vengeance, but as soon as Osric's men came, he'd be all meek and kowtow-ing. Now she understands why. What choice did he have? If he'd been banished to the island alone, he might have put up a fight or refused to make the firetongued swords or tried to escape. But with Isla and Blue living on the island along-side him, he must have lain awake at night weighing up one trouble against another. Perhaps he planned for all three of them to escape together. Perhaps he waited too long and ran out of time. Isla wishes she'd asked him more questions. She wishes she'd been kinder.

"Father says this last firetongue has been . . . difficult," she says.

"It's not finished?" Thorsten has raised his voice. Sweat has gathered along his top lip. A vein on his temple throbs.

Blue looks up in alarm.

"Father says the iron you sent was not good," Isla says, turning her back on Caius to ignore the look she knows he will give her because the iron that Caius brings them is always good.

The word "trouble" still hovers darkly in the air.

"Not finished? The Gathering is two days away, woman. Two days. There are boats traveling up the Great River, wagons on the roads all the way from Dumnonia, pigs, cows and chickens butchered, flagons of mead brewed, even a boatload of wine coming in from Gaul. You want me to go back to Lord Osric and tell him the firetongue is not finished? That there will be no dowry gift for his son's betrothal feast? Am I to tell him he has to send every one of those ships and carts and wagons and soldiers and lords back to where they came from?"

Isla thinks of the blade up there on the shelf in the forge. Father had twisted and plaited the molten rods and forged on the handle, but she still has to raise the pattern up the length of the blade with the hammer, forge on the cutting blade, temper the whole and then polish. The hilt is complete, but there are still the jewels to set. It is at least two days' more work.

"One more day," she says. "Father said one more day."

"Show it to me." Thorsten grabs Isla's hair, yanking her neck back so hard that she cries out in pain. She sees Caius turn, his hand on the hilt of his sword. She can't see Blue at all now.

"The trouble is . . ." she stammers, gasping for breath, "the sword is in the forge and without Father here, I can't take you in. I don't dare." She lets her words tail off. Thorsten releases her hair.

"You don't dare?"

But he isn't looking at Isla anymore. He is staring at Blue. His skin is gray. He looks down at the mead, then back up at Blue.

Blue, sitting on her stool in the corner of the hut, has taken one of the hares from Caius's bundle, looped it onto a rafter hook and run a knife down between its teats. Now she is hooking out its insides with her hands so that they slither down into the bowl on her lap. Her fingers are red from the blood, her face and hair smeared with it.

With all of them staring, Blue whistles suddenly for her bird. Wrak appears at the open hatch in a flurry of oily black, then flies across the room straight over Thorsten's head to land on Blue's shoulder, dipping his head to take the hare eyes from her fingers before disappearing back out the window. If the Exactor had been minded to tell Osric about the beauty of the Great Smith's younger daughter, Isla thinks, he's going to think better of it now. She's a mess of entrails and blood.

Thorsten stares for a long time, saying nothing. He tries to stand and reach for his bag but stumbles and slumps forward onto his knees. The mead has done its work.

"Is he ill?" Isla says, when Caius steps forward to help him. She can feel the sweat dripping down her back. "Perhaps it's too hot."

"I must see the Great Smith," Thorsten stutters. His eyes drift to the rafters as if he's seeing something perched up there. "What the devil is that thing?"

"Perhaps," Caius says, "your father might be fetched?"

"Father told us we were to stay inside the hut until he returned, sir," Blue answers from the corner, her bloodied fingers hovering and pointing in midair, her head cocked to one side just like Wrak, eyes wide. "Otherwise, we would be glad to fetch him, sir. But Father has rules. We must stay in the hut, at all times, unless we are with him. He will be angry, sir, if we leave the hut without him and when he is angry, sir, especially since the night of the . . ."

Blue, her face smeared with the hare's now darkening and crusting blood, gives them all a look of terror. Her eyes dart about. She is shaking.

When Isla and Blue go to gather firewood in the wood and Isla is cross or tired, Blue sometimes plays a game to put Isla back in good spirits. She turns herself into a dragon or a bird or an animal from one of Old Sive's stories to make Isla laugh. She can conjure people and animals and worlds with a single look or a gesture of her hand.

Isla watches her sister weaving her threads about the Exactor now. Her voice has a crow note in it. Her shoulders hunch over like her bird. But this isn't a game played in the wood. This is dangerous. Isla has no words for what this is.

"Take Caius with you," Thorsten says to Blue, blurring one word into another just like Father used to do after drinking the mead. "Take Caius to the Great Smith. Fetch him back from his, from his . . . Where is he?"

"Father would not like that either, sir," Blue says. "He might be anywhere. There's the woods and the shore near the bee skeps and the weir near the fish traps. Sometimes he goes out to the Sun King wreck on the mudflats to trap for eels. It might take us a long time to find him. It is better for us to stay here and wait with you. He does not like to be fetched."

"But the tide," Caius says, helping Thorsten onto a stool at the table. "We don't have long."

Blue brings the bowl of entrails to the table. Slowly, piece by piece, she begins to lay out the hare's shiny insides on the table in front of the Exactor, just as they've seen the soothsayer do in the camp. She prods at them. Thorsten lifts his head and peers at the bloodied mass.

"Father is a man of very short temper, sir," Blue says, shaking her head and then tutting as if she does not like what she sees in the entrails on the table. "Oh, that's not good. That's not good at all."

"Stop that," Thorsten says, waving his arm through the air as if brushing away invisible things. "Just stop doing that."

Wrak is back on the other side of the hut, dashing himself up against the walls, his wings catching the light through the cracks. *Wrak-wrak*, he cries. Thorsten jumps in fright.

"What in hell's mouth is that?"

"It's just the bird, sir," Isla says. "You mustn't mind him."

"Something's coming," Blue says, rolling her eyes up into her head to turn them almost white for a moment.

Isla is afraid she will burst with laughter or terror, split her skin like a ripe plum.

"Wrak knows," Blue says. "He always knows. He can see."

"Where is the sword?" Thorsten roars again.

Blue sweeps the entrails from the table back into the bowl as if she wants to scrub out what she's seen. She shakes her head again, shudders, then lays the old cloth across the bowl.

"There's been sorcery in the making of that sword, sir," she says. She clutches the glass ball to her chest as if she is warding off bad spirits. "No good will come of it."

"What kind of sorcery?" Thorsten's voice has a tremor in it now. Caius steps forward, his eyes narrowed, intent on Blue too. For a moment Isla might have said she saw a smile flicker around the edges of his mouth, a glint in his eye.

"Dark magic, sir," Blue says. "I hardly dare speak of it. The things we have seen here on this island, sir, just last night, you would not believe. Father is lost sometimes, sir, lost in the fire. He is not himself."

"Blue," Isla says, her voice cracking, "you mustn't. Father said you weren't to say." But the Exactor puts his hand up to command her silence.

"Go on," he says, turning back to Blue. "What have you seen? Tell me," he roars.

"Sometimes we do not see him for days, sir," Blue says, as if she can't help herself. Thorsten keeps glancing up into the rafters, twisting the rings on his fingers. "And when he comes out of the forge, sir, his eyes are dark with flecks of fire. There have been creatures abroad here, on this very

island, first on the edge of the wood, then in this yard—
even in this hut. Beasts that not even Father has seen before.
One of them came up from the marsh, sir, up from the mud
itself, covered in . . ."

"Covered in what?" Isla sees Thorsten tremble. She sees
him shake.

"Scales, and horns, and . . . feathers."

"I knew it," Thorsten says, turning to Caius. "I knew it.
You can smell it. Can you smell it?"

Caius nods, raising his eyebrows at Blue.

"Blue," Isla says. "Father said we were never to speak of
these things . . ."

Blue puts her finger to her lips as if she has been scolded.
Her eyes blaze.

"Beasts?" the Exactor says, draining his cup again.
"What kind of beasts? Not . . . ?"

"We saw her," Blue whispers, leaning forward, her eyes
mad and wide, pointing to the window in the direction of
the river. "We saw her, sir—on the night of the storm. Rising
up out of the mud. Right out there."

Wrak-wrak, the bird calls again, beating his wings
against the sides of the hut, making Thorsten drop his cup
and clasp his hand to his chest.

"Here?" Thorsten says. "On the island?"

Blue nods.

"From the mudflats," she says. "It was a terrible sight.
Her eyes were like the lightning. Her teeth, sir . . . She . . ."

"From the mud?"

Isla's face burns as if she's leaning right into the forge
fire. Blue is describing the marsh demon, the one that the

Seax call Grendel's mother, the gorgon that the Norse call Gefion and that Isla has heard the Briton women call Jenny Greenteeth. The Exactor knows her. Of course he does. Everyone knows her. Their cousins will not let their children go near the mudflats alone for fear the marsh demon will snatch them. They say she spares nothing and no one.

"Blue," Isla says again, raising her voice, watching the look on the Exactor's face. "Father said we were not to say . . . He said no one must know. No one." She steps toward her sister.

"Go on," Thorsten hisses.

"I can show you where, sir," Blue says. "I can show you where her fire left marks on the rocks on the beach. Let me show you where we saw her first, sir, out on the mudflats. Let me take you there. You can still smell her, even now. Sometimes it's like bad eggs, ya, sometimes like shit. She must have come right into the yard last night, because when we found the goat this morning, sir, his coat had turned from black to white."

Isla bites down on her lip hard, so hard she tastes blood. Musk is white, just as Blue has said, but Musk has always been white and though Thorsten might not know that, Caius does. Blue's gone and done it now. She's given the game away. Isla fixes her eyes on a knot in the wood beneath her feet and makes herself count backward silently, waiting for the sky to fall.

"This morning?" Caius says.

The Exactor's hand is trembling now.

"Caius," he says, "we have tithes to collect at the camp.

We must be back at the palace before sundown. Lord Osric's orders."

"Osric—" Isla begins.

With a roar the old man lunges at her, pushing her up against the wall, his hands round her throat, levering her head up so hard she has to stand on the tips of her toes to breathe. His fingers press into the hollows of her neck as if he means to stop her breath altogether.

"Lord Osric," he says. "Lord Osric to you, girl. Who do you think you are? Stuck-up, high and mighty, know-it-all . . ."

"Lord Osric," Isla stutters. Each time she tries to free herself from Thorsten's grip, he digs his fingers deeper into her neck. The lights from the windows stretch and fade. She opens her eyes wide, turning them on Thorsten, looking straight at him. He gasps and looks away.

"Damn you," he says, taking his hand from Isla's throat. "Don't do that." When she falls to the floor, gasping for air, he kicks at her, hard, blow after blow, cursing and spitting. Then there's a scuffle and the kicking stops.

"Sir," she hears Caius say. "The girl's eyes. Take care."

Isla braces herself for more blows. She prays to Freja that Blue will have the good sense to get through the door and make it down to the reed beds.

"Her eyes? What of them?" Thorsten roars.

"The first augury that Crowther gave Lord Osric," Caius is saying. "The time his father took him to the Sun King temple on the Walbrook stream? When he was a boy. Remember?"

Crowther? Isla feels a chill pass across her skin at the

sound of the old soothsayer's name. She strains hard to listen. As children, she and Blue would crawl under the Mead
Hall table on feast nights, hide down there among all their
cousins' legs and feet and dogs, just so they wouldn't miss
any of the stories about the great soothsayer their cousins
called Crowther.

"Can Crowther fly, then?" Blue had whispered one night
when the stories began. "Does she have a special pouch on
her back for her wings? If she can turn herself into a wolf,
can she turn herself into a butterfly as well? How small can
she go?"

"How am I supposed to know?" Isla had hissed back.
"She might not even be real. She might be made up. One
day, when we're bigger, we'll ask Nonor."

"Augury?" Thorsten says now, dropping his fist at the
mention of Crowther's name. "What augury?"

"Didn't Crowther tell Lord Osric that two sisters of fire
would come up the river?" Caius says. "Didn't she say one
of them would have eyes of the storm? The other a bird?"

Isla turns her head just enough to see Caius whispering
into Thorsten's ear.

"Crowther told him that?" Thorsten says. "You're sure?"

"I have heard Lord Osric tell that story many times."

"Then he will want to see these sisters for himself."

"He will."

Isla stays where she is on the floor. It hurts to move.
Then she hears Blue's voice:

"Father says my sister and I must bring the sword to
Lord Osric. It is the only way we'll get it over the river to the
palace, he says. The only way to stop . . . the trouble. Send

us a boat and we will bring the firetongue to Lord Osric in time for his feast."

"So be it," the Exactor is saying, waving his hands as if he's cutting himself out of the threads that Blue has spun around him. He turns to the door.

"Send them a boat," he mutters to Caius. "We'll soon see what Lord Osric has to say about all of this."

Isla watches the two men's boots move toward the door.

"It must be a strong boat," Blue is saying. "It might be a wild crossing. If the sword, sir, is as Father thinks, there may be trouble."

But Thorsten is already out through the door, Caius behind him.

"On the flood tide, tomorrow," Blue calls after him from the doorway. "It must be the flood tide."

6

Look at your poor hands, Isla. They're shaking. Look how they're shaking. You're bleeding."

"What did you just do, Blue? How did you just do that?"

"I got us a boat."

"You did. You just got us a boat. Now we can go home, Blue. We can go home."

Blue smiles her sad smile.

"We can't go home, Isla," she says. "You know we can't. Our cousins won't let us."

Isla doesn't want to argue. She hasn't the strength.

"You frightened me," she says.

"I did?"

"Your face. It was like . . ." But, Isla thinks, her sister's face wasn't like anything she has seen before. Nor was her voice. It had made Isla's insides turn.

"Sit down," Blue says, putting a stool firmly in front of the hearth and pulling a wolfskin rug around Isla's shoulders. "Sit. I'll clean you up. You have to finish the blade, but first we have to draw out those bruises."

Before she begins Blue puts her hand back into the mess of entrails in the bowl and makes a fresh red smear across her nose and cheeks. Isla starts back, seeing the blood on Blue like that.

"You look just like Mother," she says.

"Say it again."

"You look just like Mother. You do. It's the blood on your cheeks. When I close my eyes, I can see Mother like she's standing right here with us in the hut."

"Keep your eyes closed. Tell me what you see. Tell me everything."

Isla says: "Father's here too. They're dancing."

"Tell me all of it."

Isla winces as Blue daubs the wound on her head with vinegar. She looks at the flickerings and pulsings behind her closed eyelids. She can see the old hut back in the camp, the fire in the hearth, clear as day.

"Can you see me too?" Blue says. "Am I there too? Can you see me?"

"Yes, you're still a baby. You're sitting up in the little

hazel basket down by the hearth, the one Nonor wove for you. You are holding the doll she stitched for you."

"Lovely Gretel. I lost her when they torched the camp. What am I doing?"

"You're staring right into the fire. From the moment you first opened your eyes, you were always looking for the fire. That's why Father called you Blue."

"After the color the fire makes when it gets a heart in it."

"Yes."

"Don't stop. Tell me. Where are they now?"

"Father is fixing a lock to the door," Isla says. "It must be when the first night raids began. He was always trying out new locks, bringing them from the forge to show Mother."

"Oh, and what is Mother doing?"

"She's talking back to him in Ikeni. They're fighting."

Now that Isla can smell the mugwort in the salve that Blue is stirring up for her bruises, she can see Nonor too, sitting hunched in the corner. Nonor used to mix mugwort into everything.

"Nonor's here too," Isla says. "She is all hunched over in her chair by the fire like she used to get when she was cross."

"What are they fighting about?"

"The hut is full of flowers, so it must be the night of the Midsummer feast. Mother's dressing. She's got out her Ikeni robe and has it hanging from the rafters. Nonor wants her to burn it."

"But that robe was beautiful. Why would Nonor want Mother to burn it?"

"Nonor is saying that Mother must break and bury her

Ikeni torc, too, the one Father made for her, and change the way she wears her hair. Father is trying to explain why, but Mother won't listen. Father says all the women in our camp, wherever they come from, and whatever language they speak, Briton, Seax, Gauli, Ikeni, have to start speaking Seax now because of Osric. He says that if they want Osric to protect them, they have to dress Seax, wear the Seax brooches, carry the Seax shields, tell only the Seax stories, worship only the Seax gods. He is saying that it's safer for the women that way. He says everyone knows who you belong to if you all dress and speak the same, and Mother is giving him this look. Oh, you should see that look she is giving Father, Blue. She says to him: 'Belong to, husband? I don't belong to anyone.'"

"I don't belong to anyone," Blue repeats, unraveling the strips of clean linen she keeps for wounds. "Oh yes. Father won't like that."

Isla shudders despite the heat from the fire. "Mother is looking straight at me now. I am sitting on the bed in the shadows with the dog, watching them. Mother is putting her fingers in a bowl and she's painting these red stripes in pig's blood—dragonfire red—like this, slowly right across her cheeks. She's looking straight at me, as if she's doing it for me. Nonor's mouth is gawping open. 'Say something,' Nonor says to Father. 'Tell her to wash it off.' But Father just laughs and puts his hand in the small of Mother's back. He tips her backward, like they are dancing, and he kisses her there on the red of the blood and she laughs right back at him when it stains his lips red."

"Dancing, yes," Blue says, clapping her hands. "I remember them dancing. I remember that. Like this."

Isla opens her eyes.

Blue is dancing round the hut, her arm out in front of her as though she is Father back in the days of the camp when he used to laugh, and while Blue is spinning around, she is holding her hand there, right in the small of Mother's back. But now that Isla's eyes are open again, they've all gone.

"He was calling her his dragon blood," Isla goes on, blinking back tears, "his Ikeni queen. He was kissing her. Mother was laughing, she was laughing, and spinning me around, round and around."

"Where am I?" Blue says. "Where was I?"

"You were watching them dance. Clapping your hands. You had the firelight burning in your eyes."

"I remember. I remember."

"Then Nonor walked out. She slammed the door behind her. The whole hut shook. I'd never seen her do that before. It made me jump right out of my skin."

"Then what?"

"I can't see them anymore, Blue. They've gone. They've all gone."

"Why was Nonor so angry?" Blue says later, as she combs out Isla's wet hair close to the fire, steam rising off her.

"She was afraid. After the raid, you know, Nonor told me she knew something bad was coming for us when Mother put the blood across her face that night."

"You didn't tell me that. I thought Nonor liked Mother."

"She did, but she said that if Mother had made herself

more Seax, if she hadn't been so proud, the night raiders wouldn't have taken her. Mother should have thought about her kin, she said. She said Mother should have thought about us."

"Why?" Blue says. "Why should Mother have thought of us? Father didn't."

"It's different for women," Isla says. And when Blue asks her why it is different for women, Isla tells Blue that she is just like Mother: always asking questions, never listening to the answers.

"Can we sleep outside again tonight?" Blue says.

"So long as the marsh witch doesn't come up off the mudflats while we are sleeping," Isla says.

"And rip our heads off. And tear our arms and our legs off and suck out our eyeballs."

"Stop it," Isla tells her. "It hurts when I laugh."

Blue is already falling asleep, curled up on the pile of reeds, facing toward the fire, Isla arched around her sister's back, by the time Isla is ready to tell her what they are going to do.

"Once Osric sends us the boat," she says, "we'll row west, upriver. At night. We'll hide out in a Sun King ruin for a few months or in the woods. We'll trade the jewels that I've been hiding away for a wagon, then head farther west, to somewhere where no one knows us. We'll change our names. Find you a husband."

"Mother wouldn't do that," Blue says.

"How do you know what Mother would do?"

"She wouldn't run away and hide. She'd go to the palace. If she was us, she'd take the sword straight to Lord

Osric and demand Kin Protection, make sure she was free to go anywhere she chose. She would."

"But what if Osric finds out about the boat burning? Or that I've been making the firetongues all this time? He'll have us strung up in the trees in one of those cages that Thorsten has Father make, leave us up there to die. They'll use us to show people what happens to women who break the Seax law. And if they don't bury us properly, Blue, if they scatter our bones, we'll end up wandering the marshes forever."

"Mother walked into the Mead Hall with those Ikeni marks right across her face. She wasn't afraid."

"What's got into your head tonight?"

"Mother. Mother's got into my head. Do you remember the hare?"

Isla remembers the hare. Of course she does. Of all her mother's stories, the one about the hare is Isla's favorite. When the Ikeni queen had marched on the Sun Kings, Mother said, she had released a hare straight into the lines of the Sun King armies facing her people in their final battle. She'd meant it as an augury, but that hare had run straight at the Sun King's soldiers' feet, fast and mad, right between all the tight, shiny rows of soldiers in armor. The fast, jittery to-and-fro of that single hare, whiskers twitching as it ran, had scattered the men, and for a while the breaks in the Sun King lines had given the Ikeni archers time to load their bows.

"Just one hare," Mother said every time she told them that story. "Just one little hare, girls," and she held up her hands as if she were cradling the animal to her face. "That's all it took to scatter a whole Sun King army. Never forget that."

Isla lies listening to the fire spit and flare, the sound of her sister sleeping, and the owls' hunting calls out on the water meadows across the creek, thinking about the hare.

There is no safe path for them to follow. She knows that. Every direction—upriver toward the west and into hiding, downriver to the palace to ask Osric for Kin Protection— end up tangled thick with snares and traps and gallows, feet swinging, and two girls wandering the marshes forever, unburied.

When Isla finally sleeps, in her dream a single hare runs up the ditch-edge of a battlefield heaped with bodies and steaming with spilled blood, sniffing the air. It runs a few yards along the ditch, darts first one way and then quickly sideways through a hole in the hedgerow into another field altogether. Isla wakes remembering the way that hare moved, back and forth, slippery, never in one direction.

She feels Blue stir.

"If we do go to the palace," Isla says, "we'll have to keep the boat burning a secret. We could say something bad happened to Father."

"Jenny Greenteeth took Father, sir," Blue says, sitting up, starting straight into it as if she's just been waiting for Isla to catch up. "She dragged him away in her teeth right across the mudflats, sir. Then we saw this great star, sir, shaped like a hammer that tore across the sky, and in the flash of lightning we saw Thunor himself. He said—"

"No. Not like that. You see, that's the trouble—it can't be like one of your stories. It has to be something Osric will believe. We'll say Father never came back from the fish traps. Then they'll think he drowned. And that way no one has to know about the boat burning."

"And," Blue goes on, "when we went down to the shingle beach, sir, looking for Father, we found these claw marks on the mud. Blood on the stones. A piece of his tunic all torn and stained with blood. And there was this bad smell everywhere—"

"I'll do the telling," Isla says. "You'll just nod. Understood?"

Blue makes her eyes roll white again to make her sister laugh.

"Do you remember what Caius said to Thorsten tonight about the augury?" Isla says.

Blue nods. "He said two girls of fire will come up the river, one with eyes of the storm. He said it was one of Crowther's auguries. A girl with eyes of the storm. That's you, Isla."

"That's what I thought he said. You know I think Caius made that story up right there and then to stop Thorsten from hurting me anymore. He was protecting us. Why would he do that?"

"Caius didn't make it up, though, did he?" Blue says. "He said Crowther gave that augury to Osric when he was a boy. And Thorsten knew about it too. He can't have made it up."

"That must mean Crowther was soothsaying for Osric's father. I never heard anyone say that. Perhaps Crowther belonged to Osric's father like Father belongs to Osric. Perhaps she belongs to Osric now too."

"I don't think Crowther belongs to anyone," Blue says.

Isla shakes her head. "No one knows what's coming for us, Blue, not even Crowther, if she's even real. What are these women of fire supposed to do anyway when they come up the river? Did you hear what Caius said about that? Did he say?"

"You have to finish the sword now," Blue says. "We don't have long."

"We did right by Father, Blue," Isla tells her sister. "We did."

"He knows," Blue says. "He does. He's gone, Isla. Back to the Old Country with Nonor."

7

I t is only when Isla lights the forge fire and piles up the charcoals carefully over the first flames that she feels the darkness settle inside her again, feels the danger of the path ahead and the weight of Father gone. She sighs, looking at the window with the view down over the river, the tools hanging on their different hooks, the bellows. There'll be no more hammering or welding for her now, no more listening to the hiss and steam of the hot metal from the barrel of river water. She'll never get to work the forge fire again. She'll never be allowed to.

Back in the Old Country, Nonor told them, women, even girls, had worked alongside their fathers and brothers in the forge. But since Nonor and Father came to live in the new Briton land, the wiccans and the Christian priests all say that when women bleed, they blunt, sour, curse, turn cattle barren, make crops fail. They say that if a bleeding woman even passes near the forge when a sword is being made, curses will settle in the iron, and trouble will follow.

When Isla asked her grandmother if this was true, Nonor had spat on the ground and said:

"What do they know? You can't put a curse into iron like that any more than you can stop the tide or move the moon from one part of the sky to another."

"Be quick," Father said, that first night when he had woken Isla and taken her out to the forge on the night of a full moon. The snow lay thick on the ground around the camp, so Father made her step in the prints his feet had made, all the way to the forge, so she wouldn't leave a separate trail. Once he'd gone in through the door, he said, "Come in, child, before anyone sees you."

Still Isla hesitated, certain that if she crossed the threshold Thunor would strike her dead or bring the Great Sickness to the village or turn the corn.

"Be quick," Father said again. "What's got into you? The fire won't wait."

Once Isla had taken that first small step across the threshold, Father pushed the door shut behind her, slipped the latch and pulled the old wolf skin across to stop the drafts. There was no turning back after that. When her eyes stopped stinging from the smoke, she saw Father standing there in his leather apron, holding the blade of the sword in one huge hand and the hammer in the other. Behind him, tools glinted on hooks on the walls: hammers, clamps, tongs and files, all lined up according to size and within his reach. Some of those tools he'd brought with him from the Old Country, but most of them were tools that Osric's men had gathered for him from the abandoned Sun King smithies.

"Don't stand there gawping, girl. The fire," he said, pointing to the high bellow arm. "I can't tend the bellows and the blade at the same time. My hands are too stiff with the chilblains tonight. You take the bellows. Get the fire back into the dark blue and keep it there until I say. Slow, mind. Don't rush it."

Isla knew what to do. She'd been building and tending the hearth fire in the family hut for as long as she could remember. The forge bellows were much bigger than the ones they used for the hearth fire, but she reached up as high as she could, closed her hand around the polished wood of the handle and put her weight onto that arm, slowly. She could feel how the air passed down through the brown cowskin bag at the back and into the funnel, hear the first great hiss and watch the fire flower. She'd show Father. She'd show him how she could work the bellows.

"That's it," he said. "Yes. Good."

Isla thought she'd stop breathing for pride and for fear that she'd wake up back in her own bed to find she'd dreamed the forge and Father's praise. But she kept on, her hand on the handle, steady and quiet, counting out the rhythms.

The first fire color that comes in after you light the charcoal and draw down the bellow arm is pale straw. Next comes yellow, brown, purple and then the blue comes in like the night goes out: first dark, then pale. Isla knew that she had to keep the fire between the purple and the dark blue so that the blade would bend and not crack when it cooled. If the blade cracked it would be good for nothing, and Father would have to start again on the next new moon. That's why Father had named Blue Blue. She was the blue in the fire he tended, the magic that made the blade. Isla was just Isla, named after Nonor, their grandmother. She had to prove herself like the steel. She'd always have to prove herself.

"Don't go too hard on that bellow arm," Father would always say, no matter how many times she'd shown him she could do it. "You don't need any more than a whisper in there." And then sometimes he'd say: "Good, that's good. Yes, just like that."

8

At noon the next day, when Isla is examining the blade patterns starting to appear under her hammering, she hears scratching at the forge door. Blue has left a bowl of stew steaming under a cloth, a pile of oatcakes and a flagon of cold water from the well. Out in the yard, Wrak sits on the edge of the rain trough, watching. Later, when Isla sharpens the blade on the turning stone, she can hear Blue singing as she packs up the hut. That afternoon, when she starts carving the double-tailed merman for the hilt, she sees her sister through the forge window disappearing off down the track to the west, Wrak on her shoulder. She knows Blue is harvesting the seeds she wants to take, walking the deer paths, pulling in the fish traps and closing up the bee skeps. At dusk, she finds a plate of fish and more oatcakes outside the door.

"Don't let the blue go over to the purple, girl," she hears Father say in the dark of that night as she tempers the blade, her eyes stinging from fire. It is as if he is standing right behind her. "Don't let the blue go over to the purple, girl, or you'll never get it back."

She feels the tears come at the remembering of him.

The following morning, when she has finished the last of the polishing, Isla opens the door and calls out to her sister.

"Is it done?" Blue says, looking up from the goat pen. "Already?"

Isla nods, too tired to speak, as Blue crosses the threshold into the forge. She shows her sister the blue-black twists and circles that have surfaced under her hammer, the snakes that swirl down the middle of the shining blade, running narrower toward the point. The firetongue pattern has come out a herringbone weave this time, mottled black against the polished blade.

"Just like fish scales," Blue says.

"Or the patterns the mud makes at low tide," Isla adds.

"Like eel slitherings," Blue says, making the shapes with her hands.

The firetongue runs down the center of the blade and, when the light catches it, it flickers and puckers as if it is alive.

"It's beautiful." Blue closes her eyes to feel the weight of it, the way it sits in her palm. "Perfect."

"It makes me sad to think that Father never got to see it."

Blue examines the smith's mark Isla has made on the tip, her own new mark.

"It's close enough to Father's mark for no one to see the difference," Isla says.

"We'll know," Blue says. "We'll always know it's your mark."

"I wish he'd seen it." Isla wipes away tears.

"Perhaps he can. Perhaps he's watching us now."

"Don't say that," Isla says with a shiver. "Why do you keep saying that? It's bad luck. He can't be here. We sent him off. He's gone. You said."

But Blue isn't listening. She has gone outside to turn the blade in the sunlight. She waves it in great circles so she can hear the sound of it slicing the morning air.

"It's the best one yet," she says.

Isla nods. "I've made the hilt a new way. I put the rivets in different places so that they won't chafe."

Blue scythes at the edge of the reed beds to test the blade's sharpness, felling the young reeds like corn stalks. Wrak sits on the thatch roof and screeches, his wings out.

"You be careful," Isla calls out, her spirits lifting. "Dark magic went into the making of that sword."

Blue turns and spins again and again, her hair and the flashing blade catching the light, laughing. Wrak beats the air above her.

"The things we have seen here on this island, sir," Isla says, mimicking Blue.

The blade scatters the seeds from the bulrushes high

and wide into the white light about her sister, on every side, like snowflakes or blossoms in the wind.

"Father is lost sometimes, sir, lost in the fire," Blue says, laughing. "He is not himself."

"That was mean," Isla says. "I had to bite my lip to stop myself laughing when you said that. I nearly choked."

"Don't you cheek me, girl," Blue says, stopping spinning and putting her hands on her hips. She sounds so much like Father it gives Isla a chill. "You'll feel the back of my hand for that."

"Don't," Isla says. "Just don't."

"What will you call her?" Blue says as she kisses the blade.

The sword? Isla hadn't thought. Osric had always named the swords. The Talon. The Horned Boar. The Master. He chose each of those names to impress the other overlords he was gifting them to. He'd choose a name for this one too. But she'd choose one first. She'd give it a secret name.

"Jenny Greenteeth," she whispers. She says it again, this time louder: "Jenny Greenteeth."

"Jenny Greenteeth!" Blue shouts into the air. "Jenny Greenteeth, Jenny Greenteeth!"

9

Isla has heard people say that if you cross the threshold into a forge, even just once, the smith will put his evil eye on you. Now that she's finished this new sword, she is beginning to wonder if Father has put his evil eye on them after all, on all of them, on the whole land, just for plain spite. After the raiders took Mother, Father had enough hate in him to do that. Isla doesn't like to remember how much hate Father had.

Now, as she thinks of Blue out in the reed beds with the sword, the seeds scattering, her hair blowing in the wind like smoke, and the way Blue had spun her story of the dark magic to save them both, she feels a clench inside her like she is soon to bleed, like something bad is coming for them. She is just tired, she tells herself. The moon is turning her inside out. She has not slept. You fret too much, child, Nonor always used to say. Fretting never helped anything. Use your wits.

Stories can work for you and then turn against you. They can double back. They can bleed. And bite. You never know how—or when—they'll turn. It had been Isla's stories that had brought them so much trouble back in the camp.

She remembers the slow bleed of those stories. She remembers the night they began. Mother had been nursing Blue by the fire. Father, coming in from the forge, had thrown himself down next to where Isla was lying on the trestle bed in the firelight. The smell of the forge fire rose off him so strong that night that Isla could almost have touched it. Thinking him asleep, she put her finger on Father's closed eyelids to trace the pale blue and purple veins that forked like lightning on his skin there. Her finger tugged at the thin skin. He smiled but kept his eyes closed. His smile made lines fork at the corners of his eyes.

"Which eye is the evil one, Father?" she whispered,

because at the washing brook that day, cousin Hermann had told her about the devil's work of the forge and talked about the Great Smith's evil eye.

When Father opened his eyes wide to make Isla jump, she started back at the sight of the quick blaze from the fire-light caught inside the blue of them. She watched as the black circle at the center opened and closed, and opened again, like a flower in the sun. She saw her own face in there.

"What nonsense are they talking now, girl?" he said.

"The boys are saying you have the evil eye, Father."

"And what does that mean?"

"That they mustn't catch your look, that in the forge there are monsters, that Blue is touched, that my eyes have curses in them. Cousin Hermann says he has seen the dragon in your right eye. And he says I am a witch because my eyes are different colors."

"That boy needs a good cuff around the ears. What did you say to him?"

"I said Father's eyes have gold around the rim of the black circle in the middle. I told him there is no difference between Father's right eye and his left eye because I have looked there and seen the gold in both. I told him that I have looked up close and there is no dragon there. That I will push him in the cesspit if he calls me a witch again. That I will hold his face down there so long he will breathe in the shit."

Father tipped his head back and laughed.

"That's my girl. You go and tell your cousin Hermann that you've seen monsters in the forge. You tell him you've seen your father take his right eye out at night and that when he does it, he screeches like the owl in the woodshed. You tell him that sometimes the Great Smith leaves his right eye in the forge fire all night."

"That would be a lie, Isla," Mother said from the other side of the room, the firelight dancing in her hair. "Don't listen to your father. He's making up stories. Shame on you, husband. You're frightening her. Stop your nonsense."

"Tell those boys that you have seen your father fly," Father whispered, glancing over toward Mother. "You tell them that your father has wings like a dragon and that when he flies, his mouth spits fire." He opened his mouth and roared. And Mother laughed then, too, and roared back.

Isla understood. Father wanted the forge to himself. He didn't want anyone seeing what he did in there, prying, asking him questions. If people in the village told stories about him, repeating what Osric's men were whispering abroad, then that kept everyone away, and that was good.

No one listened to her stories much at first. But later the stories that Isla told cousin Hermann about the things she had seen and heard grew and spread. They blotched and stained into the women's whisperings and mutterings at the washing brook, glances in the herb garden, nudges in the fields. Those stories seeped away from her grasp. In time, little by little, her stories turned all their cousins against them. Soon people were saying that Isla's family was to blame when a crop failed or a baby died from the Great Sickness. Soon their cousins were saying that they all had the evil eye.

That, Isla thinks now as she sharpens the sword one last time, that must have been where the first threads got tied in, the threads woven by the Fates that brought them here to the island on the mudflats. Other threads must have webbed out from those first stories; or perhaps, she thinks, they were weaving even before then. Perhaps they wove all the way back to the time Father had made the firetongued sword in exchange for Mother, before either Blue or Isla had been born. Father didn't have to make the firetongued sword. He knew the trouble it might bring once people knew he was a Great Smith. Nonor had warned him. But he had made that firetongue because he had wanted to rescue Mother from the slave trader. And later, even though he knew Isla wasn't supposed to work in the forge, he had still asked her to come with him that night. And she could have said no. But she didn't.

10

The next day the sisters are sitting perched on the old sea chest that they've dragged down to the shingle beach when they see Old Sive's boat crossing the flood tide toward them, a second boat tied behind it.

"There it is," Blue says. "Sure enough. Here he comes."

Isla has rounded up the chickens into baskets covered in old nets and tethered Musk the goat to a pole she's staked into the shingle ready for Old Sive to take back to his wife Cathleen at the camp. He bleats into the wind that comes off the river.

"He knows he's for the chop," Isla says.

"He doesn't. I've told him he's going to Cathleen. You're mean."

"Cathleen always liked you best. It was always you she wanted on her lap at the Mead Hall feasts. Where's that sister of yours, she'd say, when I went to collect the charcoal for Father. Tell little Blue I have honey cakes. Tell her to run over later. She never offered me any."

"I ate so many once I was sick."

"You never said."

"She smelled of rotten eggs."

"When Old Sive gets back to the camp, she'll ask after you. Not me. 'How does that pretty little Blue look now that she's grown into a woman?' she'll say."

"Old Sive crosses himself when he sees me up at the mound now. He doesn't think I'm pretty anymore."

"He won't look at me at all."

"Those poor motherless girls," Blue says, mimicking the lilts and tilts of Cathleen's voice. "She was kind. I liked Cathleen. She had soft hands."

Cathleen wasn't like the other women. Blue is right. She'd laugh at Old Sive when he talked about ghosts and marsh witches and soothsayers. Nonor said Cathleen came from far west, an island, where they had fogs and banshees and where bodies came up out of the mud every full moon.

"What would Cathleen think of us now—if she knew what we've done?"

"If she knew you've been making the firetongued swords? She'd probably march right on up the hill to Nonor's grave, put her hands on her hips, like this, and tell Nonor she raised another Great Smith and she should be proud."

"Do you think Cathleen's been keeping Nonor's shrine

lamp lit?" Isla says, feeling the heat rising in her face like a fever, aching for Nonor. "And tending the wild roses? She said she would. She promised."

"I don't know," Blue tells her. "People make promises sometimes that they can't keep."

As Old Sive gets closer, Isla thinks they must look to him like a fine pair of sisters, sitting out there on the chest on the beach waiting for him. Blue had gone to find the tunics and cloaks that Isla had packed away all those years before, the clothes Osric had sent them. Cast-offs from his whores, Father had said, but Isla didn't care who'd worn them. She and Blue had laughed when they'd lifted them out of the trunk. They knew there'd be no use for such fine clothes on the island. They'd snag them on a twig or bramble. They'd shrink in the rain. They'd billow in the wind, get caked in mud, collect seed heads.

"We'll store them away in Nonor's old sea chest for a better time," she had said, running her hands over the cloth, and that had set Father off again, muttering about how there'd be no more better times, that the bastard gods had seen to that.

If they were going to get an audience with Osric now, Isla said that morning as they started to pack up, it was time for the tunics. Blue had jumped up and down at that, clapped her hands and howled like a wolf.

"Can we? Can we?"

Isla had forgotten how fine the weave and colors were, soft against the skin, a patterned braiding running around the neckline and sable along the edges of the cloaks. The green tunic fitted Blue better, so Isla took the blue one.

They fixed those tunics on their shoulders in the Seax way, using the two pairs of five-pointed star brooches that Father had designed and cast for each of them. Then Blue braided their hair in the Ikeni way, the way Mother had shown them. She wove strips of rabbit fur and crow feathers into their plaits and twisted them up on the top of their heads. Isla sewed leather ties inside their pockets and sheathed their short swords there—in case of trouble, she said, so they could reach for them easily, and keep them out of sight. Then they stitched on their veils, carefully pinning them back for the river voyage, and put all their Sun King rings back on.

In the sunlight, Isla thinks that Blue looks like a Seax queen, but also a bit of a wiccan, too, all mixed up. A bit of both. Blue said Isla looked like the old Briton cunning woman who had come through the camp once, selling posies, but, she said, Isla didn't smell as bad as the cunning woman had smelled. Isla had thrown an egg at her sister for saying that, but it missed her and hit the flagstone near the door, and went everywhere, and Blue said that was bad luck, but she had laughed when she said that as if she wasn't scared of bad luck anymore.

When they'd cleared away the mess they'd made, they went to look at their reflections in the goat trough. It had been too long, Isla said, since they'd dressed up like this, too long since they had last looked at themselves.

"You've got Nonor's eyes, see," Isla said. "And her forehead. And I'm starting to look like Father. Look at my mouth." She frowned to make herself look cross.

"When you do that to your chin—see," Blue said, "you

look like Mother. Her chin used to wrinkle up just like that when she was trying not to laugh. I remember that. I think I look like Father now. One day I will grow a long beard like his. All curly and matted."

"You can't grow a beard if you're a woman."

"Who says I can't?"

"Women can't grow beards."

"Maybe in the west they can. Maybe women have wings there, too."

"Nonor would have said."

"There are lots of things that Nonor didn't know."

"And how would you know that?" Isla said. "You think you know better than Nonor now, do you?"

"There are many things, ya, that we don't even know we don't know," Blue says, making the long slow sounds that Nonor used to make, scratching her chin just like Nonor used to do.

"Will you stop with that kind of talking?" Isla says, trying not to laugh. "It makes my head hurt."

"Your face is pretty when you smile, see." Blue pointed at the trough.

"I wasn't smiling."

"You were."

Blue brought her hand down flat on the top of the water with a smack so that water splashed in Isla's face and before she had time to blink or roar, Blue ran off to hide in the clearing.

"See—you're smiling now," she called back. "I see you."

"We don't have time for this . . ."

"We don't have time for this . . ." Blue echoed back.

"Will you stop that?"
"Will you stop that?"

They had quarreled about the animals. Isla wanted to gift them to Thunor to make sure he protected them on the journey, but Blue said they'd already given Thunor the Great Smith, and that anyway it was Freja who you were supposed to gift something to before a journey. Isla said they should bury the animal bones and the rest of the good scrap metal down in the well just as Nonor had said she'd done when they'd left their farm in the Old Country. But Blue said they could leave other gifts for Freja. They didn't have to kill the animals. They should go to Cathleen. Freja liked shiny things more than she liked dead things, she said. If they spared the animals, she said, she'd dig holes around the edge of their hut and place ten of her best Sun King coins in each instead. She said that should settle things with Freja. That would be enough.

Isla wasn't sure at all, but she didn't want to upset her sister, not then, not with Father only just gone, and him taken right in the middle of making a sword like that, and not having said his goodbyes or made his peace, not with the journey that they had ahead. She and Blue would need to work together if they were going to cross the river and get to the palace. Once Blue had rounded up the chickens into baskets and fixed the old nets from the fish traps across the top to keep them safe, she packed up the old sea trunk with clothes, bread, the last of the goat's cheese and some mead, and the seeds she'd chosen from her store. On top of all the folds and tucks and layers, she had placed the sword, Jenny Greenteeth, wrapped in the length of fine blue linen Osric had sent.

Last of all, Isla used the bucket of river water to pour over the embers of the forge fire as she made her prayer to Thunor, asking him to look over the Great Smith's daughters on the river and to help them get Kin Protection. As the steam hissed from the charcoal, she was sure she could hear Father's voice still in there, muttering and roaring. When the door slammed behind her, she was sure it must have been Father, but whatever it was, she kept it to herself. There was no use letting Blue think Father was still roaming about.

Now, Old Sive's boat comes larger with each dip of his oars. Soon the old man is wading through the shallows toward them, calling out for them to fetch the Great Smith. He looks afraid, Isla thinks. And she wonders what it is that frightens him. Most times he's visited them before, he's stopped to talk, even if he has always wanted to stay in the shallows and not step ashore. Now he is keeping the second boat far out behind him, letting out and tugging at the rope to make sure it stays right out of reach.

And then Isla remembers: Thorsten and Caius went to the camp after they left the island. They must have told everyone Blue's story about the dark magic and the marsh witch. Now Old Sive doesn't want to step out of his boat onto shore because he is afraid of the island, because he is afraid of them.

"He thinks Grendel's mother is still here," she whispers to Blue. "Look what you've gone and done. Poor Uncle. He's frightened of us now."

"He's always been frightened of us," Blue says.

Old Sive had been like an uncle to them in the days when they lived in the camp. On the coldest of winter nights, Blue and Isla and the other children used to steal away to the charcoal mound to listen to his stories. The ground steamed and cracked from the heat of the fire down there, under the smoking soil and turf piled up over the slow-burning wood. It was the best of places to be on a winter's night. The children would lie alongside each other in a hollow in the warm ground like a pack of wolf cubs, and Isla, lying among them, couldn't help thinking of the fire down there underneath them, smoldering red deep in the dark soil, like the roar inside a sleeping dragon.

It had been Old Sive's job to mind the mound. Still was. The whole camp depended on him, Mother used to say, not just for the charcoal that he'd harvest, but for their lives, because if that fire broke through that mound—and it was always trying to—the dragonfire down there would shoot up in great blue shafts and set the whole wood aflame, and it would take the camp with it.

So, when Isla listened to Sive's stories as a girl, she'd also be watching out for the fire cracks in the dark of the charcoal mound, for a glimpse of the dragon's roar. And though some of the children would always fall asleep before the end of the story, with the warmth of the ground and the sound of Old Sive doing the voices of all the Seax warriors and heroes, not once did she see Sive sleep out there at his mound. Not once. He told those stories to keep himself awake.

Old Sive is the last of the camp folk they have seen for years. When he brought the charcoal and the dried meat and grain over to them on the full moon, he'd sometimes sit on the beach and tell them news of babies and quarrels, weddings and feast days, funerals and the boys from the camp who'd been lost on Osric's battlegrounds and in his hill forts.

But now he won't land on the island at all. He is too frightened.

"Father says you must leave the boat with us, Uncle," Isla begins, shouting over the wind.

"And you have to take the animals to Cathleen," Blue adds. The wind off the river is making her veil twist up behind her like smoke.

"Blue's made more salve for your swollen foot, Uncle, like the one we sent you before, the one you liked."

"That wasn't my orders," he says, slugging a drink from his flagon, still holding back, the current in the river pushing and tugging at his legs. "The Exactor said to bring this fancy boat of his to the Great Smith, not to his daughters. And I don't want your salve."

Isla's never seen Old Sive act like this.

"You have brought the Great Smith the boat, Uncle," she shouts back. "Father will make sure Lord Osric rewards you. There's not much time. Be quick. Throw me the rope. The sooner we have the boat, the sooner you can get back to Cathleen and your dinner."

Still he comes no closer.

A few feet away Blue sighs and draws herself up to her full height, putting up her arm and clicking her fingers so that Wrak flies to her hand as she has trained him to do. Old Sive cowers as the bird takes off again straight toward him.

"That there is a bird of ill omen," he says as Wrak circles above him. "Send it away." He is turning back toward the boat. "Send your devil bird away or you'll not get your boat."

"Wrak knows, Uncle," Blue calls out. "Wrak sees. He knows where Old Sive builds his mound in the clearing in the wood. Wrak sees you, Old Sive."

Wrak perches on the prow of the boat and turns his face slowly toward the old man, cawing again. Old Sive reaches for his oar and prods it toward the bird.

"Get off there. Get off."

"Keep watch," Blue calls, as Wrak lowers his head, and launches himself back into the air. "Keep watch now."

Isla splutters, quickly turning the sound into a cough. Keep watch now, these were the words the old soothsayer used to his bird in one of the sagas that Sive used to tell. Poor Sive has forgotten. Blue hasn't. Wrak takes a high branch in the lightning-struck oak at the back of the beach, and caws again loudly, *wrak-wrak*, as if to say they might all now continue. Isla thinks of all the stories she told to keep people out of Father's forge, the stories that got away from her grasp. Are they going to have to pay dues for Blue's stories now, just as they had paid for hers back in the camp? She puts the thought from her mind. Now was now. Later was later. What choice did they have?

"You're to take our animals back in your boat," Blue calls

out again, as Sive draws his boat a little closer into the shallows, hesitating still, the larger boat tugging along behind.

"Father says you are to take them to Cathleen," Isla says. "Come on now, Uncle, pass me that rope."

She slips off her sandals, hitches up her skirts and begins to wade out toward him. The river water ripples about her feet. She is glad of the cool of it in the rising heat of the day.

"No one told me nothing about that," he says, clutching the edge of his boat, still struggling to stay upright in the currents. He puts himself between Isla and the boat. She knows about the swelling in his feet, how much he hates the heat of the sun on his bald head. She knows all about his fear of leaving the mound in his son's charge for too long and about Cathleen chiding him for idling on the river. She knows he can't keep this up for long. The tide is going to turn soon. He wants to be off. But he's going to face questions back at the camp if he comes back with the Great Smith's animals. What is he going to do? He is caught between one trouble and another. Just like them. She feels bad for him.

She wades farther into the water, one slow step at a time, feeling the water soft now up around her thighs, the weight of the wet tunic. She keeps her eyes down so as not to frighten the old man into bolting.

"Keep back," he says. "Don't come any farther. Fetch your father. Damn you, girl. Stay back."

Shingle gives way to river mud, slippery against the soles of her feet. Little fishes shoal down there. She feels the current's strong pull against her knees. The tide is beginning to turn. The waves are moving both ways at once around her. Behind her is all swells and eddies over the mud beneath.

She watches him glance behind her to where the path winds uphill through first the reeds and then the trees toward the hut and forge on the mound. She turns to look where the broom fringes the edge of the dark wood. Blue stands up there now, Wrak back on her shoulder, quite still.

"Did you hear that, sister?" Blue calls, pointing toward the darkness in the hollows of the scrub behind her, her eyes wide. "Did you hear it?" When Isla turns to look, she sees her sister down on her haunches as if she is bracing herself against a blow.

"What's that?" Old Sive shouts back. "What was that? What did you hear?"

Blue is chanting words Isla can't understand, her eyes closed, arms reaching for the sky. Then, as if she has heard some new sound, she pulls her short sword from her belt and turns toward the edge of the woods, as if she is preparing to fight.

"What is it? What are you seeing up there?" Sive yells, his voice wild. He is shaking. Isla is afraid for him. "Is it her?" he says.

"It's nothing," Blue calls back, her voice cracking. "Nothing at all. It must have been the wind in the reeds. You'd best to be quick with that boat. And be careful. Don't move too fast."

"Sooner you lot are gone, the better," Sive mutters, throwing Isla the rope at last, his eyes narrow, keeping his hand on his short sword. Isla lunges for the rope, grasping it firmly in both hands.

"Dirty witches. Why don't you take your devil spirits away from this place and go? Leave us alone."

That stings. Their cousins would be better off without them. Isla knows that. She can't bear to think of it, but it is true. For five years Osric has been sending his cloth, grain and game directly across to the island, but he's also been making their cousins send a share of their food and their charcoal out to them once a month, too. Keeping the Great Smith and his daughters in food and charcoal must have been hard for them, especially through the winter months. The children will have gone hungry sometimes so that they could eat.

There'll be no going back to the camp now. She can see that. They'll be stoned if they try to beach at the bend in the creek after this. However dangerous it might be for them to go to the palace, they have to go to Osric and petition him. This new boat is their only chance.

With Blue chanting on the shingle, Isla drags the boat through the shallows and up the beach, listening to the old man's curses fade away. The boat is lighter than she expected. It slides easily over the shingle. There, she says aloud to Freja, god of edges and dawns and second chances, wiping away her tears, it's done.

"There's a bell next to the tiller," Old Sive calls out, turning for the last time. "Thorsten says your father is to ring that bell when you come within sight of the landing stage. Three rings, then silent for four counts, then three again, then stop. The bell will tell the soldiers you come with Osric's say-so. You understand?"

"Yes," Blue shouts back. "Now you must come back

ashore and load up the animals. They are to go to Cathleen."

He is silent.

"For Cathleen," she calls again.

But Sive is already back in his boat. He's taken up the oars.

"No chance," he shouts. "I'm not taking those animals of yours anywhere near the camp. And Cathleen won't want them neither."

And then he is off, rowing east with the outgoing tide toward the camp smoke rising on the other side of the creek. Soon he is no more than a speck. Isla's never seen Old Sive row so fast.

She feels a great sadness wash over her then. She and Blue are alone on the beach. The forge is closed up. Its fire is out. Father's ashes are shoaling in the river. When Blue comes to stand beside her, she slips her hand into Isla's and leans up against her, nuzzling into her shoulder.

"He wouldn't look at me," Isla says, her eyes stinging with tears. "He wouldn't even take the animals. It's like we're lepers, Blue. It's like Uncle hates us."

"Sooner you lot are gone, the better," Blue says, mimicking the sounds of Old Sive's voice. And then she says it again as if she is trying to get the patterns of Old Sive's voice better still, deeper: "Sooner you lot are gone, the better."

Isla has seen lepers on the road heading to the leper camp, their bells tolling in front of them to warn people away. She's seen the children taunting them. She always thought how cruel it was that those poor people had already lost an arm or a leg, but then they had to lose their kin as well.

Nonor, Father, Mother—all gone. Over on the other side of the creek, their cousins no longer own them as kin. The camp children would certainly stone them now if they ever approached from the river or from the road.

There is no going back. There is no staying. There is no home.

She thinks of the nettles growing tall in the herb garden, dust settling on the bottles of tinctures in Blue's still and on the tools in the forge, birds nesting in the thatch, ants stripping the last of their food, and the trees closing back in on their little island clearing.

"He called us dirty witches," she says.

Blue laughs. "Dirty witches," she echoes.

"We're without kin now, Blue. Cut off. We're all alone."

"But we are kin, Isla. You and me. We are dirty-witch kin."

"I was supposed to get you back to the camp. I promised Father I'd—"

"I had another dream last night," Blue tells her, as they heave the sea chest into the boat together.

"You and your dreams. Sometimes I wonder if you wake up at all. What did you see this time?"

"Stone walls rising above miles of reed beds, facing out to sea. Round huts built on stilts right out in the marshes, hidden in the reeds. People in them, Isla. Children."

"They must be Mother's people. The Ikeni. Mother said they lived in round huts in the marshes. But she also said the Sun Kings burned all their camps after their queen attacked their cities. She said the Sun King soldiers killed them all."

"Mother said they killed the queen, but she didn't say what happened to the queen's daughters, did she? You know: the poor girls that the Sun King soldiers raped. They might have escaped after the battle. They might have got away to the marshes. Mother had sisters, too, didn't she? Didn't she talk about her sisters? If the Ikeni were all killed, then where did Mother come from? There must be some left. We could find them. We could try."

"If there are any Ikeni left," Isla says, "they'll be slaves or married into Seax like Mother, not living in round huts on stilts in the marshes. If there was ever an Ikeni camp or a palace, it will be just a few rocks in a field by now. If we travel north out of Osric's kingdom, we'll only come into the land of a new Seax lord, or a Briton lord who might be even worse yet, and beyond that there'll be another and another. Father said all the overlords want more land now, and to get more land they have to have more soldiers and slaves to fight each other, and to get more soldiers and slaves they have to have more tithes, and so it goes on. There's no escaping it. There's no getting outside or around it."

"You sound just like Father," Blue says.

She does. She sounds just like Father.

The light is falling over the river; the geese landing their heavy bodies back onto the water ready for the night, honking and rustling up their feathers. Isla thinks of the tethered animals. Now that Sive has refused to take them, they'll have to gift them to Freja after all. They'll have to sacrifice something. Isla wonders how much luck the blood of a goat and seven chickens will get them. She reaches for the knife on her belt.

But while she has been staring out across the river, Blue has slipped the rope from the goat. She's taken the lid off the chicken basket and she's tipping the birds out, scattering them on the shingle. They strut and squawk and ruffle their feathers. Blue is clapping her hands and chasing them across the beach, whooping and flapping. Musk is already nuzzling the driftwood at the high-tide line, hunting out rotting fish. They'll never catch him again.

"What did you do that for?" Isla says. "They'll all be dead by morning. They'll be picked off by the fox or the marsh harriers. What's wrong with you?"

"They're free, Isla. Listen."

Everywhere, the birds are calling to each other, the rushes are whispering. A single nightingale begins to sing up on the mound. The two of them stand together in the dusk, listening to the birdsong, hardly breathing.

"Look," Blue says.

The moon is rising over the Ghost City. A dark shadow crosses it, a black shape against the white circle, and behind it, where the night sky is patterned just like Isla's new firetongued sword, a shooting star fires north and is gone.

"Is it a sign?" Isla says. "You were talking about the huts in the marshes and now there's the shadow on the moon and the star moving north?"

"Mother would know," Blue says. "She knew everything about what the stars mean."

"But we can't ask her what they mean anymore. And if

we don't know what the stars mean, we'll have to keep our eyes on the ground," Isla says, "so that we don't trip up."

But in the half-light Isla can see those walls in Blue's dream, clear as day, the round huts in the marshes. She can't put them out of her head. After they get Kin Protection, she is thinking now, perhaps they should go north. With Kin Protection they will be able to go anywhere. Perhaps Mother got away north, too. Perhaps she'll be waiting for them there.

On the flood tide, two days before the great spring Gathering of the Seax clans, the two daughters of the Great Smith sail the dark waters of the great river, heading east, across the creek toward Osric's beacon; not away from the eye of the storm, but straight into it. With the Great Smith dead, laws broken and secrets to keep, Isla knows they are taking a dangerous leap into the dark, but they have no choice. Osric is their only hope now. The gods have seen to that.

TWO

+

1

While Blue settles at the tiller, Isla rests the oars on the dark water, letting the tide tug the boat out into the faster current. Just a few yards from the beach, she takes one last look back to the little cluster of huts on the mound, ringed by the dark curve of oak trees. The hut all boarded up. The well closed. The animals roaming the woods. The forge fire out. Now that they are on their own out on the dark river, Isla is afraid of what lies ahead. She whispers a prayer to Freja, god of journeys and rescues, then takes a deep breath and lowers her oars into the river.

To stop the boat running aground on the mud spits that finger out from the smaller islands in the creek, Isla has told Blue to steer them directly north at first, out into the deepest currents of the night river toward the north bank. Once they are far enough away from the mudbanks, Blue is to turn the boat east, close to the walls of the Ghost City. They'll pass the gap in the wall where the Walbrook stream empties into the Great River. Only then will it be safe for them to turn back to the south bank, straight toward the fire of Osric's beacon tower and all the little lights beneath it.

Soon they are right up close to the flint stone walls of the Ghost City, closer than Isla has ever been. The walls loom above them, high and jagged and moonlit against the night sky, behind a tangled black mass of rotting wharves and jetties. All along the line of the waterfront landing stages, the remains of old barrels and broken pots lie scattered about.

At the first gate in the wall that they come to, the great doors, thick with creepers, hang creaking on broken hinges. A single swan raises its wings and hisses at them, before they glimpse another, startling white in the dark, her skirts wide over a nest built right into the broken wharf.

Soon they have reached the break in the river wall where the Walbrook stream enters the Great River. Willows and alders hang thickly over the marshy banks. A white mist hovers low over the water. Now that the stream has silted up again, it is hard to imagine that Sun King soldiers and traders ever sailed up there, as Caius had told them, taking goods to and from the north of the Ghost City. But Isla can just make out the masts of the old Sun King wrecks still moored to the rotting jetties in the distance, deep in the reed beds now.

Suddenly a wail comes from the mist upstream, a call then an answer, one from the west, then one farther north. *Piaooooow. Piaooooow.* Not quite a child's wail. Not quite a child's cry. Not quite human at all. Isla has heard those shrieks before, first in the camp and then out on the island, but always from far away, carried on the wind, always from somewhere inside the walls of the ruined city. She pulls her cloak around her. A burst of wings clips the side of her head, but it is only Wrak. He takes his perch on the front of the boat, his feathers ruffled, his eyes beadier than ever, darting in every direction. She has never been so glad to see him.

Blue points to a bull's skull hammered onto a thick wooden post sunk deep into the riverbed at the entrance to the Walbrook stream. Someone has hung bead necklaces over its horns. A bird has made a nest of leaves and moss in one of the eye sockets.

"Look," Blue says. "Someone's been here recently. See. That's a Seax bull. Look at its horns."

"That's probably been hanging there since the Sun King days," Isla says, although from the shape of its horns she can see it is a Seax bull, too, and that the glass beads, catching the light from the moon, have been strung in a Seax pattern.

"Now we're here," Blue says, "we could moor up. Go and look around. We could go on to Osric's palace at dawn tomorrow instead."

Isla shivers. "We'll lose the tide," she says. "We have to go now."

"You're scared," Blue whispers. "You are. Isla's scared."

"I'm not. It just gave me the creeps, that's all. That smell. It's horrible."

Blue turns the boat and they head south again toward the glow of Osric's beacon tower. Isla picks up pace with the oars, quick to put some distance between them and the bull's skull and the dark, mist-shrouded tributary where the air hangs thick with the smell of sulfur and rot. It still seems to linger about them even now as they reach the middle of the river, as if it has got into the boat and into their clothes and hair.

"Rest up," Blue says at last. "Look."

As they turn the bend of the riverbank, the white curve

of a torch-lit shingle beach comes into view, directly beneath
the beacon tower. Boats of all sizes, some rigged, some
upturned, lie beached just above the waterline. A walled
walkway zigzags up the mound from the beach, torches lit
at crumbling watchtowers at each corner, up to a great stone
building that looks to Isla as if it must have been a grand
Sun King villa once. Its windows glow with flickering lights.

"You ready?" Isla whispers.

Blue nods.

There is no turning back now even if they wanted to.
They've been seen. Men are shouting. A bell is clanging.
Someone has sounded an alarm. Wrak has taken flight
again, protesting.

"The signal," Isla says, remembering Old Sive's instruc-
tions. They'll soon be within reach of the soldiers' arrows.
Blue gropes about for the leather cord of the bell, but it is
dark and with the boat tipping about, the tiller abandoned,
Isla dares not pull in the oars to help her. Instead, she
sets them flat on the water. This rights the boat, gives it
some balance, but the current is pushing them nearer the
beach.

"Who are you?" a man's voice calls out. "Where are you
from? Show yourselves."

"Just ring the bell," Isla hisses to Blue. "Ring the bell.
And get down."

When a single arrow whistles past her shoulder, she
pushes Blue down into the boat and throws herself on top
of her.

"Hold back," the soldier roars to his men. "I said hold
back."

Isla prays in a whimper down there at the bottom of the boat, prays to Freja and Thunor and Tuw, all of them at once. Blue is quite still beneath her, trembling, humming one of Mother's songs.

"Show yourselves," the man shouts a second time.

Isla clutches the sides of the veering boat and peers toward the lights. A tall man stands on the beach at the water's edge a few yards away. The torchlight reflects in the metal of his helmet and breastplate, and with his visor down, Isla can see nothing of his face but the dark hollows of his eyes. He stands, feet wide, looking straight out to them. He holds his arm high in the air, a signal to the soldiers gathered behind him on the shingle and to the archers stationed at the watchtowers on the hill, bows raised. Nothing will happen while the captain holds that position. No one moves.

At last Blue finds the cord.

Three rings. Four counts. Three more rings. Then silence.

Now the captain makes some new signal. As the soldiers pass the command back from line to line, the black and flattened shapes of soldiers all along the walls lower their bows, slipping arrows back into their quivers. Isla takes a deep breath and drags Blue up from the bottom of the boat. As the captain lifts the visor of his helmet and begins wading toward them through the shallows, holding his torch high above his head, river water spraying up around him with each stride, Blue and Isla scramble back to their seats. Isla takes up the oars. The boat is still tipping in the waves and taking in water.

"Pull in your oars, damn you," the captain says, and as Isla turns toward him, she hears Blue say: "See, Caius, we've come."

2

D rop your veils and keep them down," Caius says in a low voice, as soon as he is close enough to take the rope from Isla. "Where's your father?" He peers into the shadows, expecting to see the Great Smith seated beneath the low awning.

"Father sent us," Isla stammers, "to bring the firetongued sword to . . . The gods willed it so. Thunor . . ."

"It's not safe for you here," he says, glancing over his shoulder to make sure no one can hear him. "Not now. Not after what you told Thorsten. Sweet gods, give me the firetongue and then turn this boat around and go home. Get out of here."

"We can't," Isla says. "We have to see Lord Osric tonight. We have . . . business with him. Father's business."

As another wave edges the boat closer to the beach, four soldiers carrying smoking torches, some dressed in a patchwork of Sun King armor, some with the rough helmets of Seax make, are wading through the shallows toward the tipping boat. Caius turns to face them.

"I told you to stay back," he says. "I gave an order."

"Lord Osric sent us," the man at the front says, stepping back. He points up to a group of figures standing surrounded by torches on the top of the beacon tower. "Lord Osric has sent for the Great Smith and his daughters."

"And I say you are to wait," Caius says. "I am in command of this beach. And I say you will wait until I give orders."

The soldiers withdraw back to the beach, pushing at each other to try to get a look into the darkness beneath the awning, whispering.

"What is the danger here, Captain?" she asks, trying to right herself. "You knew we were coming. You sent the boat."

"I didn't. I told Thorsten it wasn't safe for you to come here. I told him to send his soldiers to fetch the sword instead. He must have gone ahead and done it anyway. Sweet gods, Lord Sigulf, Lord of the East Canti, has arrived with his bodyguard and most of his army. There's to be a betrothal feast to seal their new alliance between Sigulf and Osric: Sigulf's daughter is to marry Osric's son. Soon scores of boats will be beaching right here, full of fighting men come to join the feasting. Don't look up at the tower. Don't. They're watching you."

"Why?"

"What did you think was going to happen here after what you told Thorsten? He's been telling stories in the Mead Hall, gilded stories, tales of marsh demons and spells and augury, each one wilder than the last."

Of course he has, Isla thinks. That's what happens when you tell wild tales. They get wilder. The stories she had told about the forge all those years ago had got away from her in just a few days. When stories get out of your hands and into the Mead Hall or down among the women at the washing brook, who is to say what they will grow into?

Blue leans forward.

"Father is dead, Captain," she says.

Her words disappear with the screech of a gull.

"Dead?" Caius is so close now that Isla can hear the leather of his armor straps creaking, see the black stubble against the brown of his skin, smell his sweat. She sits very still, her eyes full of tears. She has never felt so small.

"Father died," Blue whispers again, before Isla can stop her. "No one came. We sent him off in a boat we found in the reeds. We made a boat burning for him."

If Blue hadn't blurted out the truth at that moment Isla might have done. Suddenly she longs to tell Caius everything, to unburden herself, to tell him about the flies and the smell and the speeches they had made to see Father off. She wants to ask him if they said the right things, if he knows what Thunor's palace in the sky looks like, if it will take Father long to get there, if Nonor might be there, too, waiting for him. She is tired of keeping secrets, tired of holding her tongue. But Caius's face twists into a grimace as if he has taken a mouthful of vinegar. He recoils.

"The Great Smith is dead?" he says.

"We burned his boat, Captain," Isla says. "We burned it."

"Sweet gods. With him in it?"

"Yes."

"What possessed you? Boat burning is against the Kin Law now. Don't you know that?"

"It was my idea," Blue says before Isla can stop her. "I made my sister help me. I broke the Kin Law. Isla didn't. You have to take me to Lord Osric now. He will punish me, but he has to grant Isla Kin Protection. He must give it to her. That is the Kin Law."

"She's lying," Isla says, trying to get her hand over Blue's mouth. "It's not true. I burned the boat. Blue didn't know anything about it."

The leader of the soldiers sent by Osric, hearing their raised voices, is losing patience. He steps forward.

"Captain," he says, nodding toward his men approaching from the bottom of the walkway. "Lord Osric has sent for the Great Smith. He does not like to be kept waiting."

Caius turns to address the soldiers. "The Great Smith has not come," he says. "He is not here. He sends his daughters to Lord Osric's court in his place. They have brought the firetongued sword. Thunor has willed it. All hail great Thunor."

Isla can see the news spreading from one group of soldiers to another across the beach and up to the walkway. A messenger is making his way toward the steps leading to the beacon tower to tell Osric.

"All hail Thunor," she hears the soldiers chant.

"Say nothing," Caius hisses. "You understand? If anyone speaks to you, if anyone asks you anything, say only that you are here to bring the firetongue on your father's orders. I'll find a way to get you out. Wait for me on the beach. Keep your veils down. Say nothing."

Blue stands up in the boat, and Caius lifts her so she can wade to shore. All across the beach the heads of soldiers turn to look at her. Isla follows, scrambling clumsily over the side to wade through the shallows after them. One of the soldiers calls out something. Another starts up a quiet rhythm with a sword on a shield. When Caius leaves the two of them alone so that he can attend to the boat and their chest, the soldiers crowd in, their faces ugly in the torchlight, clambering to get a closer look. Soon the men have made a close circle around them.

"Blue," Isla hears one of them whisper, "they say she's called Blue. What kind of name is that?"

"And the other one?"

"Brown and green eyes they say."

They are engulfed so quickly, before Isla can call out for Caius, before she can gather herself, that she has no time to reach for the blade hidden in the folds of her tunic. She doesn't need to. Blue reaches up to take a torch from a soldier's hand. He gives it to her. Someone laughs and jeers. Another elbows him silent.

Blue walks right around that dark wall of soldiers, Wrak now flying in to perch on her shoulder, wings out, cawing so loud you can see his fat black tongue. Blue lifts her torch to look closely at each face, as if she is making sure to remember every one of them. Those moments are as slow as the snowmelt on the edge of a thatch, a bee drunk on its own honey, the fall of a seed head on a day without wind. One by one, as Blue passes them, muttering nonsense in one of her made-up tongues, each of those soldiers takes a few steps backward. The line recedes.

When Blue thrusts the handle of the torch deep into the shingle, her face is aflame with red and gold light. She takes Wrak from her shoulder, and, cradling him in both hands, throws him high into the air. The soldiers gasp. One man, watching the screeching bird as it disappears upward, loses his balance and staggers forward before steadying himself with his spear. Wrak does not come back.

"Didn't the Exactor say?" Isla hears one of the soldiers say as they part to let them through. "Didn't he say that they raised the marsh witch, old Jenny Greenteeth . . ."

"I heard it was Grendel's mother."

"A child has been born with two heads far north, they say, up near the wall."

"What was the young one doing with that bird? Was she sending a message? Where did it go? Where is it now?"

Isla thinks of Osric and Sigulf, the visiting lord, watching from the top of the tower, seeing their soldiers cowed and dulled, the bird circling the beach and disappearing into the darkness. Don't look up, she tells herself. Don't look up. Let them look. Let them see her.

When Isla reaches for her sister's hand as they walk up the beach together to find Caius, flanked by the soldiers, Blue's palms are wet with sweat.

"There's too many of them," Blue says, breathing heavily now.

"It's going to be all right," Isla says. "Caius will keep our secret. I'm sure of it. Tomorrow we'll see Osric. We'll tell him about Father not coming back, like we agreed. We'll ask him to help us. He's going to give us Kin Protection and a wagon, you'll see. Then we can go. We won't be here long."

"There's more coming," Blue says. "Up the river from the sea. Downriver from the west. Too many."

Isla turns to look. Storm clouds are gathering, metal gray against the black of the night sky. They have already blotted out the moon. The wind is up, bending the trees along the shore.

"It's only a storm," Isla says, as she used to whisper to Blue when the wind and rain rattled the walls of their hut in the camp at night. "It will pass." But she's seen the first of the painted sails out there, billowing tight white against the storm clouds, and rows of oars moving together, all heading toward the shingle beach and the beacon tower that is pluming black smoke and fire up behind them.

3

The prows of the first boats are already nudging up onto the shingle on the other side of the beach. Scores of soldiers, heavy with blades, shields strapped to their backs, are climbing out to wade through the shallows, pushing and heaving the heavy boats up the shingle to make room for others coming in behind. Everything is loud: the sounds of swords, armor and shields being unloaded, horses rearing as they're coaxed onto gangplanks, men calling to each other. The air smells of sweat and smoke.

"You'll be protected," Caius says when he comes to find them. "I've seen to that. Osric has given you rooms in the palace, away from prying eyes. He's posted a guard."

"You'll get us an audience?" Isla says. "Tonight?"

"One thing at a time. Let's get you out of sight first," he says, passing them a pair of soldier's cloaks to cover their tunics. "Put these on.

"Your father," he adds, his voice sad. "I had those iron blooms to show him from across the sea. I had the garnets from Saxony that he asked for, too."

"Blooms?" Isla says. "Father didn't think he'd see iron blooms again in his lifetime, not from a working mine. He thought he'd have to use re-smelted Sun King iron or poor-quality bog iron for the rest of his days. And now there's blooms from a working mine and poor Father died before he got to see them."

Isla stands too long looking out at the boats, thinking of Father's stories of the days when, back in the Old Country, a good smith could make a mountain of nails in a day using iron from blooms from one of the open Sun King mines, when you didn't have to try to work up a half-decent blade from a heap of scrap metal pulled out of Sun King ruins. But that had been in the days when the Sun Kings ran the mines, and when the Sun Kings went, their mines stood empty, and the scrub and grasslands closed over them.

When she turns, Caius and Blue are already halfway up the walkway deep in talk. She runs to catch up with them but can't get through the tide of soldiers coming from the beach. She can hear Blue calling her name. A horse has stumbled. Not knowing her for the Great Smith's daughter under her cloak, men coming up behind her shout out and jeer and shove.

"Get a move on. Move yourselves. We haven't got all night."

Above her head, four corpses hang suspended from the walkway walls, faces black and maggoty, clothes in shreds, wooden signs strung round their necks. How long, she wonders, how long before someone finds out about the boat burning or the firetongues? What if Caius is lying or breaks his word? What if Blue blurts out the truth? How long before the two of them stand in shackles listening to the roll call of their crimes while soldiers jeer and bay for punishment?

Making swords at the forge. Against nature. Forbidden.

Laying curses on the swords. Against nature. Forbidden.

Lighting a funeral pyre without a wiccan present. Against nature. Forbidden.

Lying to the lord. Against nature. Forbidden.

And after all, even if they are allowed to defend themselves, what is there to say? They've broken the Kin Law. Osric is not going to pardon two kinless women, not even the daughters of the Great Smith, for such crimes, not in front of his warlords and his war band. If Osric doesn't believe their story about Father going out to catch fish at the weirs and not coming back, or if Caius breaks his word and tells Osric about Father's death and the boat burning, then, by the next full moon, she and Blue will both be hanging up there on ropes suspended from the tower walls, bodies slashed to make the blood run, red kites, crows and buzzards fighting over their carcasses, signs around their necks. And then much worse: they'll be lingering and lost, stuck wandering the marshes or woods with all the other Unburied Ones, forever.

"Go now," Caius had said, before they came ashore. "It's not safe." And just for those few moments, sitting still in the boat, oars within reach, they could have gone, they could have handed over Jenny Greenteeth and turned the boat around, slipped back into the darkness and taken their chances upriver, but the gods cut that thread off. Right in their faces. They could have gone, and they didn't. And, Isla thinks, there's going to be some heavy dues to pay for that.

At last, Isla has pushed her way up the walkway and through the arch into the wide, walled, torchlit courtyard outside the old Sun King palace. Smoke from the campfires and the food wagons drifts in every direction, making her eyes smart. Torches flare and hiss. Boys hawking food and beer run at the heels of the soldiers, shouting in snatches of Seax and Briton and Latin and other languages she can't follow. She is relieved to see that with the hood of her cloak pulled up over her head, no one is taking any notice of her. The newly arrived soldiers behind her are too busy looking for a space to pitch a tent, or a hatch to buy mead, or a stable hand to stall their horses.

When she climbs the steps up onto the old palace walls to get a better look for Blue and Caius, it isn't the scale of the city walls over the other side of the river, closer up now, or its moonlit whiteness that makes her gasp. It is the crows. Hundreds of black shapes fly up together from the Ghost City walls like scraps of burning ash over a bonfire, a scattered squall against tonight's storm clouds, and settle back down again in a corner of the wall. The long line of wharves and waterfront are black with birds. They sit in rows, hundreds upon hundreds, still and silent, facing toward Osric's camp, as if they are waiting for something. Every now and again a few dozen scatter up into the sky and drop back one by one into place again.

"We thought we'd lost you," Blue says, climbing up behind her, her face stained with tears, Caius following. "We couldn't find you. Where did you go?"

"It's summer," Isla says, pointing toward the birds on the ruins. "Crows don't roost like that until winter. Is it the storm? Why are they doing that?"

"They are saying it's a bad omen," Caius says. "It's upset the men."

"What does it mean?"

"Crows before battle. My great-grandfather saw them gather like this once, far up north along the Great Wall. They sat in rows just like this then, too, facing toward the battlefield."

"They know," Blue says.

"I've seen them strip the bones of the fallen soldiers in a week," Caius says.

The wind whips the beacon fire into a great blue twist of flame behind them. To the north, behind the city walls, black clouds have begun to roll toward them, turning like the edge of a wave. The Plow has gone under now, and the Red Star with it.

"The Ghost City is so big," Isla says. "I had no idea how big it was."

"There are bigger ruins in the deserts of Afric," Caius says, "built by people much older than the Sun Kings. After storms, my grandfather said, great white stone palaces nudge up through the sand, statues as big as mountains, giant lions with the heads of women."

"Was it the Great Sickness?" Isla asks.

"The Great Sickness?"

"That made the Sun Kings go?"

"They had sickness enough, no doubt, in the last days," Caius tells her. "But they had other troubles too: raids and rebellions here, raids and rebellions back in Rome. My grandfather said that the Sun Kings had to give up this land and all the cities they'd built here because they couldn't hold it anymore."

"Look." Isla points to the waterfront over the river. "There's someone standing behind the wharf, just next to that winch arm. See? It looks like a boy. He must be wearing something metal. It's catching the light from the moon. Can you see?"

But the figure has already disappeared.

"No one lives in the Ghost City now," Caius says. "Osric's orders. The moonlight can play tricks on your eyes."

"It wasn't the moonlight," Isla says. "There was some-body there. I'm sure of it. There must have been thousands of people living in the city once. Where did they all go?"

"Perhaps they all turned into crows," Blue says.

"They say the Sun King emperor called all his legions back to Rome," Caius says. "They had trouble back in Rome, too. They had trouble everywhere."

"Rome?" Isla tries hard not to ask all her questions at once. "Legions? What is Rome? What are legions? What kind of trouble?"

Caius laughs. "Your father said you knew everything."

"He did?"

"My Isla, he would say. She knows everything. Ask her anything and she will give you an answer. Ask her where swallows go in winter, or why geese fly in the shape of val-leys, or where to find the best bog iron on the marsh."

"She can," Blue tells him, her eyes wide. "She does."

"I know nothing," Isla says, feeling the blood rise in her face, trying to hold back the questions that she longs to ask Caius before the doors close on them again. "I know nothing. But I want to know everything. What is Rome? What are legions? Tell me."

"Rome was the Sun Kings' home, the place of their ancestors. It was a hundred times bigger than our city. They say it stretched across seven hills."

"Can we go there?" Isla asks. "Is it far?"

Caius laughs again. He turns and points south, down past the wall of Osric's camp into the great dark forests beyond.

"If you walk south from here and keep walking for many days, you'll get to the edge of this island."

"The sea," Blue says. "Yes, yes, the sea, the sea."

"And if you row across the sea for a whole day, still heading south, you'll reach the edge of another kingdom."

"The land of the Franks." Isla remembers the drawing of the Old Country that Father made for them on the piece of old birch bark, and how cross he was when Blue painted dragons and ships and sea monsters on it. "We know that."

"If you walk for a whole summer south from that shore—" Caius says.

"A whole summer?" Blue interrupts. "How can anyone walk for a whole summer?"

"Every hour, every day, still walking south, through the Frankish Kingdom, through the Kingdom of the Great Forest People, down through Aquitanica, traveling the old Sun King roads and crossing their bridges, always toward the sun, you'll see more Sun King cities, all with stone walls and forums and amphitheaters and temples and forts. Most of them are three or four times bigger than our Ghost City, they say, all of them crumbling now. It gets hotter. As you walk from one mountain pass to another, the soil turns yellow, then black, then red, then black, then yellow, then black again. The birds are colors you can't imagine. You see animals and birds and lizards you've never seen before, white-topped mountains, valleys so hot they shimmer like shoals of silver fish. Then you come to Rome. Built on seven hills, with temples and statues the size of mountains. You can see it from miles away."

"You talk as if you've been there," Isla says. "Have you?"

"My great-grandfather was billeted in Rome before Londinium. He told stories to my grandfather. My grandfather told them to me."

"Londinium?"

"It's the name the Sun Kings gave to your Ghost City."

"Londinium," Isla says, feeling the word in her mouth. "Londinium."

Then, coming back to herself from the valleys of silver fish and the statues pushing up through sand, she goes on: "We must see Osric tonight. Before the feasts begin. Can you take us to him now?"

"You know that if you tell Osric about your father and the boat burning, he'll—"

"We're not stupid," Isla says, cutting him off. "We'll tell him that Father disappeared, that he went out to trap fish at the weirs and never came back. They'll think he drowned. He'll have to give us Kin Protection, then. He will, won't he? He has to. It's the Kin Law."

"It's hard to tell what he will do. He is not what he was. I can get you out of here but not yet. It's too dangerous. And Osric will want to see you for himself. I have to think. Talk to some people."

"We have to get Kin Protection. We won't get anywhere without it. We have to see Osric."

"And then? Where will you go?" Caius asks. "To Rome?"

"North."

"We're going north?" Blue says. "You didn't tell me that."

"We have cousins there," Isla says, trying to sound steady and sure. "With Osric's Kin Protection, we'll be safe on the road. We'll ask him for a wagon and two oxen, too. Tomorrow? We can see him tomorrow?"

"Where are these cousins of yours?"

"We don't know exactly. Blue had a dream."

"A dream? How will you find this place, then? Will you dream yourselves a set of directions for the road, too?"

"We have no kin, sir," Blue says. "You mustn't laugh at us."

"I'm sorry," Caius tells them. "Look, Osric has given you the palace rooms he picked out for your father. You'll be safe there. Now that you are here, you will have to trust me. And make sure you are ready to leave when I come for you."

"Why not tonight? Why not take us to him now?"

"He has been drinking all day. He does not keep good company. Tomorrow."

Caius leads them across the courtyard toward the beacon tower and the palace walls. They weave their way through a sea of tents and cooking fires. In one corner, a few old men are dancing to the sound of a lute. A man is trading a great pile of old Sun King cremation urns from a stall for use as cooking pots. A mangy-looking bear on a chain sways backward and forward to the sound of a drum. Chickens hang by their necks from stakes. Others squawk from covered baskets.

Soldiers cross themselves as the sisters pass, or they point, clustering in to whisper and mutter. A woman stirring a cooking pot over a fire looks up and smiles. A young woman comes to the entrance to a tent, naked to the waist, her face flushed. She stares first at them, then at the storm clouds and the row of crows gathering along the palace roof. She spits on the ground and curses. "Dirty witches," she says.

4

Richly colored rugs hang on stone walls in their new quarters, but although there are carved stools and polished furniture, a side room with low beds, and a cauldron hanging over the hearth fire, Isla has seen the metal rings bolted into the walls and deep gouge marks running the full length of the walls. Over in one corner someone has scored marks into the wall as if counting out days.

"You didn't say we'd be under armed guard," Isla whispers to Caius. "This is a prison."

"Osric's orders. He wants you protected."

"Protected? From what?"

"The soldiers are telling stories about auguries and omens, crows, screech owls and babies born with no heads.

They're drinking. It's best if you stay here, out of sight. Don't forget: you are the Great Smith's daughters. Because no one here has seen your father, only his firetongues, people picture him a hundred feet high, with wings, or with two heads, living on an island made of fire. They think he is a god. They haven't decided what you are yet."

"I saw Father touch the stars once," Blue says, settling at the table with the game board. "When we were children, looking up from his knee, he'd line up his hands with the stars. It made him look like he was a hundred feet high. But it was just a trick."

"Whalebone," Caius says when he sees Blue try out one of the gaming pieces on her teeth. "Sun King." Blue moves the pieces backward and forward on the board, white on one side, black on the other, King in the middle.

"Lord Osric's women will send someone to cook and to help with your clothes," Caius says.

"To watch us, you mean?" Isla asks. "To spy?"

"Isla," Blue says. "You sound like Father."

"Isla's right," Caius tells them. "Be careful what you say in front of Merig. Osric will question her about you."

"Why are you helping us?" Isla says. "Why put yourself in danger?"

"Your father was my friend," he says, but Isla has a feeling he's done this before. These people of his. The ones he has to talk to. Who are they?

Caius nods to the far wall where their chest has been placed on a table. "Osric sent for the firetongue," he says. "He's taken it."

"He shouldn't have done that." Isla is cross and cornered. "It wasn't his to take. What is happening here in the palace, Captain? You have to tell us, because if something happens to you, we'll have to fend for ourselves. Something's out of kilter. The soldiers are not just upset about the crows, are they? You have to tell us something."

He checks the door then takes a stool, gestures for Isla to sit.

"Osric's second wife brought a Christian priest with her when she came from Gaul," he begins.

"Everyone knows that." Blue lifts her head from the board. "They say Osric has two altars in his private temple now, an altar to the Christian god at one end, at the other a shrine to Mithras."

"Osric has bad dreams." Caius leans in and lowers his voice. "In his dreams, he drowns. One night his boat is ship-wrecked. Another night a river bursts its banks, sweeps him away. Sometimes he is locked in a tower and the water is rising. He can't get out. When he wakes from these dreams, gasping for air, he swears he will conquer all the hill forts between here and the land of the Dumnonii. He prays to Thunor and then to Christ. He calls his wiccan, then his priest, then he has them both thrown out. To secure more land, he is making alliances. Now he has arranged the biggest of all: an alliance with Sigulf of the Canti, sealed by a betrothal between Sigulf's daughter and his eldest son, Vort, so he can take more lands to the south. He doesn't trust anyone. 'The water keeps rising in my dreams, Caius,' he said to me this morning. 'Someone must want my crown.'"

"Did you say Vort?" Blue drops a gaming piece that skitters across the tiles. "His son is called Vort?"

Isla hears the catch in her sister's voice. What can Blue know about Vort? Did Father tell her more things that he didn't tell her? How many more secrets is Blue keeping to herself?

"Osric has eight sons," Caius says. "They are all dangerous. But Vort is the worst of them. He has his father's ear now. No one else is allowed in Osric's bedchamber. It was Vort's idea to make this alliance with Sigulf. Vort says Lord Sigulf hates all Christians, so he has insisted that Osric banish his priest. And now that the priest is gone, Osric's wife, the mother of his youngest son, is threatening to return to Gaul, which, of course, is what Vort has wanted all along. And every night Osric has more bad dreams. He walks the palace gardens at night rather than sleep. He has sent out men to find Crowther, the great priest of Isis, so he can ask her about these dreams of his, but no one can find her. How soon before he hears what all the soldiers are saying: that you are the sisters of Crowther's augury?"

Isla laughs. "You tell the soldiers that they've been played for fools if they think we are the women of that augury of Crowther's. We didn't come up the Great River. We crossed it. Eyes of the storm? What kind of riddle is that? It could mean anything. And anyway, no one can say what is coming for any of us. Even Crowther didn't say, did she?"

"She told him the women of fire would bring him to a new kingdom."

"See? 'Bring him to a new kingdom,'" Isla says. "What's that supposed to mean? Crowther was probably making it up to save her skin, or just making mischief."

"It's too late now." Caius lowers his voice. "Whatever Crowther might have meant by that augury of hers, no one can ask her if they can't find her. We've looked everywhere."

"How many soldiers are telling these stories?" Isla says.

"More every day. And not just here in the palace. Upstream, too, in Osric's brother's camp."

"What does that mean for us?"

"I wish I knew. Right now, those stories they're telling are like the first small flames on a dried-out heath. They might blow out. They might flare up. Depends on the way the wind blows. But I'll tell you something," he whispers, drawing in closer. "If Osric gets to hear what his soldiers are saying, even if it is just a few stories whispered in the Mead Hall, he's not going to give you Kin Protection and send you off with a wagon and a pair of oxen and a few crates of chickens."

"If he hears?"

"Vort has spies everywhere."

"What will Osric do? If he hears?"

"Call back his priest? Consult his wiccan? Go looking for Crowther? Cut the throat of an ox? Hang a few soldiers? Burn you? Who's to say? Depends if he's had any sleep. Depends on what Vort has whispered into his ear that morning. We have to get you out of the palace as soon as we can, but with Osric the way he is, we have to pick the right moment. If enough people believe that the daughters of the Great Smith are the sisters of Crowther's augury and Osric has you killed, then who knows what will happen among the Seax lords, or their men, out there across the Seax tribes of the South Lands. There'll be war."

"Ah," Isla says. "So it is not our skin that you want to save, then. You're thinking about your own skin."

"Your skin and my skin and the skins of my men."

In the Old Times after the Sun Kings left, Mother used to say, no one had minded what gods you whispered to, or what shape your shrine was, or whether you walked wither-shins for your incantations, or walked with the sun, so long as you left others to make their prayers their own way. Incomers and Outcomers and Strangers, those from north of the Rhine, those from south of the Rhine, those who spoke Seax tongues or Gaulish or Canti, Briton or Frisii, they'd lived together and farmed together. They'd gone their own ways to pray back in those days, to sacrifice, to keep the children well and the crops growing, the dead buried or burned, and the rain coming. They'd all used different charms and incantations for the leechcraft, too. And though some of the women kept their remedies and their incanta-tions secret, most exchanged them or traded them for new ones.

But once a Christian priest has made his bed in a chief's palace, Mother said, soon enough all those shrines—to Isis, Thunor, Tuw or Freja—will be smashed or burned, the heads of the statues hacked off. And when the young ones, all fire-eyed, go over to the new Christian god, with the three heads in one, the Old Ones call out in their sleep, because they know there'll be no one to talk them down into the Next World or to look after their shrine in the cemetery, keep the lamp lit, sweep off the leaves, or chase off the wild dogs. It's not the Christian priests who are the trouble, she said, or what they preach, it's the promises they make about the Next World and what they expect in return. One god only, they demand. Everything else is devil worship.

That, Isla thinks now, must be the trouble in Osric's camp just as it is across Osric's kingdom. Didn't Mother always say that when the priests come, the Old Ones grow fearful and hide their statues of the old gods beneath their floorboards, keep their prayers to themselves, close their doors on their neighbors. Not war and bloodshed, just a quiet kind of rumbling, like the fire under the charcoal mound. You have to watch and feel for it to understand it, Mother said. And no good would come of it.

5

Time was when they used to leave babies out in the woods," the old woman, Merig, tells Isla as she lifts Isla's chin to examine her eyes. "Those born with limbs missing or with witch's marks on them."

"It isn't a witch's mark." Isla pushes Merig's hand away.

"I didn't say it was, child. I'm just telling you how things used to be here with my people, before the Sun Kings came. How they used to do things. The old ways."

"The old ways aren't always the right ways," Isla says.

"They tried to do that with Isla," Blue says, throwing the dice onto the table again. "When she was born, they took her deep into the forest and left her there. But a great black bear brought her back, carried her in his mouth, put her in a pile of washing left at the brook. Not a mark left on her."

"Not a single mark?" Merig asks. "From a bear?"

"Not one," Blue says, throwing her dice again. "Not a scratch. Another seven. That's seven sevens I've thrown now, just this morning."

"Bless you and may the gods protect you," Merig says. "And may they protect me first."

As Merig busies herself with the cooking pot at the hearth, she tells them stories of cockfights and bear fights and archery competitions out in the camp and down on the shingle beach and off in the forests. There is no end to her talking. Blue sits on the floor at her feet, preparing vegetables, turning the quern, asking Merig new questions whenever she stops to take a breath. The feasts are getting bigger every day, Merig says, and the fights bloodier. She tells Blue about the geese, the gallons of mead the guests are drinking, the pies, the bread, the cheese, the wagons of firewood that Osric's soldiers are having to bring in from the woods. The palace cooks have never seen anything like it, she says. Scores of hunters have gone west to the marshes for swans and geese. Soon there'll be no firewood or geese or salmon or swans left in the whole land.

And when Isla tries to tell Merig that they don't need her to look after them, that they are not used to having people do things for them and they can wash and mend their own clothes and cook their own food and they are used to dressing their own hair for each other, Blue says: tell me about the kitchen, or tell me about the lord, or the priest, or the lord's wife, and Merig starts right up again.

The betrothal feast is to be the biggest ever seen, with music, she tells them, and roasted boar and swans, and wine imported from Gaul. The Great Smith's daughters, she says, have been given a seat just tables away from Lord Osric's table, which is the greatest of all honors.

"Once the families are joined, Lord Osric and Lord Sigulf will control all the land south of the river together." Merig's eyes shine with pride as though Osric's lands will be her lands, his glory and kingship and all his new grain stores and slave markets hers to share. She doesn't say anything about the tithes and the way the Exactor takes his dues, or Osric's dreams or Vort's plotting, or the bodies strung up high over the palace gates.

"They say," she continues, lowering her voice as if she might be overheard, "that Lord Osric has plans to take on the Dumnonii. Soon he will be king of all the lands of the Britons south of the Great Wall."

"We should never have come," Isla whispers, when Merig has slipped away back to her hut and the firelight is dancing on the painted walls above their bed.

"Do you think anyone asked Gudrun?" Blue says.

"Who?"

"The girl. Gudrun. Sigulf's daughter. The one who's getting married. Do you think they asked her if she wanted to marry Osric's son, the one they call Vort? She might not like him. He might not be kind."

"Does anyone ever ask girls like her what they think?"

"What do you mean—like her?"

"Her father's an overlord, isn't he? She has to marry who her father tells her to marry. She doesn't get to choose."

"Hengist and Horsa, the first Seax brothers, were the sons of Guictglis, and he was the son of Guicta, who was the son of Guechta, and he was the son of Vouden, son of Frealof, then Fredulf, then Gregor, then Foleguald, and then Geta," Blue says all in a rush.

"How do you remember these things?"

"Old Sive can go back and back, from one Seax king to another. But where are the women? Who is going to remember them?"

"Maybe Gudrun doesn't want to be remembered."

It is only after Blue slips into sleep that Isla remembers she'd meant to ask why Blue's face had darkened like that when Caius talked about Vort, why her voice had that catch in it, what made her drop the gaming piece. She thinks about how quiet Blue has been, and how that dark sad look is back in her eyes, but, she asks herself, just as she falls asleep, is it any wonder, now that Father is dead, now that our lives are in danger, that Blue is not herself?

6

They are woken early in the morning by the sound of a hammering at the door. A tall soldier is carrying a sick boy of about four or five winters. When Merig opens the door the soldiers on duty gesture for him to go in, glancing around to make sure he's not been seen.

"Why didn't you send for me?" Merig says. "I told you to send for me if he got any worse." She has tears in her eyes.

The boy's arm has been bandaged and hangs limp across his body. His face is red and swollen with fever. Merig puts her hand on the boy's forehead.

"My grandson," she explains. "He has a fever."

The boy turns his head slowly toward Isla, his eyes glazed and bloodshot.

"They're saying you and your sister fight with dragons," he says.

"Sometimes we do," Isla says. "But only when they take our chickens without asking. What happened to your arm?"

"Dog. Big dog. Big teeth." He bares his teeth at her, but when she laughs, he turns his head away and begins to whimper.

"Is my son going to die?" the soldier asks Isla, laying him on the trestle bed that Blue has dragged close to the hearth. "His mother died. They say your sister has the Touch. They say she can help him."

Blue strokes the boy's hair, but when the others are out of earshot she whispers to Isla that the boy's wound has turned, that she can already smell death on him. Nonor used to say that Blue could smell death before anyone else did. She'd go and sit at the feet of a dying person, like a dog. It was another of those gifts of hers.

When they first came to the island, and Isla started to work alongside Father at the forge, Blue took on Nonor's work at the still, mixing the remedies and tinctures that Nonor had taught her. Before long, if Father woke with a scratchy hot throat, Blue would have already made something for it before he got out of bed. If Isla went foraging in the hedgerows and got slashes from bramble branches all across her legs, Blue would have a salve prepared before she got home. As for wounds going over, Blue can smell them now before there is a fever or even a swelling. She says the smell comes in on the skin at the back of the neck first. Like wet leaves left in a pot outside all winter, she says, and she wrinkles up her nose as if the smell is still there. Nonor could do these things too. But Nonor is gone.

"They say you have leechcraft," the soldier says now, looking at them both.

"It's not allowed," Isla says. "You have medicine men here in the camp. Ask them."

"There was a sick boy," Merig says. "Just last week. They gave him something bad to drink. He died. If you could just . . ."

"He might have died anyway," Isla says.

"I'll need a copper kettle," Blue says. "And plants from outside the camp."

"Bless you," the soldier says.

"No one must know," Isla tells him. "No one. You must promise."

"I promise," he says. "You will help him?"

"What's your name, little one?" Blue asks. But the boy doesn't answer.

"We call him Stefan," his father answers. "Little Stefan."

When Merig lays the boy out on the bed, his face hot and red and swollen, his body shivering and his eyes rolling, they are all afraid. Isla pulls the rug up and around him, but he throws it off. And then he is quiet. Blue and Isla both know that quiet is not good.

Blue sends the boy's father back to his men. She tells him to come back in the morning, that Stefan will be safe with them. She sends Merig to fetch water from the spring—it has to be water from the spring, she says, not the well, that is important—but Merig protests, saying the spring is a long way off and with her bad leg it might take her too long to get there and back. Isla insists that she go, and says there isn't much time, and that for their leech-craft to work properly the water has to be fetched by kin, and Blue tells her to make a prayer offering at the spring and tie a piece of cloth around the nearest oak tree. Both of them want to keep her away for as long as possible. Merig runs off so quickly she forgets to lock the door behind her.

Isla looks out through that open door to the empty courtyard beyond, thinking that they could run, head away from the river and follow the paths south into the forests, but when she turns back, Blue has already unwound the muddied bandage on the boy's arm and seen the marks. It is too late. A new guard comes to take up his post, sees the door open and closes it. There is no leaving the boy once they've seen that rash. The chink in the wall has closed again.

They've cauterized before—when a wolf mauled Musk's leg—but never with a child. You never cauterize a wound unless you have to. But Blue says they have no choice. The infection is too far gone. Isla takes the boy onto her lap—he is limp, light as a feather. She soothes him while Blue cleans the wound with vinegar. She holds his shoulders and legs down while Blue brings the poker from the fire to the wound. When he screams, the boy's back arches like a sprung bow. His bloodshot eyes open for a moment and then close. His body slumps.

By the time Merig returns with the water, Blue is already binding clean linen to the salved wound. She drops her curing stone and a new sleeping draft into a cup of buttermilk and warms it in the embers of the fire.

"He'll sleep now," Isla tells Merig, after they've said the prayers and incanted the spells. "But we have to keep him here with us. To watch him. Just for a few days. Until the fever breaks."

"Bless you," Merig says.

She leaves the door ajar again behind her. Isla pulls Blue over to the doorway. They watch Merig talking to the soldiers on guard. She is sending them to fetch the boy's father. She is going with them. Now no one is guarding the door.

"I say we run now," Isla whispers. "Take a boat, then make our way to the marshes. The boy will live. We might not."

"But we have to wait," Blue says, leaning up against the doorframe and gazing out into the courtyard. "It won't be long now, see?"

The crowd of soldiers has fallen quiet, most of them turned toward the south, some of them pointing. Along the thatched ridges of the huts all around the villa, crows are gathering, coming down to land one by one, thick and silent as black snow. Four becomes six and six becomes ten.

Isla shivers. "What is it?" she says. "What can you see?" But Blue turns to go back inside to tend the boy. She says they must keep on wiping him down with cold water to break his fever. She says she didn't mean anything. She says Isla can run if she wants to but she's not going to.

Isla would have taken her turn through the first night, but Blue tells Isla to sleep. She and Merig take turns to watch and bathe him that night. Each time Isla wakes, she hears voices whispering, sees shapes flickering across the ceiling, hears the crows, always the crows, a thunder of crows.

When she wakes after a few hours, the boy has lost that swollen look. The night is silent, other than the faint sound of the guards outside the door playing dice. The boy's forehead is cool and dry. He opens his eyes, drinks a little of the water that Blue offers him, smiles a weak smile. At dawn Blue drags herself into the warm hollow Isla has left in their bed and sleeps.

Isla wakes again a few hours later, slumped on the floor next to the boy's bed, to the sound of the soldiers camped outside their door quarreling. In the gray of dawn, she hears scuffles, the sound of people pushing each other. While they are washing the boy down again, Blue says she sees a hand trying to get the shutters open on the high window.

"I'll talk to Caius," Merig says when an eye appears at the crack in the shutters. "We'll get more men on the door. They're saying you have the Touch."

"Tell her there's no magic in these potions of yours," Isla whispers to Blue. "It's just good leechcraft. Tell her."

"She won't believe me now," Blue says. "You know that."

Blue is right. It's already gone too far. If Isla had stopped to think, she might have realized that using leechcraft like this would only stoke the stories that the soldiers were telling. But she didn't stop to think. They'd only wanted to save the child.

Isla listens to the soldiers talking outside the door. The sick child, they say, has told his father he dreamed of a bird with a pig's head and eyes of different colors. The woman who tends the herb garden had described the plants that Blue sent her to find. These were no ordinary plants, she said. These were plants she'd never seen before, plants with flowers and leaves that Blue had drawn out in the sand, plants with no name.

"How could she know?" Isla hears them say. "How could the Great Smith's daughter know that the plant she wanted would be growing on that part of the old wall of the old Sun King garden, exactly in the spot where she said it would be? What kind of knowing is that?"

If Blue had let her, Isla would have told Merig and the soldiers that it was Nonor, that Nonor had taught Blue about the plants that grew back in the Old Country: where they grew, what they did if you boiled them, dried their leaves, ground them and mixed them with other leaves. There is nothing different about what Blue does, she would have said, than what your medicine men do. Nonor had learned all these things from her mother, and she'd learned them from her mother back in the Old Country. It's not magic, she'd have said. It's just that sometimes old things get forgotten and you have to find them again.

But Blue shakes her head. "Too late," she says.

Blue is right. While they are locked away, there is no stopping the stories that the women are telling in the palace kitchens, about the bird with a pig's head that the sick child saw, the strange plants that breathed fire, the copper kettle that dripped blood. The Great Smith's daughters, they say, bring children back from the dead. Soon Isla and Blue are no longer the Great Smith's daughters, they are the daughters of the Great Smith and the marsh witch that some call Jenny Greenteeth. Soon, Isla hears Merig say, a child has sworn he saw Blue fly.

7

On the night of the betrothal feast, Caius brings two men to their quarters, their faces hidden beneath their cloaks. When Caius whispers a few words to Merig, she is quick to be gone. Only when the door is locked behind her does one of the men take off his hood. He is an old man, tall and broad with a white beard plaited in the Seax way, blue-green eyes beneath heavy brows, sallow skin, dark shadows under his eyes. Except for the fact that he wears a sword in the sheath on his back, he is dressed like most of the older soldiers whom Isla has seen in the camp—a simple tunic of a rough weave, a few Sun King rings. So when Caius introduces him as Lord Osric, Isla gasps. At last. They have their audience. At last she has a chance to ask for Kin Protection. Perhaps they will be able to get away before the feast after all. Before she can take a step back, the old man takes her jaw in his huge hand and holds it fast.

"It's true, then," he says, peering closely at her eyes. "Vort, come and see."

"I don't doubt the stories, Father," the second man says. "In Afric they say purebred horses with eyes like that fetch their weight in gold."

"Blue." Isla grits her teeth. "We have visitors."

"Lord Osric the Mighty," Blue says, stepping away from the gaming board and coming to stand by her sister. "Lord Vort," she says, nodding her head.

Only now does the younger man lower his hood. He is wolfish, not like his father at all, thin-lipped with a long black beard, a deep scar beneath his right eye. He does not step forward, nor bow. As he takes in Blue, Isla watches his nostrils flare.

"You look just like your mother," he says. "You look very like her."

"You knew our mother?" Isla asks, but Blue is looking straight at Vort now, her eyes narrowed, and he at her. He tips his head at Blue in a kind of question before he turns to Isla.

"Knew your mother? Did I know your mother? Not exactly. No. Not knew her. I remember her hair. So much hair. Like the mane of a wild horse." He smiles.

Blue stiffens.

"You play?" Vort asks, smiling. He stands behind Blue now, too close, reaching over her to move the pieces idly around the board, his arm brushing Blue's shoulder, all the time his eyes on Caius. Isla can see that Vort is goading Caius, watching for a crack in his defenses. Why would he do that? And why use Blue? The room is full of storm.

"Most people play too fast, you see," Vort continues, his eyes still on Caius. "Most people are too eager to move in on the prize. They see a path. They rush it. If you wait, you win. Isn't that right, Caius?"

"I don't play."

"Caius says the two of you are not like other women," Vort says, as Osric gestures for them all to sit. "He says you have grown quite wild out on that island of yours."

"We have?" Isla feels for Blue's hand and gives it a squeeze. Not long now, she tells herself. Not long.

"You have made quite a stir among the soldiers," Vort says. "Where is this bird of yours?"

"Wrak doesn't like to be locked inside," Isla explains. "He will find us again when we are on the road."

"How do you like this old palace of ours?" Osric says. "It was one of the finest of the Sun King hill forts. Next year we'll tear it down and build a new palace in its place in the finest wood—huts and halls and temples. But for now these old walls keep out the wind well enough. How do you like all this stone?"

"I prefer to hear the wind whistling through daub and thatch, sir," Isla says.

"And you prefer flies in your thatch, too, I suppose," Vort sneers, "and mice in the grain?"

"You can't keep the flies from the thatch or the mice from the grain, sir. They'll find a way in when they want to. Stone walls don't keep flies and mice out any better than wooden walls do."

"Well said, girl," Osric says. "Well said. You like a good riddle, then?"

"I was talking about mice and flies, sir. Not riddling."

"Not quite beasts of the field, then, eh?" Vort winks at Caius.

"I did not say they were, sir," Caius says.

"Enough now," Osric says. "How old are you, girl?"

"I have twenty winters, sir. Twenty-one. I forget."

"And your sister?"

"Seventeen winters, or thereabouts."

"They're saying the young one is not quite right in the head," Vort says. "Looks that way to me."

Caius's hand is on the hilt of the sword on his belt. Isla sees Blue give him a look. It's a look that says: not here, not yet.

"They say the mother was the same. Not at all right in the head."

"I said enough," Osric tells his son. "Caius, take the younger girl for some air. We'll do our business with the older one. Make sure you guard her closely mind. We don't want her coming to any harm."

The time has come, then, Isla tells herself, rising to her full height. She must make her petition here and now, and alone. She is not ready. She has not prepared herself or thought what words she will use. But she must speak. It is their only chance. And with Blue and Caius out of hearing, she will find her way more easily.

"It's all right, Blue," Isla says, squeezing her sister's arm. "Go with Caius. This won't take long."

"Your father is getting old, lady," Osric begins when Vort has locked the door again. "He must struggle in the forge with no one to help him. It is heavy work."

"Yes, sir. But Father is the Great Smith. He does not need help."

"No strikers to carry the anvil, work the bellows, hold the clamp when he twists the molten rods. He could make more firetongues if he had strikers to help him, no?"

"Father prefers to work alone."

"And where is the Great Smith now?" Vort asks. "Caius says he is ill. You say he went out to the weirs. How can he be ill and well enough to trap fish?"

"Vort . . ." Osric puts his hand on his son's arm. "Too strong," he says. "Leave it to me," he says. But Isla can see it is too late. The sluice gate is up. There is no stopping the rush of white water now. The father cannot bridle the son. She must stand her ground.

"The trouble is, you see," Vort goes on, his mouth tight, "our soldiers, my soldiers, went out to your island this morning. They have spent all day looking for the Great Smith, down along the shore, in the huts, in the woods, at the eel and fish traps on the weirs. All day. Poor men. In this heat, too. Do you want to know what they found? Someone has closed up the well and the bee skeps, they say. Whoever left the island, they tell me, did not mean to come back. They found the remains of a goat on the shore, a chicken roosting in the woods."

"Father went out to the weirs, sir," Isla begins, making sure to keep her forge-scarred hands out of sight under her tunic.

"He went out to the weirs," Vort says. "Did you hear that, Father? What a man. He can make himself invisible, too, it seems."

"We waited for him," she says. "We looked everywhere for him, too. Everywhere. We fear, sir, that he might be drowned."

"I say you are lying," Vort says. "I say you are a liar."

"And what do you say?" Osric asks, turning to Isla. "Where is the Great Smith? What happened out there? We will take care of you here. We will keep you and your sister safe. But you have to tell us where the Great Smith is. He is an old man. He may need our help."

"We came here to ask for your Kin Protection, sir," Isla says, steeling herself. She can only get them out of this hornet's nest of a palace once she has secured Kin Protection. She must hold her ground. "Father went out," she repeats. "He didn't come back. We waited. We searched for him for days. He . . . he may be drowned, sir. He may have slipped at one of the weirs. We didn't know what to do. The Kin Law says—"

"The gall of it, Father," Vort sneers. "The girl talks of the Kin Law. If there is no Great Smith, Father, if the Great Smith has escaped, there won't be any more firetongues. If there are no more firetongues, there are no more alliances. If there are no more alliances, there will never be a kingdom."

"The Great Thunor will send us other smiths."

"There are no smiths south of the Great Wall, Father, none who can make firetongues. Believe me. We have sent out men. We have spies in the ports. There are no other Great Smiths for Thunor to send us."

"What's to be done, then?"

"If the Great Smith has escaped, if he's hiding, if someone has taken him in, he'll turn up sooner or later. No one will hide him for long. They don't dare. And when he does, we'll hunt him down with our dogs. This time we will whip him and then hamstring him properly just as we should have done from the start."

Isla flushes with rage. "Our grandfather made firetongues for the great lords of the steppes and the high kings of the Seax. Who are you to say that you will hunt Father down like a dog to be whipped and hamstrung? Be careful what you say. Thunor protects him."

She had meant to keep her hands out of sight, but anger had got the better of her. She slides them behind her back too quickly.

"Show me your hands," Vort commands.

"My hands?"

"Yes, show me your hands."

Isla holds them out. She is trembling. "They are rough hands, sir. My sister and I have no one to help us at the washing brook or to chop the firewood. I am clumsy, sir. Father says so. I am always breaking things, cutting myself."

Vort does not answer. He turns Isla's hands over. He looks at her palms. He strokes his finger slowly along the edge of a deep burn that runs like a gorge through the palm of her left hand. Vort's face is close to hers now. His eyes blaze.

"I don't see cuts here, Father," he says. "I see burns. Look for yourself. These burns are not from the hearth fire. They are from the forge. See? Your sister, too?" he says, turning back to Isla.

"No," Isla tells him. "No. Blue has never been inside the forge."

"I don't understand," Osric says, banging his fist down on the table. "What does this mean? Will someone explain what all this is about?"

"If the Great Smith escaped or drowned weeks ago, Father, then tell me: who made your new firetongue?"

"You don't mean her? This runt of a girl? How could she make a firetongue? You think the Great Smith taught her? How can that be? It is against the Kin Law." Osric looks ill. He looks like Father staggering back from the woods after drinking the mead.

"The gall, Father. I told you we should have hamstrung that man years ago."

"Father needed a striker," Isla says, cursing herself. How could she have been so careless? How could she have thought they'd get Kin Protection or that Osric would believe their story about Father's disappearance?

"Was Caius in on your little secret, too?" Vort says.

"No, sir. No one knew. We were careful."

"All five of the firetongues?" Osric says, pacing the room

now. "Every one of them? Sweet gods. What happens when Sigulf finds out we are giving him a cursed blade to celebrate his daughter's betrothal? And what about the other lords before him? What happens when they find out that we've gifted them cursed swords?"

Isla does not answer. She is watching Vort. Vort isn't pacing.

"They won't find out," Vort says slowly. "They must never find out."

"We'll have a trial," Osric says. "A hanging. When the priest returns from Gaul, we'll get him to cast out the demons in the blades. We'll explain. None of this is of our doing. We didn't know."

"We'll lose our hold on the land," Vort says.

Isla hadn't reckoned on Vort, or on Osric's bad dreams, nor on the son playing the father. And now the secret is out, and Blue is off somewhere with Caius.

"The seas are rising on us, Vort. This is what my dreams have been telling me. Didn't I say? What will we do?"

"We go on, Father. We behave as if nothing has happened. Leave everything to me. I will fix this."

"We must find Crowther. Send for Crowther. Ask her what this all means. Send the men out to look for her again. Do it now."

"Listen to me, Father. Keep your head. We don't need a soothsayer. We will go on just the same. After the feast, while everyone is sleeping off the mead, I will take this girl back to the island. I will see to it. I will personally see to it—I will make sure—that she can't escape."

"You're going to hamstring her?"

Isla gasps but she lifts her chin, fixes her eyes on a spot on the wall. She must not show her fear. She thinks of Mother with the smears of red on her face walking into the Mead Hall.

"With your permission, Father. It's the only way to be sure she doesn't escape like her father. If he is still alive and hiding out there somewhere, then once he hears what we've done, he will come for her. My soldiers will be waiting. We'll keep the younger one here with us in the palace, to make sure her sister does exactly what she is told. And you will do what you're told, won't you?" he says, his lips up close to Isla's ear. "Your sister is so very pretty. So very like your mother."

Isla nods.

"And while we wait for your father to come for you, you are going to teach two of my best young smiths how to make firetongues. When those boys have made their first sword, we'll throw a little party."

"My name is Isla," she whispers, clenching her fists. "And my sister's name is Blue."

"You breathe a word tonight, Isla," Vort says, his hot mouth up against her ear again, "and you won't have a sister to call by any name. By the time I am finished cutting the sinews in your fine legs you won't remember your own name. I can be slow. Oh, I can be very slow. You will beg."

"The women came for your sister," Caius says when he arrives later. "Osric wants her to present the sword at the feast. What happened here? Are you all right? You look sick. You didn't tell them about the boat burning?"

"No," Isla says, gathering herself. "I told them Father is drowned, just as I said I would. Osric says he will give us Kin Protection. It is done. It was easy. Where did they take Blue?"

"He told you that? They said that?"

Isla longs to tell Caius everything, about how she kept her head, how she did not beg, about how Father always said she must be careful not to burn her hands but that the poker would have hit his foot if she hadn't grabbed it that day, leaving a scar like a gully in the palm of her hand. With Blue gone, though, she is walking on blades. She has made too many mistakes. She can't make another. She needs to think. She needs to gather herself. She needs to pray.

"They are lying," Caius tells her. "Why else would they take Blue? We have to get you both out tonight, after the toasts, when the soldiers are drunk. I'll see to it."

Caius slips his short sword from his belt, the one with the carved boar's head on the handle. He places it on the table between them.

"Attach it to the back of your belt, under your cloak."

Isla reaches for it, but as soon as she has her fingers round the handle, she takes her hand away again. "Who are you? What do you want from us?" she asks again.

"I say the Great Smith's daughter, the one with the eyes like the storm, makes the finest firetongued swords in all the lands north of the Rhine. I say she's been making them for years, just as Crowther said she would. I say Vort knows that, too, now. And if I am right, and this is what has happened here tonight, I say you and your sister are in trouble and you need all the help you can get."

"Women can't work in the forge," Isla tells him, feeling the blood rise in her face, keeping her hands out of sight. "It's against the Kin Law."

"Take my blade," he says.

"If anything happens to me, will you get Blue out?" she asks. "Will you promise me that? You'll try? At least you'll try to get her somewhere safe?"

"Have you ever watched the first pieces of a midden start to slide and you know the whole pile is going to follow," Caius says, "but you can't say exactly when?"

"Don't talk in riddles. Promise me you'll get Blue out."

Now she can feel the heat of Vort's breath up against her ear again: *I can be slow. Oh, I can be very slow.* And she knows that no one will hold her head and look into her eyes as Blue had done with their first goat back in the camp when Father made them hamstring it. Caius catches her when her legs buckle. He helps her onto a stool.

"They didn't promise you Kin Protection at all, did they?" he says. "And Vort has threatened Blue, hasn't he? That's why you won't speak."

Isla takes the dagger from his hand and slips it into the pocket that Blue had sewed into her tunic on a morning that now seems like hundreds of winters ago.

"Promise me," she says. "If anything happens to me, you'll get Blue out?"

"Yes," he tells her finally, "you have my promise."

8

The hall of Osric's Sun King palace is perhaps ten times the size of a mead hall, but longer and narrower, reroofed with thatch. Laid out for the banquet, it glows with candles and wall torches. From the door, where she and Caius are standing waiting among the crush of soldiers, Isla looks for Blue but it's difficult to see anything clearly. Seax masons have hacked hearths straight into the Sun King walls. The room is full of smoke. Behind the long tables of soldiers, soot stains have almost blotted out the Sun King wall paintings. The candlelight has turned the walls to water and fire but she can just make out the old wall paintings of Sun King women running in and out of those shadows, flowers braided into their hair, flowers scattering behind them, pursued by men with dogs. In one corner a woman is turning into a tree, her arms half branches, her round mouth open in a silent scream.

Beneath those walls, hundreds of soldiers sit crammed around long tables, dogs at their feet, tables piled high with joints of meat and great plates of bread and cheese and pies, and flagons of mead and jugs of wine. Osric sits at the center of the far table, flanked by his sons, up on a raised platform. A bronze headdress covers his eyes, with the face of a horned boar rising above it. When Vort sees Caius standing at the door, he signals across to a table just to the side of the platform.

"Take my arm," Caius tells Isla. "Keep your head up. Don't show your fear."

As Isla and Caius walk down through the hall together, the men are singing on each side, banging their cups on the tables. Some of them turn their heads to stare, nudging each other—"Is that her?" "No, that's the other one."

Still there's no sign of Blue.

"Keep your wits about you," Caius says. "When things get out of hand, and they will get out of hand, you have to be ready."

"You told me Blue would be here. Where is she?"

"She's still with Merig and the other women. I've spoken to Blue. She knows what to do."

When Blue finally slips into the seat beside Isla, her hair dressed, wearing a simple dark tunic, her face is white. She reaches for Isla's hand underneath the table.

"Did they hurt you?" Isla says. "Are you all right?"

"Listen to me. We don't have long," Blue whispers. "See the painting of the girl turning into the tree on the wall up there? There's a door just to the right of it. Can you see the door?"

Isla nods, then takes a gulp of mead to steady herself.

"After I've presented the sword, a fight will break out among the soldiers. While everyone is distracted, you are going to walk to that door and wait for me just on the other side. Don't be afraid. I'll be right behind you. If I don't come, if anything happens to stop me, then you have to follow the road out of the camp and take the right fork down to the river. You mustn't look back and you mustn't wait. There's a jetty and some upturned boats. Caius has people waiting for us there. You must do what they say."

"I'm not leaving here without you."

"The right fork—do you understand?"

"The right fork. Yes."

"That road leads straight to the river. Keep going until you get to the upturned boats. Isla, what is wrong with you? Are you listening to me? Have they given you something? Isla?"

The mead must have been strong, Isla thinks, blinking. She takes another sip. First it is sweet, then it is salty. She is thirsty. She drinks again.

"I've been thinking about Caius, Blue," she says, her face hot. "How do we know we can trust him? It could be a trap. We can't make another mistake, not now."

She does not know the right path. A fog is rising. She can hear the slur in her voice, feel the slow swell of her eyelids, the great weight of her arms and legs. Blue looks down at Isla's cup. They both see the white powder staining the rim.

"They mean to do it tonight, then," Isla says.

"Do what tonight?"

Isla holds her tongue. Blue must get away even if she can't. She dares not speak. She cannot speak.

A roar goes up from the men—Isla can't hear Blue's voice anymore, though she can see her trying to say something. The men bang their fists on the table and keep on with the thumping until an old man starts to sing. His voice is beautiful, mournful. He sings of the dead on the battlefield, the sound of mothers lamenting their sons. Isla's legs are as heavy as lead. She wants to put her head on her arms and sleep. The men are calling for the sword.

Here and there beneath the scattering of straw at Isla's feet, hundreds of tiny pieces of colored stone gleam. There are pictures. A single eye stares up in one corner, and close by there is a woman's mouth. On the other side, a woman with a fish's tail swims next to what looks like a sea monster.

"Listen to me," Blue is saying. "Look at me, Isla. All you have to do is walk to that door when the fight begins. I'll meet you there. Can you do that?"

"What if they catch us? Blue? What if they catch us?" Isla can already feel the cold steel of Vort's blade against the backs of her legs. She will not beg. She must not beg.

Blue takes Isla's hand and kisses it. "Don't be afraid," she says. She kisses Isla's cheek. "Pray to Freja, Isla, and to Mother, and to Nonor. Keep praying. Make them all hear you. And be ready to run."

Merig appears and beckons Blue to an alcove in the side of the hall. Isla tries to snatch for her sister's hand, but her arms won't work. Blue is already gone.

Isla watches with a sickening feeling, her tongue thickening in her mouth, as Osric's women place a headdress of gold work on her sister's head and the cloak of seal skin and crow feathers around her shoulders. Two soldiers lower the fire-tongued sword into her hand, the one they had called Jenny Greenteeth back on the island, the one with Isla's mark on it. When Blue grasps it, raises it to her face and kisses the blade, the men cheer. One of the women leans forward to tuck a stray lock of Blue's hair back into her headdress. Another lifts her train of feathers. The feathers are flickering gold and black.

As Vort begins his speech about the Great Smith and how the new sword will bless the union of Seax tribes, and how the blood it spills will cleanse the soil of the new kingdom, Isla watches Blue taking her first slow steps toward the raised table, toward the men with their horned head-dresses. All Isla can do is watch.

"Soon they'll show us Gudrun," Merig is saying, slipping into the seat next to her. "Soon they'll unveil her. They say she is very young."

Isla sees the two soldiers who have been posted to watch her. She looks over at Caius on the other side of the room. He is staring down between the rows of soldiers. His brow is furrowed. He is watching Blue start her slow procession. He is expecting trouble. He is braced for it. She must be ready to run. She must try to run.

As Blue, sword in hand, reaches the middle of the room, flanked by Osric's women, Vort glances over to where Isla is half slumped over the table. One of his bodyguards has made a joke. He is laughing. They are raising their tankards in her direction.

Blue is standing at the long high table now, piled high with pies and roast swans and roast boar and flagons of mead, sword raised in her hand. Osric turns to smile at his son, delighted to see the Great Smith's daughter in the gleaming black feathers, making her tribute, presenting the sword that he has waited so long for. He claps Vort on the back again, and the men begin to cheer.

But now something is burning. The thatch is on fire. There are men shouting. Tables are turning. Dogs are bark-ing. And though Isla still feels her legs heavy as lead beneath her, she knows she has to move them. She knows she has to get to that door.

As Isla lurches and stumbles closer to the tree girl, the girl's arms seem to stretch wider still, all leaves and scrub and red and dripping branches stretching around the room and to the door beyond. As she and Blue run, hands in each other's hands, Isla sees the colors of the Sun King hall smear and twist. She sees Blue shaking off her cloak, the feathers long streaks of gold and silver as they fall.

Outside at last, Isla and Blue begin to run into the rain-soaked darkness, toward the road, through the low, scratchy scrub. At last Isla feels the cold and the wet and the soak of the rain bringing her back to herself. But soon they both hear the sound of the thunder of horse's hooves behind them.

"I said you'd give us sport tonight," Vort yells from his saddle, cutting them off from the road, his eyes red from the hunt. "Caius is right. You girls have run wild. Just like your mother did. Oh joy. You thought you'd take our firetongue too. Silly girls. Silly, silly girls. What were you thinking?"

He grabs Blue's hair from his saddle. She has the sword out of its sheath. Then he's off his horse, twisting Blue's arm up behind her back. She is cursing. He is trying to wrestle the firetongue from her hands, but she won't let it go. Then Wrak appears out of the inky darkness, cawing. He is beating the air around Vort, lunging for his eyes, all feathers and slashing beak on Vort's face and hair. At last Blue has pulled herself free and she still has the sword. She is running into the shadows beyond the trees.

"Isla, this way!" Blue is shouting. "Isla, run. Where are you?"

But Isla cannot move. She cannot speak. Her legs, her tongue, have turned to stone. The air is thick with feathers ahead. Vort has the bird in his hands. He has his bleeding hands around Wrak's neck. He is looking straight at her. He twists. Then Wrak is still. Slumped. When she looks into the rain and the feathers there are men everywhere, men with nets. Torches. Dogs. Mouths. Noise. There is nowhere to run.

"Hold her still, boys," she hears Vort shouting as she hits the ground. "You know how this goes. When was the last time we had ourselves a little hamstringing?"

Isla's on all fours now. She's whimpering, but the sound is coming from somewhere else. Vort is pulling up her tunic. She can feel the cold tip of his sword running up her legs. Then she sees him step back to sharpen the blade on his whetstone. "First things first, eh?" he says.

But when she glances sideways, bracing herself, the men are falling back.

First there's the sound of a blade passing through air, then a single cry, a sound from the battlefield, and then a thud. When Isla turns again, Vort is falling to his knees, his mouth open in a silent O. He is cradling his arm. His white tunic and his face are spattered with blood, the whetstone and the blade are in the leaves and there's something else down there too, something twitching. It's his hand. Blue has cut off his hand.

None of those soldiers step forward to help him. They are all watching Blue. Blue with Jenny Greenteeth. Blue slashing the air with the sword. Blue growling like a wolf under her mane of hair.

"Now, Isla," she says. "Get up."

Blue's hand is back in Isla's. Isla's hand is back in Blue's. Blue is carrying the limp bird wrapped in her cloak. She has the firetongue. She has Jenny Greenteeth. They are running, Blue wrenching her on. Isla can feel her hands and feet now as she lumbers, although the dark forest is still swirling and shoaling and smearing around her. Her tongue is swollen. She can taste blood.

"Kill the young one!" Vort is howling at his men. "Catch me the older one. Catch her. Use the nets. And someone get me a fucking horse."

Blue and Isla are gone, up the road, running toward the bridgehead, running for what feels like forever, through the rain, Isla's legs like wood or stone beneath her, down that old Sun King road. The furrows in the stone made by the old cart tracks are turning to rivers of rainwater under their feet. They scramble over the rotting carcasses of old Sun King carts that block the road, over the trunks of fallen trees, until they are scratched and bleeding and soaked to the skin. The sound of the hunting dogs is growing louder all the time behind them.

"Where is this jetty?" Isla yells, her tongue free at last, when the road comes to a fork and they stop to catch their breath. "How are we supposed to find it in the dark? Can't we hide somewhere? I can't run any farther. I just can't. I can't see. I'm going to be sick."

"The dogs have our scent now," Blue says, tucking the dead bird more closely into her cloak. "We have to keep going, Isla. It's not far now."

Blue's rain-soaked tunic is brown-dark with bloodstains. The braids of her hair, loosed from the pinned coil, snake across her face.

"I promised Father I'd get Kin Protection for you," Isla

sobs. "I tried. Why is Thunor so angry with us? Why won't he leave us alone?"

She can't go on.

"Forget Thunor," Blue says. "Just run. Keep running. It's not far now."

"I promised Nonor I'd look after you."

"I'm not a child anymore. You don't have to look after me. See. There are the upturned boats, Isla. See? We must be nearly there."

Isla can just make out the shapes of Sun King boat hulls in the dark scrub, now mostly rotted away, piled up in a clearing in the trees.

"Caius said there'd be people here waiting for us," Blue says. "He said."

"And I said we shouldn't trust him. We should never have trusted him," Isla wails.

"There must be a path here somewhere. He said there'd be a path."

"Go." Isla struggles to catch her breath. "You go on. You go. Leave me here. Let me sleep."

"Get up." Blue grabs Isla's arm roughly. "Get up."

Isla follows Blue down a paved path she's found between the boats, a track wide enough for a cart, but now overgrown. The track leads down to the river, past the remains of burned-out stone buildings, to an old waterfront. There's a girl, her face smeared with mud so she can't be seen in the darkness, next to a boat pushed out into the shallows, cradling a pair of oars.

"You took your time," the girl says.

Behind her, in the moonlight, the wooden Sun King

bridge arches right across the river to the walls of the Ghost City on the north bank, its posts, the trunks of ancient trees, holding their place in the rushing storm-wild water.

"You've brought friends, then," she says, nodding toward the sound of the dogs barking in the darkness behind them. "What happened? What did you do to bring down this much trouble? Can you run?" They are desperate. They have no choice, Isla thinks. They have to trust her.

"What do you think we've been doing?" Isla says, clasping her side and struggling to catch her breath. "Where are we supposed to run to now?"

A line of torches is fringing the jetty along the shoreline path from the west. There is shouting. Osric's men are all around them now, in front and behind. Isla sees the first of the dogs in the torchlight as it lurches from the trees, leashed, its jaws slavering. She sees the men with their nets.

"The bridgehead!" the girl shouts. "We have to get to the bridgehead. This way."

Blue and Isla follow her through the undergrowth back up onto the road, scrambling between charred stone buildings, mud and reeds, soaked to the skin as the rain grows heavier yet. And before Isla has a chance to protest, they've followed her out through the stone gateway and bridgehead right out onto the half-rotten boards of the bridge that span the dark water below, disappearing into the gate of the Ghost City on the other side. The three of them run on, leaping the holes and the broken planks, the swollen river rushing below their feet, Blue still clasping Wrak's limp body and dragging the firetongued sword. But when the soldiers reach the stone arch behind them, they stop.

"Why have they stopped?" Isla says, gasping for breath.

"They're afraid," the girl says. "They think the bridge gate marks the opening to the land of the dead. No Seax soldier or mercenary will cross that threshold. They can't. We've made sure of that. They won't cross it. Trust me. Come on."

"Fuck you, daughter of the devil," one of the soldiers calls out after her from the crowd gathered at the bridge-head gate. "You'll wish we had caught and killed you soon enough. You'll be begging for it. Begging."

There is a roar of laughter and another volley of insults.

"What did you and your sister do?" the girl asks again. "What did you do to bring down this much trouble?"

When Isla turns, she sees Blue with her arms up to the blood moon, her face lit, her eyes closed, holding up the firetongue with one hand and clasping the bird to her chest. It looks for all the world to Isla as if Blue is playing some game in the woods again, not just about to die in the middle of a bridge in a storm. But none of those men are jeering anymore. None of them can take their eyes off Blue, holding up that blade to the gods.

9

Nonor used to say that a new moon changes things. You can't be sure what kind of change is going to come, she'd say, but you can be certain things won't be the same afterward, as sure as night follows day. It has been a new moon and a red moon all in one tonight. It brought the storm in, made fire branches of the sky, a sea from the river, a waterfall from the crows, and brought Thunor up and out with all his weapons at once.

Isla, Blue, and the girl are halfway across the bridge when the arrows start to whip through the air past them, thudding into the wood on either side, or arcing down into the river. All those winters ago, the Sun Kings had built their bridge wide enough for two carts to pass each other, but now the walls are long gone and the whole structure is no more than a heap of wet and half-rotten timbers over the water to the gate into the Ghost City. It is not safe. Nothing is safe. After what Blue has just done to Vort nothing will ever be safe again.

The girl runs on ahead, her clothes soaked through, leaping across holes and missing planks, never falling or slipping. Isla and Blue come up behind, Blue just ahead, trying to follow the path the girl has taken and keep hold of Isla's hand at the same time, the sword strapped into the back of her belt. The planks thud and judder beneath them. The river is a long way below, the sky black with thunder and then white with forked lightning, and the red eye of the moon is sailing in and out of cracks in the sky.

"Don't look down," Blue yells, when Isla jerks to a stop to peer through the gaps in the planks. Blue tries to haul her forward, but Isla can't move.

"Just don't look," Blue says, but Isla has seen the corpses down there, face up and arms out, twisting and spinning about in the brown current, some wedged between great uprooted trees.

"You can't stop now," the girl shouts. "We're almost there. Come on."

Then a thud and a howl of pain. The girl is down on her knees, her head tipped back and howling like a wolf, an arrow in the upper part of her arm, blood pouring from the wound. Behind them the soldiers are cheering. They think they've got her. They think she's done for.

But she gets back up, ties her belt tight above the wound, snaps the shaft right away from the arrowhead, all the time cursing like Isla has never heard anyone curse before. By the time they've got close enough to help her, the wind gusts up and wrenches off the whole of the middle section of the bridge just a few feet ahead of where they are standing, twisting the planks high into the air and down into the water, leaving only a jagged edge hanging right out over the swirling brown river below. More cheers go up behind them. They're trapped.

Now, Isla thinks, none of us can go on.

But there's nothing for it. The girl shouts "jump," and without thinking, they jump. Off the bridge into air. Into wind and rain. Into the hurly-burly. Legs flailing, the girl baying and whooping.

They hit the water. First Blue, then the girl, then Isla.

All that noise—the thunder, the crows, the soldiers behind them—stops. There is only the rushing of water. Isla's ears pound with the cold shock of it, down, and down more, until she thinks she must have crossed into the Next World, that this is the end, that she's crossed the line.

But she isn't going to let Thunor take Blue. He's going to have to take her first if he wants Blue. Blue hasn't done anything. She's the one who made the firetongues. She's the one who broke the Kin Law. Thunor must take her, not Blue. But where is Blue?

When she surfaces and takes her first gasps of air, the posts of the Sun King bridge are still towering up out of the dark. They are still holding their own in the wild and brimming water. She is not dead, then. The walls of the Ghost City are still up there ahead. The wharves, gleaming in lightning flashes, are now only a few hundred yards away. Whatever Thunor is up to, whatever is going on up there that is making him so cruel and wild and vengeful, the Fates are still shuttling Isla backward and forward on their loom. And, she remembers, nothing is written in stone. Take me, she shouts to Thunor. Just be done with it. If you have to take your dues, take me, but leave my sister alone. She hasn't done anything. I made the swords. Take me.

Isla gets her arm over the trunk of a birch tree wedged near one of the bridge posts. She catches her breath, shivering and spitting out river water, before she starts looking around for signs of Blue and the girl. But there is no one to be seen. There's nothing but trees and branches and broken pieces of Seax boats and fish traps spinning past her. It is darker and wetter than she ever remembers a night being. The world has turned to dark water and broken wood, rain slanting in sideways in slashes, waves rolling and gusting in every direction.

She scrambles up onto the ledge beneath the nearest bridge post, thinking she'll see more from higher up, but there's so much storm debris gathering there—sticks and broken trees and branches, the bloated carcass of a dog—she's afraid she'll get trapped. There's no use in shouting. The wind is too high and blowing in the wrong direction. The arrows have stopped. The men are gone. They must think the three of them have died in the storm river. Peeling off her wet tunic down to her shift, she ties the clothes into a bundle on her back with her belt and slips back into the water to swim the last hundred yards to the foreshore of the Ghost City.

Each time another wave nearly takes her under, each time the sleep rises on her, Isla makes herself picture Blue safe with the girl, inside the Ghost City, up there ahead on firm ground. They will have made a shelter from old bits of wood. They will have lit a fire. There'll be steam rising off their wet clothes, meat turning on a spit. And somewhere just beyond the fire there'll be that arched gate she saw in the river wall, the one with the doors hanging off their hinges. As soon as the storm is over, Isla promises herself now to keep herself going; once they've all had some sleep and dried off their clothes, she'll get the girl to take her inside, to have a look around. They won't stay long. As soon as they've gathered themselves, she and Blue will get on the road. They'll get far away from Osric and his soldiers and find a place to hide. But first they must say a prayer for poor Wrak and bury him deep in the dark earth.

But she's so tired. Mother is waiting, and Nonor. In the Next World. Where it is bright and there are no shadows. Just as sleep is closing over her, as she shuts her eyes against the night, she pictures Blue again, Blue crouched over a pile of earth in the night wood, dirt under her fingernails, her face white in the moonlight. "Leave that thing alone," Isla is saying to her. "Just leave it alone."

She does not want to see that thing in the leaves and the mud. She must not see it. She forces her eyes open again and lets out a howl.

Someone is calling from a mass of stormwood gathering ahead between her and the wharves.

"Over here!"

It comes a second time.

"Help me. Give me your arm." It isn't Blue. It's not her voice.

It's the girl, one arm up, struggling to stay afloat in the middle of a great mess of wood and fences that's turning in the storm currents near the wall. Her face is badly cut. She's going under.

It doesn't take Isla long to swim to her. The fence panel is strong, woven with thick enough hazel to bear the girl's weight, but not for long. It's already getting caught up in another tangle of stormwood. She's going to get washed away any moment or crushed. Isla won't let the river spirits take the girl either. Or let Thunor have her.

"Don't fight them," Nonor used to say. "Just wait and see what the gods want from you. Do what they want. Always do what they want."

Isla is done with waiting to find out what the gods want. She is done with petitioning and prayers and offerings. She is done with the gods. She will never pray again.

"Let go!" she shouts at the girl in the water, once she's

got her arm around her waist and the other over the trunk of a heavy tree. "Put your arm around my shoulder. I'll take your weight."

"They must have tipped the arrow with poison," the girl says. "I can't feel this arm at all. I can't breathe."

"You're nearly there. Don't give up now. Talk to me. Stay awake. If I can stay awake, you can. What do they call you? Tell me your name." But the girl's eyes are beginning to roll. Isla wrenches the log free from the rest of the storm wreckage and pushes out with her legs toward the wall of black wood at the waterfront.

"Just hold on. Keep your head up."

Soon Isla has got the tree trunk with the girl still slumped across it right up against the dark mass of the wall of wood that fronts the river at the foreshore under the Ghost City walls. She's wedged the tree into a gap between several broken stumps of wood. It is cold. Something horrible, a stoat, a river rat, scurries across one of the cross-beams, so close Isla can see its nose twitch and its tail thrash. It leaves a smear of oily color behind it.

With the girl's head down like that, her forehead pressed up against the wet bark, Isla can't see if she's still breathing. She can't get a grip on anything. Every time she tries to clamber up onto a cross-beam, her hands are so stiff from the cold that she slips straight back into the water. Just as she decides to push them both back into the river and float them downstream to take their chances out there, the girl stutters: "No, no—it's there—there's a door—just below the winch arm."

But Isla can't see a door or a winch arm. It is too dark.

She is about to give up, her hands torn and bleeding with splinters from the wood and covered in green-black slime, sleep rising on her again, when she sees a glint of light through a chink in the wood, hears faint voices shouting from the other side. A panel, no bigger than a large door just above the waterline, cranks open and then, in the darkness and the rain, arms are reaching out for her.

THREE

✝

1

Isla slips in and out of sleep and wake like there's no edge to them. One moment she's close to waking, then she's swimming through dripping, scratchy undergrowth, looking for Blue. She can see her sister ahead sometimes, beckoning, her face like the moon through clouds, blood smeared across her cheeks, but she keeps on disappearing again behind the trees. Then Blue is crouched down over a mound of earth digging with her bare hands and Isla is saying: "Come away from that thing. Leave it alone." She can smell the smoldering timber of the camp. Blue's face turns, her eyes wet, and she's saying: "The foxes have got to her, Isla."

"What did you do?" the girl is shouting somewhere. "What did you do? What did you do to bring down this much trouble?"

Let me wake up back in the Old Times, Isla whispers to Nonor, keeping her eyes closed against whatever terror might be on the other side of sleep. Let me wake up back in the before: Father hammering in the forge, the sound of the geese down on the shingle beach. Then everything will be right side up again. There will be the chickens to feed, and water to be fetched, and breakfast to be eaten and Blue will be baking the bread.

But what about the girl?

Perhaps she was just one of Nonor's river spirits, come to fetch us for not paying our dues. Or a banshee. Maybe she was a banshee.

She wasn't a banshee.

But if we wake up back in the forge again, Isla, Blue is saying, then Father will still be roaring and clouting, and we'll still be feeling sad.

Isla shakes her head, trying to make the voices disappear, but they don't.

There's no going back. The forge island is a great river's roar and a burning boat away.

Have you gone and lost your sister again, child?

There'll be wolves out there, Nonor, and holes to fall down and snakes and broken stone and tree roots to trip over. Don't make me go looking for Blue again. I don't want to.

Just get on your feet and go and find her, child.

I'm not a child anymore. And I don't want to keep going out to find Blue. Someone else can go this time. Someone else can help. I'm not going back into that night. I am not going into the wood. You can't make me.

"Isla," Blue whispers, "you're talking in your sleep again."

When Isla opens her eyes, there's a nightingale sitting on the painted branch of a painted tree on a wall a few inches from her face. On every side there are birds:

nightingales and egrets, robins and starlings. When she gasps, she sees them all take off into the air in a great clatter-burst of wings. It's only when she's sick over the side of the bed into a bucket standing on the tiled floor that the room comes right side up again and the birds stop flying about.

"You'll have to clear that up," Blue says. "You can't leave it there. They won't like that."

Isla turns herself over onto her back slowly, toward Blue's voice. Her body aches. She's hot. Her head is sore. Everything from her fingers to her eyelids feels heavy like she's still underwater. As she turns, the room turns with her in great smears of dragged color.

"Where are we now?" Isla asks. Blue pulls the rug up over their heads.

"I don't know," she tells her sister. "It's a hut made of stone."

Isla slips the rug down and peers out. They are lying on a low bed pushed up against the wall of a high-domed stone room, dusty and dappled with light from high windows.

"It's a Sun King building," Isla says, blinking. "We're inside the Ghost City, Blue. Inside. First we were in the river. Now we're in the Ghost City. How long have I been asleep?"

"The birds," Blue says. "How did they make them look so real?"

Blue points out chiffchaffs and robins and willow war-blers and blackbirds and herons. The plaster has faded and flaked and fallen off here and there in great chunks, but it's still beautiful.

"Is that a tree?" Isla says, looking up into branches under

the dome of the roof. "It can't be real—look, it's growing right up through the hole in the roof."

"It's an oak. I can see it, too. And if we can both see it, then it must be real."

Someone seems to have patched the roof-hole around the top of the trunk with thatch and then pulled sailcloth over that, but the thatch has fallen away and the sailcloth must have come loose in the storm. It's flapping about in the wind.

"What was I saying?" Isla says. "In my sleep?"

"Don't make me go," Blue repeats, turning onto her belly to mimic the sound of Isla's voice. "Don't make me go, Nonor. There are spiders out there."

Isla laughs. "Stop it," she says. "You're mean."

"Are we dead, Isla?" Blue whispers, pulling the rug back over their heads. "Do you think we died in the river? Is this, you know . . . ?"

"No, it's not bright enough. Nonor said the Next World would be bright and very white. That's how you'll know, she said. There'll be no shadows. This place has shadows, see? And I don't think they'd have trees growing through their roofs. And we'd know, wouldn't we? We'd know if we were dead. What is that horrible smell? I think I'm going to be sick again."

They sit up.

Over in one corner a huge stone water trough, built into the wall, big enough to stand up in, carved with leaves and creatures—half man, half goat—spills over with rotted leaves, brackish water and mud.

With the lower windows boarded up, the light pierces

the room in shafts. Swallows dip in and out through the hole in the roof, between wreaths of dusty cobwebs, to nests they've built high in the rafters. The tiled floor is littered with fragments of glass, broken Sun King bottles and cups, feathers and twigs fallen from nests.

"I must have dropped the firetongue," Blue says. "I lost Wrak too," she adds, covering her face with her hands. "I lost him in the river. I couldn't swim and hold him at the same time. I had to let the sword go first, and then Wrak. His wings fanned right out in the water, like this, wider and wider, as if he was flying, and then I couldn't see him anymore. Caius said you don't need to bury birds. He said they fly to the Next World. Do you think that's true?"

"Caius? When did you speak to Caius? Was it a dream?"

"He pulled me out of the river last night. He had a boat."

"Where is he now, then? If he pulled you out of the river, where is he?"

"I don't know. I was so cold, Isla, even after he wrapped me in his cloak on the boat. I kept falling asleep. Wake up, Blue, he kept saying. Tell me what happened to Isla. Tell me what happened back there. I tried to speak but I couldn't. I was so cold. Then I woke up here. Isla, we have to pray."

"You can pray," Isla says, remembering the promise she'd made in the river never to pray again. "You'll do it better than me."

Nonor always did the praying in their hut. Nonor always knew what to say and which god to say it to. She'd pray before eating, pray before sleeping. She'd pray during a full moon, when the seeds went into the ground, and when the last sheaf of barley or rye or wheat came up out of the fields.

Great Thunor, thank you for the blessing of the new fire-tongue. Gracious Tuw, thank you for this day and for the food in our bowls. Sweet Freja, thank you for the safe return of the men from the hunt, for the rain on the fields. And all the time Nonor was praying, Isla would be looking down at the food and wondering how much more there would be to be thankful for.

After Nonor died, although Isla had tried to remember the kinds of things she'd heard her say, she could never be sure if the gods were listening. And when you don't think they're listening, it's hard to speak to them in a way that sounds like you mean it. They always know, Nonor had said, when you don't mean it.

Isla won't pray again. She's done with the gods. All of them. Thunor and Tuw and Freja, all of them with their tricks and broken promises. She won't let them get away with any of their cruel games again. She'll be on her guard.

"We are alive, great Freja, goddess of journeys and rescues and second chances," Blue says, "and the storm has passed. Thank you for making everything stop turning. Thank you for dry and for Caius and for Senna. We send you Wrak. He was a brave and noble bird, the finest of all crows. He—"

"Good," Isla says. "That's good. That's enough, I think. Who is Senna?"

"You know," Blue tells her. "The girl on the bridge. Where did they put our clothes?" Blue is down on her knees, looking under the bed. Someone has dressed them in tunics stitched from something that feels like sailcloth, tunics held up by their own brooches, and gray leggings. Blue finds two pairs of old boots under the bed, hobnails on the soles and the leather rubbed thick and shiny.

"Sun King," Blue says, pulling the smaller pair on and threading through the straps. "Soldiers' boots. Creaky. Listen to that, Isla. That's good leather. Decent boots at last. Not like the leaky ones that Osric used to send us."

But when Isla wakes up again, she is on the floor, her head cradled in Blue's lap.

"You stood up too fast," Blue says, stroking her hair, "and then you fell down. Stay where you are now. Don't get up."

The strange cries that come from the Ghost City—*piaooooow, piaooooow*—are louder and closer now than Isla's ever heard them before. The night keeps coming back to her in splinters: the men in the wood with nets and dogs, the white hand in the leaves all bloody and twitching, Vort clutching his arm, his howl: *kill the young one, catch me the older one*—the water, the girl's head down, the whispering voices of women, the sound of her own voice wailing.

"Vort," she says, trying to blink fast enough for the room to stop moving.

"Yes, Vort." Blue nudges the rolled-up rug under Isla's head before easing on the second boot. "He must have put something in your drink last night. It's probably henbane. We need to get you water. Lots of water. Stay where you are. Don't get up, I said. Not yet. I'll take a look around."

"Be careful," Isla says, as she hears Blue moving about in another room.

"There's two more rooms out here," Blue calls out. "Both of them stacked with barrels and wooden crates right up to the ceiling. And there's a big entrance door. But it won't open. I can see crossbars on the other side through the crack. Looks like we're locked in."

Isla can hear the sound of Blue pushing and shoving, groaning and cursing. Who would have locked them in? And why? Have they escaped Vort and his men only to find themselves in even more danger? What might Thunor have in store for them now?

Blue comes back cradling something in her hands, thick and shiny black as charcoal. "Most of the barrels in there are full of nails," she says. "Thousands of them. See?"

"They're Sun King nails," Isla says, sitting up slowly. "Look at the shape of them." The henbane is making the nails crawl around in her sister's hands like beetles. "How long before this wears off?" She shakes her head. "Can't you give me something?"

"Do you remember the day Caius brought the nails for Father?" Blue asks, her face all lit up, laying the nails out on the tiles.

Isla remembers. Once Caius unloaded that boatload of iron for Father, he called her and Blue over to the woodshed to show them the nails.

"Feel the weight of them," he said, shaking the bucket. "That's good iron in there. You don't see many Sun King nails around these days. They're hard to come by now. Take a good look."

"Where do they come from?" Isla asked. "Where did you get them?"

"Osric's salvagers go into the Sun King ruins," he said. "First they pull out all the doors and furniture they can find. Then they make a great pile of the wood and burn it. After a day or so, when the embers have cooled right down, they sieve through the ash for the nails. Thought you might want to see some."

"Are they from the Ghost City?" Isla asked, glancing across the river to the walls, and Caius laughed.

"No. No one's allowed inside the Ghost City walls now," he said, "not even Osric's men. There's a law. It's too dangerous. People have gone missing. There's sickness and curses in there, they say."

"Some say ghosts," Blue added, her eyes wide.

"Some say, indeed," Caius said, glancing at Blue, a tremble around his lips—as if he'd been about to say something more, Isla thought for a moment, but had stopped himself.

"No," he said, "these nails are from the small Sun King ruins out in the woods and along the old roads. Osric has them all fenced and ditched off now. Only his salvagers are allowed to work them."

"Why does Osric get to have all the scrap?" Blue said. Isla elbowed her, but it was too late. The words were out.

Caius gave Blue a look then, full of mischief. "Be careful what you say," he warned. "Questions like that will get you into trouble. Lord Osric gets to have all the scrap because he can trace his kinline back through Hengist and Horsa to the mighty Thunor himself."

"We know," Blue said. "Oh, we know all that. This land is Osric's kingdom now. All the way from the river, west to the mountains, south to the hills, east to the sea. Osric the Great, Osric the Mighty, Osric the Almost-a-God. Ya. Ya. Ya."

Isla, her heart thumping, had grabbed her sister's hand and lugged her right across the yard to the hut. But when she turned to look back, Caius was standing there, leaning against the woodshed watching them, a smile wide on his face. Isla had wondered then about how a man might say one thing and his face say something else. And now she's wondering how much more he might have been keeping to himself all this time. After all, if he thinks the Ghost City is out of bounds and dangerous, why did he bring Blue here after he had rescued her from the river?

Now Blue is climbing up onto the old stone trough, to see if they can get out through one of the windows. She is putting her face up close to a crack she's found in the boards.

"Can you see anything?" Isla asks.

"There's some kind of a garden out there. And on the other side of the garden, there's this long stone building with a porch. Lanterns hanging all along the edge of it. Rugs and stools scattered about. Looms up against the walls. Loom weights hanging from the rafters. There's a row of Sun King carved heads arranged on the top of pots all along the edge of the porch. They're all upside down. There's a white cat curled up asleep on the steps. It's twitching its tail."

"What about people? Can you see any people?"

"No people."

Blue climbs down again and finds a metal pole to lever off a piece of the boarding. Once she is back up on the trough, she smashes the pane of glass on the other side, knocking out the whole panel. Isla winces at the clatter she's making.

"Can't you be quieter? They might hear you."

"You ready?" Blue asks, hauling Isla to her feet, hitching up her tunic and tucking it into her belt. "I'll go first. It's not far to jump. Just climb onto this crate first. Then onto the trough. Slowly. Here. I'll help you. Don't go falling down again. And watch your ankles when you jump."

Isla follows Blue, landing in a patch of nettles. Her sister is already down on all fours, slipping through the long grasses ahead toward the porch, keeping low and out of sight. Isla watches her creep up the steps on her hands and knees. There's cuckoo spittle clinging to her legs. The white cat lifts its head, blinks and yawns. Now Blue is edging through the leaned-up looms, under the stone loom weights swinging in the sun.

The bright sunlight is making Isla dizzy. By the time she lowers herself down onto one of the piles of bedding on the porch, she can feel sleep rising up on her again like water across the mudflats. There is no stopping it.

When she wakes again, it is dusk. The light has gone all silver. The colors have bled out. The white cat is gone from the step. The crows are up scattering about, and the moon is rising. The domed building that they've escaped from— hours or days or years before—is bathed in silver light across the other side of the courtyard, the oak tree sticking right up and out of the broken tiles of the roof against the moon. A barn owl, sitting at the top of the tree, its shape black in the moonlight, unfurls its wings and takes off into the night.

Whispers. There are whispers.

On the edge of the porch steps a few feet away, Blue is sitting next to a tall man. His shoulder is against hers, hers against his. There is no space between them. They are whispering. Now Blue is laughing at something he has just said. He offers her his cloak and she lets him drape it around her.

"You frightened me when I pulled you out of the river," he says. "I thought I'd never get you warm."

"Who's that?" Isla says, her voice croaky with sleep. "Blue—who are you talking to? Who is that?"

"You're awake, then," the man says, turning. "Didn't think I'd see the three of you alive again after that mad jump from the bridge. What were you thinking?"

"It's Caius, Isla," Blue says, coming to sit at Isla's knee and passing her a cup of water. "I found him asleep in one of the rooms up there. He did get me out of the river. See. It wasn't a dream."

"What are you doing in the Ghost City?" Isla asks him. "You said it was against the law. You said no one was allowed in here."

"The others are up mending one of the causeways that went down in the storm," Caius says. "They'll be back tomorrow. I made stew. And there's fresh water from the spring. I'll fetch you some."

"The others?" Isla asks. "What others? You said . . . Why did they lock us in?"

"They didn't want you going wandering off. You need to stay here until I can get you out. It's the only place you'll be safe after what Blue did to Vort back there."

Now Isla remembers the blood, the white hand, the sharply severed edge of it, the blood pulsing out of the veins and into the leaves, the way it twitched. She thinks she might be sick again. "Did Blue?" she says. "Vort? Did she really . . ."

"Yes," he says, running his fingers over the stubble on his chin. "She did. With one blow, too. Took his whole hand off." Isla can see the look on Vort's face, the O of his mouth.

"He was going to hurt Isla," Blue tells Caius. "Someone had to stop him."

"I know," Caius says. "Believe me, if I'd been there, I'd have done it or tried to. A moment later and he'd have hamstrung her. A single blow. I've seen that on the battlefield, but a woman with a firetongued sword . . . That sword is heavy."

"And now?" Isla tries to get to her feet, hearing the howl of Vort's voice from the wood again, the horror of it, remembering the feel of the tip of his sword running up the back of her leg. "Where is Vort now?"

"Don't try to get up," Caius says. "You're not well. The soldiers have gone back to the palace because they're too frightened to enter the ruins. You must wait here until I come for you. Your trouble is our trouble now, so you have to wait for me here. Do you understand? It might be days. It might be weeks. But you'll be safe here. No one comes inside the city walls anymore. They've seen to that."

"He . . ." Isla's words keep slipping into dark holes. "Vort. He was . . ."

"I know. But he can't hurt you anymore, Isla," Caius says. "Not here. None of the soldiers will come in here."

"If you give us a wagon," she says, "then we can go tonight. Then, once we are gone, our trouble won't be your trouble anymore."

When Caius laughs it has a darkness in it. "Osric's soldiers will be on horseback crashing through all the camps upriver and down, searching every grain store, every last hut and woodshed. They've got dogs. Even if you get through one of the gates without anyone seeing you, you won't get far along any of the roads. No one in the camps will hide you now. No one will risk it. And you are not going anywhere. Look at you. You need to rest."

"How long will you stay?" Blue says. She puts her hand on Caius's for a moment, and then, seeing Isla's expression, she takes it back.

"I can't stay," he says. "I have to go back. Otherwise people may suspect that I know where you are."

Isla sees the tremble in Blue's hand, the heat in her face, the look she gives him. She's seen that look before: on the night that Caius had stayed on the forge island to see the star storm. At the fire, under the great starbursts of the night sky, Caius had told Father one of his ancestor stories about the horses and the race through the desert and about the white mare that wouldn't be tamed. Blue sat still then, as if turned to stone, staring at Caius, her eyes full of fire.

Not Caius, Isla whispers to Nonor. Don't let him be the one to snare Blue's heart. A captain in Osric's army? After what Blue has just done to Vort? That would be salt-in-a-wound cruel. So cruel only Thunor could have conjured it.

2

Isla has seen Sun King ruins before, back in the days before Osric fenced and ditched them all off, before he set his soldiers to guard them, back when she was a child living in the camp. She and her cousin Godric found one crumbling in a forest, covered in ivy, another near the crossing place of two Sun King roads, a long way outside the Ghost City. But none of the buildings she's ever seen before have had more than a wall or two left, perhaps a broken statue, some carvings. People in the nearby Seax and Briton camps had always hacked and dragged or carted away the stone to make hearths or pens for their animals. She's never seen any Sun King ruins with the whole of the walls still standing and the roof still on, not until Osric's palace, all patched up with wood and thatch.

And now, sitting here on the porch, she can see stone and flint walls in every direction. There are the remains of rotting wooden buildings dotted among the stone ones, but most of the still-standing walls are stone. Some of the walls are patched with daub, others are green with moss and plants, others interlaced with layers of red-mud tiles. The Sun Kings, she thinks, must have used a whole mountain of stone to build this city of theirs.

She had asked the peddler once, long ago, back in the days of the camp, why the Sun Kings had built their houses in stone, not in wood, like the Seax and the Britons did. He had taken his cap off and scratched his head.

"It must have been so much work," she said, "to cut all that stone out of the mountains and hills and carry it on wagons and boats. Even when you got it where you wanted it, you'd have to chisel it to the right shape and then mortar it into walls or into roads. Why didn't they just use wood like we do? There's so much of it. All you have to do is cut it down. And it doesn't crack. And it's easy to mend and patch."

The peddler said it was a riddle to him, too, and that maybe it was just what their ancestors had taught them to do and they'd just gone on doing it.

"Were they giants?" she had asked. "Some people say the Sun Kings were giants."

He laughed. "If they were giants, they'd have built their doorways higher, wouldn't they? Otherwise they'd have been banging their heads all the time."

"Maybe they could turn themselves into giants when they wanted to."

"Maybe they could."

The peddler told her about the Great Wall that the Sun Kings had built to keep out the Painted People from the north. It stretched, he said, from one sea to another, across whole river valleys and mountains. It was a wonder, he said. A sight to behold. He'd met a man once who had walked along part of it. Or so the man said. People like to tell stories, he added. You can't always believe what people say.

"But that great wall of theirs didn't work," she said. "It didn't stop the Painted People, did it? They could just get in their boats and sail right round it. You can't build a wall across the sea."

"They built roads and walls and bridges across anything."

"But why? Why did they want to do that?"

The peddler shrugged and reached for Isla's mead jar, saying all her questions were making him thirsty, but she snatched it back, nodding at him to go on.

"They had slaves," he told her. "Thousands of them. They could make them build anything they liked. When their slaves broke or died, they buried them by the side of roads, and went and bought hundreds of new ones, or captured them."

And when Isla asked what the Sun Kings bought the new slaves with, and what they might have traded for a man and a shovel, and how they slept at night treating people like that, the peddler told her about the coins.

"The Sun King emperors used coins like promises," he said. "The soldiers took the coins to the markets. They exchanged them for bread or boots or chickens or for women or slaves."

"But why?"

"Why what?"

"Why didn't they just exchange one real thing for another real thing, like we do? Like four bolts of cloth for a handcart. Like six eggs for ten cabbages. Why bother with the coins?"

And the peddler said little girls shouldn't ask so many questions because they made an old peddler tired and thirsty. And Isla stomped off to the woodshed and closed the door, taking the mead jar with her so the peddler couldn't have it.

She laughs in her sleep, remembering how cross she had been, and wakes herself with her laughing.

+ + +

Now she is still sitting on a pile of bedding on the Sun King porch, her back leaning up against the wall, but Blue and Caius have gone. They've pulled a rug over her, tucked it around her, like she's an Old One. They've left her the water jug and a covered bowl of stew, but she's still too sick to eat. They've gone off together alone.

Caius. Blue's hand hovering above his. The tremble on it. Her blush.

Go and find your sister, child. You can't let her go off alone, not now.

But she's not alone now, is she? She's with him.

Isla's on her feet and shuffling down the porch like an Old One.

Blue, we have to go now, she's saying. *We have to go before they come back. For the sweet gods' sake, where have you gone off to now?*

Inside the first door off the long porch, rush beds make a half-circle around a domed furnace built of baked mud and tiles. Inside, the logs are still smoldering. Boxes and baskets lie open on some of the pillows. Combs, pairs of tweezers, small glass bottles, ribbons, knives and hairpins spill and scatter across the floor.

People have slept here. Seven or eight of them. Maybe more. They've drawn pictures on the walls: runes, and birds, and five-pointed stars, and a woman with a bird's head.

Blue—this isn't a game. Come out now.

In a side room, the embers of a cooking fire still glow on a raised platform of tiles. Sun King pots stand in rows along shelves, most cracked and repaired, alongside chipped glassware, lamps and a few wooden plates. In the warmth of the room, the drying herbs hanging from the rafters give off a bittersweet smell, mixed with the scent of hung meat and woodsmoke. It's the smell of the Mead Hall and the hearth, Mother's clothes, Nonor laughing. Isla puts the neck of the jar to her mouth and drinks all of the mead in it, spilling most of it down her tunic. Thinking they'll need food for the road, she refills the jar and stoppers it, wraps up a couple of loaves, a dried ham and a cheese from the cold room, as well as some candles and a flint, stuffs it all into a sack and slings it across her back.

Aside from the cooking room and the furnace room with the beds, most of the other rooms off that long corridor are stacked with crates and barrels and sacks. Whatever this fine stone house had been built for in its first days, now it is being used as a storehouse for scrap metal. Isla has never seen so much Sun King metal, nor so many kinds. If only Father could be there to see it. He would smile and rub his hands together at the thought of all the things they'd be able to make from it once they'd smelted it down. But Father isn't there to see it. There is no one but Isla to see it.

Blue. We have to get away before we lose the light. Stop playing games now.

The next door opens onto a room that looks like a forest with the sun setting behind it, stacked vertically with waterpipes and gutters. Carved chests full of buckles, brooches and bracelets, another with grates, grilles and hooks; boxes of hinges, boxes of iron clamps, door and shutter handles, a cupboard for spoons, pot stands and bucket fittings, one for field tools, scythes, hooks and hoes. In the last room there are fifteen lead window frames, two of them complete with glass, and a pile of dead pigeons.

Blue. You have to see this.

Where the narrow corridor turns a corner into the north wing, the high stone walls have buckled inward as if a giant has been pushing up against them from the other side. Someone has shored up the walls with some of the old lead pipes, but where the props meet the wall, brown peaty water is leaking through the cracks, flowing down through bright green moss and black mold into pools between the floor tiles. That wall isn't going to hold out much longer.

Opposite the buckled, swollen wall, hidden behind a pile of broken window frames, there's one last door. There are no more inside places to look for Blue now. She must be behind that door.

Blue. It's Isla. It's me.

Is that someone whispering?

Isla puts her hand to the back of her neck where something cold and wet has dripped and run there, but her hand is dry. She counts backward, makes herself think of the Mead Hall and the women laughing.

Keep counting, she tells herself.

She remembers telling Blue once, when they first went out to explore the old Sun King hulk on the mudflats, that there was no such thing as lingerers. And Blue said she should be careful what she said out loud like that. There were Unburied Ones everywhere, she said, not just inside the walls of the Ghost City, or in the woods or in the Sun King wrecks, but everywhere and always. Mother said it, too. She was always siding with Blue. Isla told them both she'd never believe they were there until she'd seen one of the Unburied Ones with her own eyes.

"You'll never see anything, Isla," Mother said, "until you stop rushing and clattering about all the time."

She remembers Mother saying that the Unburied Ones were always about us. "Briton, Seax, Gaulish, Afric and Sun King," she said. "All living together. Just like people did in the days before the Seax warlords came, before people started digging ditches and building fences, and asking where you were born and who your people were and which gods you prayed to. Some of the Unburied Ones speak in languages that no one understands. Some are white-skinned with yellow hair, some have brown hair and skin. And some of them have beautiful eyes like yours, Isla, with different colors. You have to listen if you want to hear them."

"But I don't want to," she had said, pressing her hands to her ears. "I don't want to hear them."

Isla remembers the way Blue starts sometimes, or shivers, or tilts her head to one side to listen, always keeping very still.

"Don't you feel it?" Blue had said the day they swam out to the old Sun King wreck and clambered down into the hold. "Can't you feel the air stirring? Don't you see anything?" And when Isla shook her head, Blue shrugged her shoulders as if there was something wrong with Isla that she couldn't hear them.

"Sailors," Blue said.

"I don't like it," Isla told Blue, as the wreck leaned in the shift of the tide. "I don't want to hear them. I won't. What do they want with us, anyway?"

"They're just watching," Blue said. "They like to watch. We make them laugh."

It made Isla shiver to think of the Unburied Ones so close, just out of sight, on the Sun King hulk, behind the trees, hiding in the huts and mead halls, everywhere, all the time, laughing and pointing at the living people. It wasn't respectful. Knowing the gods were watching from somewhere was bad enough, but we must be walking through the Unburied Ones all the time, she thought. We must be brushing right past them. She didn't like to think about that. It wasn't right for them to be watching, seeing everything the alive people did, all the private things, the blood between her thighs, her hands under the covers, her squatting over the cesspit. Some things were just not other people's business to see.

"It's rude to stare," she said.

If it was up to her, Blue had muttered, the Unburied Ones could stare all they liked. And Isla said it was a good thing that it wasn't up to Blue because then everything everywhere would be completely wrong side up and inside out.

Once Isla has got the last little door open, the first thing she sees in the half-light, pushed up against the far wall of the tiny side room, is a white marble table, its base carved in the shape of a cat. On that table a single carved hand, the height of a small child, glows white in the half-darkness, its fingers pointing upward as if the person who had once owned it had been in the middle of a speech or petitioning a crowd.

"Sweet gods, don't wake me yet if I am dreaming," she says aloud, just as Nonor always used to say when she saw something strange or beautiful. She turns slowly around on the spot. Arranged on shelves round every one of those four walls are scores of hands, hands hacksawed or axed from Sun King statues, some as tiny as an acorn, in gold, in bronze, in iron and marble, others several feet high. Hands suspended from the ceiling on threads. Hands pointing, clasped or beckoning. Hands in marble, or in wood or in metal. Some several times life size, others so small you could put them in your pocket.

She slumps down in a corner with her head up against the wall. There are no more doors to open and Blue is off somewhere with Caius again when they should be heading north.

You've had the stuffing knocked right out of you, girl, Nonor would have said, and Isla knows, as she feels the sleep rise on her again, that she has never understood what that feels like until now.

3

There you are."

When Isla's eyes grow accustomed to the light, she can see that the tall, dark-skinned woman standing in the doorway is the girl from the bridge. It's morning and that must mean another whole night has gone, another night wasted when she and Blue could have been heading north.

The girl from the river, it seems, isn't much older than she is. She's dressed in dark green thick-weave wool with a gold torc at her neck, a sword on her belt and a woven basket on her back. She seems to have no wounds. How long can it have been? How long has she been asleep this time? Long enough for wounds to heal?

"Don't get up," the girl says, carefully easing the basket off her back and placing it over in a corner. "You gave us a fright."

"You locked us in. No one came."

"You broke the glass. You didn't need to break the glass. That's good glass."

"We broke the glass because no one came."

The girl laughs. "See, it's a riddle," she says. Round and round and no way out."

"It's not a riddle, it's true."

"They call me Senna," she says. She's standing near the door as if she thinks Isla might bolt like a frightened animal.

"I know. I'm Isla."

"Your sister told me your name. It's a good name. I see you found my collection. What do you think?" She gestures at the shelves. "One hundred and seven hands at the last count."

"Where's Blue?" Isla asks.

"With Caius. They're out looking for you. You gave them a fright wandering off like that. These were my first," she says, pointing to a row of three tiny white hands on a shelf. "I dug them out of the mud in one of the ditches up near the forum. Then the others started bringing me the hands they found. Anyway, Olga's cooking. There's bread and the rest of yesterday's meat. Are you hungry? You must be hungry."

Senna helps her to her feet and onto the stool.

"My head hurts," Isla says, slumping down. "I can hardly see. And I keep falling asleep. What's wrong with me?"

"It's probably the henbane. But it might have been nightshade. Nightshade lasts longer. He likes nightshade."

"Who does?"

"Vort. He likes to use nightshade before a hunt. It slows his prey. Prisoners. Escaped slaves. Poachers. He's not choosy. First, he'll use the nightshade to confuse them, then he gets them to run. Caius says it was different with you. He says Vort had a hamstringing planned for you, but you got away because of your sister. Are you all right? He didn't hurt you?"

There's a cry from the basket in the corner, soft like a kittiwake. It makes Isla jump.

"Is there something alive in there?"

"Certainly is." Senna lifts a swaddled bundle out of the basket, pushes aside the edge of the cloth to show Isla the baby's face. "We found him a few nights ago in a covered basket left at the east gate. A wagon train must have gone through last night. We thought he was dead. So little. Red hair, too. Blue eyes. You should see his fingers. It's my turn to mind him."

Now Isla is certain she must be among night witches, perhaps even the Strix themselves. Didn't Old Sive say that the Strix live in the Ghost City, feed on stolen babies, and fly through the woods at night? Turn into moths? Or is it mayflies? Or was it the banshees who turn into mayflies? She can't remember how the story goes anymore. Perhaps Caius is a Strix, too, in disguise. And Blue is out there somewhere with them, with *him*.

The Strix are clever, child, she can hear Nonor saying, wagging her finger; they are clever and ugly. You be careful out there. But Senna isn't ugly. Senna is beautiful. There's a sheen on her skin that glows even in the thin light of the morning.

"Your eyes," Senna says, leaning in closer. "Were they always, are they . . . ?"

"Yes, always," Isla says, opening her eyes wide, her face hot. "Born that way."

"They're different colors. I knew that. But there's this gold ring round the black bit when the sunlight catches—" She blushes. "What was I saying?"

"The wagons. You were talking about the wagons."

"Yes, oh yes," Senna says, climbing up onto a stool to peer out through the high window as the light turns from thin rose to gold. "Some nights the Briton wagons pass right by the east gate. The mothers know we'll take the babies. They know it's their best chance. Trouble is, the wolves know where to look now, too. We have to check every day when there's wagons going through. We have to get to them first. As if we don't have enough to do."

"How . . . many?" Isla's words are still slipping down holes. They won't hold.

"Babies? Five this last summer. When the camps move,

they go quickly. It used to be the sickness driving people west, but these days, with all the blood feuds, it's usually a raid or a warband that they're running from. There isn't room on the wagons for everyone. Poor people have to make hard choices."

"Where are they all going?"

"Most of them are heading west, looking for land they can farm that way without being tithed to death by over-lords like Osric. Crowther says she's seen more wagons on the road this spring than ever before. She says it's the young Briton boy over to the west, the one who won the battle against your people. People are heading out to join him. She says whether those boy soldiers are Seax, Briton, Jutish or Canti, they're all the same once they've got themselves a sword, a warband and a blood feud. Some of your people are the worst, she says. Your people want to own every last hedgerow and hill fort and field, like you'll never feel safe until you've got your names on everything, ditches dug, fences up and soldiers everywhere."

"Crowther?" Can she be still dreaming? Isla wonders. How can this woman know Crowther the old soothsayer? How can she have spoken to her? Can she be talking about a different Crowther? Someone named after the Old One?

"Crowther says your people came here because the sea rose up and took your huts and your fields. Is that true?"

"People here," Isla says, "talk about our people as if we are all the same, think the same thoughts, speak the same language, pray to the same gods, but we're not. It all depends what part of the old Seax lands you come from.

"The Rage," she adds, remembering Nonor's stories of

the flooded fields and farms, the coastal camps that had all disappeared into the sea. "My people call it The Rage."

"Crowther says we'd have gone looking for new land to farm, too, if we'd been Seax and lost everything to the seas and rivers and storms like that. She says we can't throw stones."

Isla remembers Nonor's story about a Seax man who climbed to the top of a mill to escape the floodwater. When he got there, he found a hundred rats up there, too. A hundred hungry rats. He carried the scars of those bite marks for the rest of his life. You never forget the floodwater, Nonor said. The smell of it. The rot it leaves behind. It stays in your clothes forever. It gets into your dreams. You dream of drowning. You keep on dreaming of drowning.

"Do you keep them?" Isla asks. "The Briton babies?"

"No. We've got too many of our own mouths to feed. Crowther sends word out and women from the Seax camps upriver, the women who have lost babies and the ones who can't have babies, they row downriver in the night. They take the babies back with them and raise them as their own."

Isla can't help herself. "I thought you were dead," she tells Senna. She wants to cry.

"Crowther thought so too." Senna throws back her cloak to show Isla her bandaged shoulder. "But see—Olga healed me."

"Do you mean Crowther the soothsayer? How can Crowther be here?"

"She lives here. Always has. Not all the time though. Sometimes she disappears, goes off. But she always comes back."

Now Isla is sure she is dreaming. "Where are we?" she says.

"We call it the Rookery. Used to be the finest brothel in Londinium. The whole west side of the Ghost City is ours now, from the Walbrook stream to the east wall."

"A brothel?" Isla remembers Mother talking about a brothel. She had once lived in one. Isla remembers her talking in her blank-eyed way about a stone cell, a wall, a high window, a chafing bed, guards at the door, a cesspit overflowing. Isla remembers running her fingers over the marks of Mother's thrall, the scars of the whip on her back. Nonor used to say that Mother made up those stories about the brothel, though Isla never understood why anyone would want to do that.

"Women, mostly," Senna says. "Boys on feast days."

"Poor people."

"Oh, the Rookery women were free to come and go wherever they liked, wear what they liked, turn men away if they wanted. Now, some of us live and sleep down in the east wing, some in the west. We've got most of it watertight, and it's close to the river. We've patched up a few of the outbuildings to make workshops. We've even got a fermenting hut now. I'll show you, once you've eaten. If Crowther says I can."

"I saw a boy on the waterfront a few days ago," Isla says. "He looked like he was dressed in metal. Is he one of yours?"

"That's Gregor. My brother. That armor of his catches the light—I've told him so many times that he'll give us away one day, but he won't be told anymore, not by me anyway. Why do you call your sister Blue? That's not a Seax name, is it?"

"Father named her after the color that the forge fire takes on when it's got the heart in it, where the metal starts to change its shape."

"Good name for the daughter of a Great Smith," Senna says, handing Isla the swaddled child. "Take him for a moment—I have something to give you."

"I can't." Isla tries to protest, but it's too late. It has been a long time since she's seen or held a baby. This one has hair that is red as a fox. When the milk smell of him rises up to her, and the child opens his eyes and looks straight at her, she starts to cry.

"Your sister should have killed that monster Vort, not just maimed him," Senna says, climbing onto a stool so she can reach the top shelf. "You should hear the stories that the Strangers tell about him. When he'd finished with one woman, he left her remains hanging from the trees. Osric used to rein him in, Caius says. But not anymore."

She reaches to the back of the shelf. "Aha. Here it is."

She uncurls Isla's fingers and places a tiny child's fist made of polished gold in her palm, a ring on its finger mounted with a fleck of a ruby no bigger than the dot of a distant star.

"I can pick you another if you don't like it," she says. "I found it in a ditch outside the temple on the Walbrook. Those ditches are full of Sun King treasures. I've never seen so much coming up on the spade. You dig out one ditch and you just find another. We've pulled out plates, earrings, swords, bracelets and coins in the black silt up there, some of them solid gold, too. It just keeps on coming up. I can take you. Show you?" Her eyes are wide. "You wash the soil

through the net in the river and it's thick—thick—with gold
and silver and jewels." She pauses. "I'm talking too much,
aren't I? I do that when I'm nervous. Do you like it? The
hand? It's gold. Solid. All the way through—feel the weight
of it."

Isla tries to pass the tiny hand back to her, but Senna
shakes her head.

"No, no, it's for you to keep. You saved me from the river.
I'm indebted to you—beholden, tied, obliged; something
like that. It'll bring you luck. And me, too. Take it. You have
to. It's a Rookery rule."

"You'd have done the same for me," Isla says, watching
Senna threading the eye on the back of the gold hand onto
a thin strip of leather. "You don't have to give me anything."

"It's not a gift. It's part of our Kin Law. It will bring both
of us good fortune. See, there, it's done. The knot's made.
You can wear it as an amulet. Keep it on your belt."

Senna puts the baby back into the basket and ties the
ring onto Isla's belt. As she fumbles with the knot, Isla
breathes in the smell of woodsmoke and scented oils on
Senna's hair, sees the berry flush of a birthmark under her
ear, the down on her cheek where the sun falls.

Then Senna is swinging herself down into the hole in
the floor, in the corner, in the gap between the barrels of
scrap metal. She disappears right down into one of the Sun
King under-rooms.

"What are you doing now?" Isla calls to her.

"Checking the flues," Senna calls back, her voice muf-
fled. "After the storm. It's my turn."

"Why did the Sun Kings build stilts like that under their

floors? Why would they do that? I've seen it in one of the other Sun King ruins."

There are so many questions Isla wants to ask. She is afraid that once she starts, she'll never stop. But she and Blue can't stay to ask questions. They mustn't stay. There's no time. They have to get on the road. She'll have to bite her tongue.

"Oh, they're not stilts," Senna says with a smile in her voice. "The Sun Kings piped in hot air down here to make the floors warm. We tried it a few years ago—lit the furnaces, rigged up some bellows—but the pipes are all broken now. The frost gets in and cracks them. We just smoked ourselves out. Just think: those Sun Kings made their slaves sit outside in the rain and the snow, day and night, stoking the furnaces to keep those fires going all through the winter, so they could walk across a warm floor with bare feet. Little precious darlings. They didn't like the cold."

"I don't like the cold. I hate the cold," Isla tells her.

"That's why we blocked up the flues in here," Senna says from somewhere under the floor, "to keep out the drafts and the rain and the hillwash. But after a storm, some of them open up again. These stone buildings. They're so much work. Every year we have to patch and shore up the walls and roofs. There's no end to it. The north wall is breaking up now, too, and if we don't do something it will collapse completely and bury all the scrap we've collected. We are starting to find hiding places for some of it—the silver and the gold—in case we need to leave quickly."

"How many of you are there?"

"Now? Hard to say. About twenty of us grew up here, raised by Crowther and the Old Ones."

"Twenty?" How could twenty people be living in the ruins? What did they live on? Isla's head is buzzing like a bee skep. Everyone had told her the Ghost City was empty.

"Then there are the Strangers," Senna adds, raising her voice over the sound of her hammer on the pipes. "Some stay. Most of them are just passing through. Sometimes the cooking pot feeds twenty and sometimes as many as thirty or forty. We've got chickens, goats, pigs and cows, looms, querns, everything we need. We trade our scrap for everything else we need at the night markets just outside the east gate, or with Caius."

"But Caius said no one was allowed in the Ghost City. He said Osric made a law."

"He did. Doesn't stop the Strangers, though. Not when they need help or shelter or leechcraft. They're not going to ask Osric for permission, are they? Not when it's usually Vort's men they're running from. They need refuge. We give them refuge."

"Where do they come from?" Isla says.

"The Strangers?" Senna's head appears from a hole in the far corner of the room, cobwebs and dust in her hair. She leans her head on the edge of the hole thoughtfully. "All over. Most of them come off the Briton wagons heading north or west: Briton women, too old or too young or too sick for the wagons. Widows with children. Girls running from a forced marriage. Lepers. Pregnant women. A few have escaped from the slave market. Some have crawled away from a night raid or one of Vort's night hunts. There's Olga. Her mother was Magyr and her father Afric. When her husband died, the Briton and Seax people in her camp blamed her for all the bad things that happened, because she didn't speak Seax properly, and because she looked different from them. When the chief's son died, they said she was a Strix. In the end they dug a pit for her, told her they were going to bury her alive and that, when she was dead, they'd dig her back up and cut off her head to stop the bad spirits she'd brought with her from across the sea."

"Scapegoat," Isla says, remembering Father's words.

"What's that?" Senna ducks back down under the floor. "What did you say? Scape what?"

"Scapegoat. You put all the bad luck in the village into one goat and then you drive it out or you kill it."

"Yes. That's it. They say poor Olga just turned and ran. And she kept on running until she got here. Didn't speak for weeks. When Olga was well enough again, and had got her voice back, Crowther put her in charge of the cooking, and after a while she decided to stay. Now she's running the place. You should see the leechcraft she makes out in the barns. Pass me that wadding. Next to the basket."

But Isla feels herself falling.

4

She is running through the woods. And there it is—the pile of leaves and fresh soil, and now the white edge of a foot, bloodied and torn, toes missing. She won't look. She mustn't look. She doesn't want to see the thing that is down there in the mud.

"The foxes have got to her," she hears Blue saying. "I didn't get her deep enough. Help me. I can't do it by myself," and Blue is pushing the soil and the leaves back over the mangled, maggoty foot, trying to bury it. But Isla can't stay. She won't help. She won't look. She's turned away and she's running again.

She opens her eyes.

"Am I sick?" she's saying, surprised at the sound of her own voice.

"You fell." There is an old woman hovering over her, necklaces of glass beads around her neck clinking and clanking every time she moves. "You hit your head. Crowther says you need rest."

The woman gives Isla herbs to drink, but they make her forget who she is. She is struggling to remember her own name or her sister's name or anything about the island or Father.

"Who are you?" Isla asks. "What is your name? Are you Crowther?"

"My name is Olga."

Isla remembers something Senna had said about a frightened Magyr woman standing looking at a hole that the people in her camp had dug for her.

"That's good," Olga says, when Isla whispers about the fog in her head. "That's good. That's supposed to happen." She strokes Isla's hand and pats it, looking at her under the tendrils of her wild white hair with eyes that make Isla think she knows and understands everything.

"You'll remember," Olga says, "when you are meant to remember. All in good time."

Isla thinks that it isn't what Olga says that soothes her, just the way her voice sounds, the way it rises and falls, and the sound of the clink and shiver of all those Sun King glass beads the old woman wears, threaded onto the leather straps around her neck.

When Isla wakes again, Olga makes her up a pile of bedding on the far end of the porch and helps her down into it.

"It's what Crowther has us do with all the Strangers with the falling sickness," she says. "It's what she did with me. You just need rest. You had a fall."

"My sister and I have to go," Isla whispers, trying to sit up. "They're coming for us."

She can see the burning huts, the men with the painted faces. She can smell the smoke. There's someone crying in the wood. *Mother! Where's Mother?*

She and Blue must get to the great north road. They must travel at night, stay out of sight. Then they must get to the huts in the marshes where the Ikeni wade on long stilts and fish for eels, the land of geese and hiding places and reed beds, the land of kin. No one will find them there in those marshes. Not Osric. Not Vort or his men with nets, or his dogs.

Olga has hung awnings around her—made from one of the bolts of Sun King sailcloth that they've fetched back from the cellars of an old warehouse, she tells Isla—and hung strings of Sun King glass beads that they've collected and threaded together with old Briton loom weights over the years, beads that blow and chime in the wind.

Isla's mouth tastes like ash. All the food Olga gives her tastes like ash.

All through the day Isla listens to the sounds of the women and the children talking and coming and going down the covered walkways and across the courtyard. She hears Canti, Dumnonii and Trinovanti, snatches of what sounds like Gauli and what might even be Sun King. And sometimes, when there is laughing, she thinks she hears Blue's laugh out there, among the others.

A woman leans over her.

"Where is she?" Isla whispers. "Where is Blue?"

But it is Senna who whispers back this time: "Blue's safe," she says. "Olga's showing her the fermenting hut. Your sister has leechcraft. You didn't say. Olga says Blue knows her plants. She says she's good."

"She does," Isla whispers. "She is."

"You scared me," Senna says, kissing her hand. "I thought . . . I thought you were . . . But Olga says you're going to get better. She says you just have to rest. I've been sitting outside on the step since this morning, waiting for Olga to let me in. I brought honey cakes, see. Your sister says you like honey cakes."

At dusk, Senna's brother, Gregor, slips under the awning wearing bits and pieces of Sun King and Seax armor stitched together with so many punch holes and leather twine that it rattles and clangs when he walks. He pulls out a bowl, grins and passes it to Isla.

"The first cherries," he says. "Good. I picked them for you."

"She's been sick," Olga tells him. "She's not stupid."

"For later," he insists, when Isla shakes her head. "They grow in the Sun King garden across the street. If you like them I'll bring you more." And then he disappears back under the awning again.

"Definitely one brown and one green," Isla hears him whisper to another boy a few minutes later. "Just like I said. You owe me that dice set." She sees Olga smile.

Isla just wants to sleep. The river is still on her, the herbs keep the dreams at bay, but Olga says she isn't to close her eyes until the moon is up above the river wall, and the lamps and fires are lit. She will bring Isla vegetables to wash and scrape, she says, grain to grind at a hand quern, fish traps to mend. If her hands are busy, she says, her mind will rest.

The next day Blue is allowed to visit. Her face is flushed.

"Oh, Isla," she says. "They wouldn't let me come before. They said you needed to rest. But they let Senna come. And that's not fair. You can't be sick. Not now. There's so much you have to see. You have to get up."

"We can't stay here, Blue," Isla whispers. "The soldiers are coming."

"But Caius said that we had to wait here until he came for us—"

"Blue," she says, trying to gather herself, "remember the night you went out to the wood after the raid and the fire? The night you came back covered in mud and—"

"Olga is teaching me her leechcraft, now," Blue says, her eyes darting about, shifting from one foot to another, moving toward the door. "She has this fermenting hut full of powders and seeds and tinctures I've never heard of. She's trying to make this thing called Gaetuli fire for the Night of the Dead. Caius gave her a recipe, she says, a secret one, handed down from his Gaetuli ancestors. Their priests used the fire at their ceremonies. You can put it in water and it won't go out. I'm helping. But she needs more quicklime. And we don't have enough here."

She goes on talking fast, ignoring Isla's question: "You have to come and see the hut, Isla. There's all these dried flowers and plants I've never seen before, and dried mushrooms and roots, all arranged in Sun King bottles and jars, on shelves that Senna made. On the Night of the Dead here, Isla, they bring out their god from this secret cave. Crowther calls her Isis, but I think it must be just their name for Nonor's Queen-of-the-Corn. Her daughter comes back up out of the earth for the summer, and then on the Night of the Dead they all have to drum her back down. It's sad and beautiful all at the same time, Olga says. And they all wear red and there's fire and torches hanging from the trees. You should see the robes that Anke is making. She's the one with the wooden leg. You have to get up, Isla. You can't lie about in here."

"What about Caius?" Isla says. "Is he gone now?"

"Yes. But he's going to come back to fetch us. He promised. We just have to wait here. It might take him some time."

There's a whistle outside somewhere.

"I have to go now," Blue says, and then she's gone. "I'll come back later. I will. But you have to get up."

That night when Isla wakes from her bad dreams she listens to the ghostly cries—*piaoooooow, piaoooooow*—blending into the other night sounds of the Ghost City: the rain on the porch roof, the wind in the trees, someone stumbling out to the cesspit and cursing, and she makes herself remember the Mead Hall and Mother laughing until she falls asleep again.

5

When she wakes the next morning, another Old One is sitting at a loom a few feet away in a shaft of sunlight. Isla takes a deep breath and tries to sit up, remembering the stories Nonor used to tell her and Blue about the Fates, how they sit at their looms and gossip and laugh. But this Old One isn't laughing. She is hunched over and her skin, brown and leathery from the sun and wind, is mud-dark against the wild white of her hair. Isla watches her through half-opened lids, watches her threading the loom, closing the frame, *clank-clonk*. She wears an amulet at her neck in the shape of a woman with wings.

The Old One is old enough to look like a little bird, old enough to have hands swollen in the joints and to need a stick to get her up from her stool. She stoops just like Nonor

did before she died. Isla feels herself trembling. She is holding her breath. But if this Old One is Crowther, she reminds
herself again, hardly daring to move, she must be hundreds
of years old. And that isn't possible. People don't live that
long. Perhaps, Isla thinks, perhaps she has been dreaming
all this time. Perhaps she'll wake up back in the hut on the
island and she and Blue will pull the covers up over their
heads so that Isla can tell her sister all of the strange things
she saw in her dream.

"We brought nails," the Old One says, when Isla stirs.
"Nails," she says again, prodding at the box on the table
beside Isla's low bed with her stick. "Your sister says you
know how to sort them."

"Are you . . . ?" Isla asks.

"Our name is Crowther." Her voice is low and leathery.
"The nails," she says again. "They need sorting."

Isla tries to stand up to show her respect, her head
crowding with questions, then feeling her knees give way,
she takes the stool. She begins to sort the nails, trying to
follow the loom-frame rhythm that Crowther makes. She
puts small ones in one box, long ones in the other. And after
they have sat in silence over their work for a while, when
Crowther asks Isla how she got to be so quick, Isla tells her
that Father once showed her how to separate the Sun King
nails so that he didn't lose the difference between the good
iron and the less-good iron.

"They say the shorter nails are made from the better
iron," Crowther says.

"It's the other way round," Isla says, before she can stop
herself. "The Sun Kings made the longer nails from higher

grade iron so that they'll drive farther into the wood. You can't use that iron for blades, you need steel for that, but it's good for pretty much everything else."

"And the less-good iron?" Crowther says, adjusting her loom weights. "Can you use that, too?"

"I don't know," Isla says, slowly, dropping her eyes. "Father didn't say. Women aren't allowed in the forge. It's against Seax law."

Crowther stops her work and tips her head to one side at that, staring at Isla's hands, as if she knows that Isla is not saying something. And she says:

"Oh, the Seax law."

When Crowther asks Isla where her family lived before the island, Isla tells her about the camp at the creek bend, downriver from Osric's palace, where her kin settled many years ago. It is a long time since she has talked like this. Her words are flowing like the weir at spring tide. Her father and grandmother, she hears herself say, were on one of the very first Seax boats that came in from across the sea from the Drowned Lands after the Rage took their camp. She tells Crowther about the Mead Hall and the goats and the little mound up on the hill where they buried Nonor. She tells her about the Great Fire and the raid and how Osric made them a new home and a new forge out on the island to make sure they were safe. But she takes special care not to say anything about the forge, or anything about the sound of the hiss of molten iron in the vat of river water, or the shape of Father's anvil, or the firetongues.

"If I close my eyes," she says, "I can still see Doe plowing out in the east field or fixing the fences."

"What else do you see," Crowther says, "when you close your eyes?"

Isla shuts her eyes and looks. She sees the forge, the tools glinting on the far wall, but she says: "I can see Willow weeding the top field, Nonor and Mother sitting outside in the sun with the looms or dipping the candles. Godric is waving from the gate as he comes in with the hunters. The dogs are barking, the puppies tumbling over each other. And there's Blue dancing in the herb garden. Old Sive is gossiping, and there's the sound of Father's hammer clanging, always clanging, out in the forge."

Crowther reaches for her stick and limps across the floor to where Isla is trying to lever one of the nails out from where it's got stuck in a crack in the floorboards. She puts her hand under Isla's chin, uncurling knuckles swollen like claws, her fingernails gnarly, yellowed ridges. She lifts Isla's head to look at her eyes. She runs her fingers across Isla's cheek.

"Your hair is so like your mother's," she says. "We saw your father once, a long time ago. Soon after his boat beached up here. The summer he met your mother. We were at the night market."

"You were?"

"Your grandmother was there, too."

"She never said."

"No," Crowther says. "She wouldn't have done."

"She talked about you, though," Isla tells Crowther. "All the women in our camp talked about you. Some said you'd left the city and gone west. Others that you were living in one of those Christian camps on one of the islands north of the

Sun King wall. I remember hearing someone saying that you had walled yourself up inside an old well shaft and the crows were bringing you food and water. I thought you were just a story. I thought you were made up. I used to think of you living inside that well and talking to the frogs down there . . ."

Crowther smiles.

"Your father made a firetongue sword to buy your mother from the slaver," she says.

"How do you know that?"

"Your grandmother told us that she knew it for a curse. She said she knew that as soon as people had seen the firetongue that your father made to buy your mother, the overlords would find him. She said they'd never stop. No one gets to have a power like that and keep it secret, she said. Wise woman, your grandmother. And now, there's you . . ."

Isla feels her skin turn cold. How much does Crowther know about the forge and the firetongues? How can she know? Her thoughts are a tangle.

"The slaver promised Father not to tell anyone about the firetongue," Isla says. "He promised."

"Secrets. Secrets. Secrets. They all come out sooner or later."

"When you told Osric about the augury . . ." Isla begins.

"He was just a boy then. He came with his father."

"Did you make it up?"

"Make it up? Of course not," Crowther says. "Back in those days, we read for anyone who came to the Temple: hands, runes, dreams. People brought us gifts in return. It helped us get through the winters, but we never made anything up. You can't do that. Not many people came, of course. A dozen at most. Most people are not curious like that. They don't want to see what lies ahead."

"And Osric?" Isla asks.

"We didn't know who he was that first time he came, or his father. We sat with him in the darkness like we do with everyone. We asked him about his dreams. He knew something. We just helped him to see it better."

"Caius said that Osric is still coming up the Walbrook to see you. Is that true? Does he?"

Crowther shakes her head. "He's not been to see us since his wife brought in the Christian priest from Gaul a few winters ago," she says. "But yes. Every few years he used to come upstream on the Night of the Dead to speak with us at the Temple. But things will be different now, now that you and your sister are come. Things will change. I have been waiting for you. Time is quickening already. Can you feel it?"

Crowther must be mistaken, Isla thinks. She must have mistaken Blue and her for some other sisters.

"We only want a bit of land to farm," Isla tells her. "Somewhere we can start again, where people don't know who we are. We don't need much. We don't want—I don't want—to be any part of that augury of yours. That's your business."

"It's too late, Isla. You don't get to decide. Perhaps you have never been deciding. Perhaps you only think you have."

"That sounds like a riddle to me," Isla protests. "I'm done with riddles and gods and auguries. I promised Nonor I'd keep Blue safe and that's what I'm going to do. I need to find my sister now. We have to leave."

"Now that you are in the Rookery," Crowther says, "your trouble is our trouble. You must wait for Caius. After what Blue did to Vort, it will take him some time. You must be patient. He will find a way to lure the people who hunt you far away from the Ghost City and then it will be time. Until he tells us that the time is right, you can't think of leaving here."

6

A full moon comes and goes. As each day passes, Isla feels herself becoming stronger and more familiar with the life of the Rookery. At first she just watches. She watches people crossing the courtyard, greeting each other or stopping to talk, shouldering firewood, or reeds, or bringing back tools from the field, or working together to load or unload handcarts with scrap. Apart from the two boys, Gregor and Gunnar, they are all women. When they walk together Blue stops to introduce Isla to everyone, adding details as soon as they are out of earshot until Isla's head is spinning: "Gunnar, the boy over there, he helps Olga in the fermenting hut. Olga's in charge of most things. No, no, that's Giselda. She's the one who lost her finger in a stoning, remember? She works in the field and makes the rushlights. That's Anke. She's from a Briton tribe. She lost her leg and her baby to the Sickness. Gregor, that's Senna's brother . . . he's a tracker. That tall one, that's Lena, she's from Frisia. She mends the fences and does the leatherwork." It is not long before Isla is remembering most of these things for herself.

Isla notices the hush that falls across the courtyard when Crowther appears from the shrine built in the river wall where she spends her days. She watches the way the women bow their heads in respect or clear a way for her or offer her a seat in a patch of sunlight.

"She doesn't seem to come out much," Blue whispers, as they watch Crowther disappear inside and pull the door closed behind her again, "but people go in there to consult her sometimes, if there's something important to decide."

Blue takes her to see the outbuildings: Olga's fermenting hut with its drying herbs and powders and vats, the wood store, the grain store, the meat larder, the workshops. Between the wall of the Rookery and the crumbling walls of a Sun King fort farther east, the land is open, with only the remains of small buildings dotted about here and there. Here the women have cleared and cultivated the stony wasteland to make a kitchen garden. They have planted a small field of barley. Now when Isla works alongside Blue in the kitchen garden, and turns her head to the sun, she could almost forget the trouble that has brought them here, her fear that they'll be found, her urge to run. Soon they will be bringing in the harvest, she reminds herself. She makes herself think only of that. They will stay for the harvest but if Caius has still not come by then, they'll have to slip away and up to the north gate at night.

Isla wishes Mother could have seen the Rookery. All these women with their different languages and gods, Strangers and incomers, working together, hunting, butchering, cutting down trees, digging wells, mending pots, weaving, doing leechcraft. There are arguments, there are even fights sometimes, but it's like the women in the Mead Hall back in the camp; the quarrels always melt away. When she asks Senna how it works, Senna says Crowther had got them all to describe the way that their Old Ones had done things back in Frisia or Saxony or Gaul, so that people could find new ways out of the old ways. They were always finding better ways to hang or smoke meat or pan for salt or preserve fruit. There are always new ways to find, Senna says.

One afternoon, Senna and Giselda take Isla and Blue up to the old stone-built cattle shed that lies in a little hollow on the other side of the field. They stop outside.

"Crowther asked us to make it," Senna says.

"Oh, Isla," Blue says, grabbing her hand.

Isla looks at the shed, the roof mended, the brambles all cut back, a new bench leaning up against the outside wall.

"Isn't it pretty?" Blue asks. "Don't you think it's pretty?"

But when Isla says: "It's a cowshed," Blue looks at Senna and they all smile at each other.

"It was a cowshed," Blue says.

They take her in. It takes a while for Isla's eyes to adjust to the darkness after the bright sunshine outside. She hears Senna talking about the old cowhides she found, how she hung them from nails across the walls and across the door because she thought they might stop the drafts. And now Giselda is explaining how they built the fire basket with straw and mud that they carried up from the river.

And they just keep on talking, one voice on top of another. But Isla needs everyone to be quiet so she can listen and think.

It's a forge. They have built her a forge.

"It's so quiet," she says, remembering how noisy Father's forge always was, the quenching and hammering, the crackle of the fire, the hissing and spitting of the charcoal.

"I made sure there was a notch for the anvil," Blue says. "Just like Father's. I showed them how he had his."

Blue hasn't just copied everything from Father's forge, Isla sees now. She has made everything better: the height of the forge fire is her height, not Father's height, and the bellows are just the right distance away from the fire.

"Blue," Isla whispers quickly when the others have gone to fetch water. She doesn't know where to begin. "Why did you tell them? What were you thinking? No one was supposed to know. It's too dangerous. You promised."

"I didn't tell them," Blue says. "Crowther did. Why did you tell her?"

"I didn't."

"Perhaps she guessed . . . look at your hands."

"I think she knew before," Isla says.

"They asked me to help get it right," Blue says. "Gregor made the bench outside like the one we used to sit on up at the mound. I drew it in the sand for him. He's made it just the same. Even the legs. Look."

Then Senna is back with the pitcher of water and she is lifting the sacking off the table to show Isla the field anvil and the tools she's collected: tongs, crucibles and molds, punches, shears, files, several decent-looking whetstones.

"For you," she says. "All for you." And she smiles that wide smile of hers.

Tools, Isla tells herself. They are just tools. Good tools. Don't touch them—it's just another trap that Thunor has set. He never lets up. What new game is he starting now? Is it just Thunor or all of the gods? She won't be played. She won't be trapped. She'll outrun them all.

"They're rusty," Senna says, "but they'll clean up."

Isla clasps her hands behind her back to stop herself from reaching out to feel the tongs. Such good tongs.

"There's this row of ruined Sun King forges," Senna continues, "on the old road south from Osric's palace. I had a poke around. I wanted to find you a field anvil small enough to carry so that you can take it with you when Caius comes for you. This one's light enough to put on the back of a wagon. Well? What do you think? We've put nails all along the rafters here, see, so that you can hang the tools where you want them for now. Will it do?"

"I won't," Isla tells Senna at last. "I can't. It's not allowed."

Down on the mud floor in the half-light, she sees Father's skewed face. His mouth has fallen open, as if he is trying to say something. Maggots are looping across his cheeks.

"We found a box of brooch molds, too," Senna is saying, her hands fluttering about, ignoring Isla's protests. She's tipping a basket of clay molds out onto the table, molds for Sun King brooches, molds for chariot mounts and bull's head mounts. "There's one with a woman with snakes for hair here somewhere. And a man with a bull's head. How hard can it be? You smelt the nails. You pour the molten metal into the molds. You have to show us how to do it, Isla. At least show me, please?"

"You can't smelt nails without a furnace," Isla hears herself saying.

"A smelting furnace?" Senna is scratching her chin. "A furnace? Giselda, didn't you say you'd seen something out the back?"

"Maybe," Giselda says, her eyes bright. "You know I can't quite remember. Perhaps I did. And then perhaps I didn't."

Blue is jumping up and down on the spot, spinning round, clapping her hands. Isla puts her hands back inside the folds of her tunic, clenches her fists.

"Can we show her?" Blue says. "Can we? Now?"

Senna nods. She smiles.

Blue drags Isla outside to the back of the forge and through an arch they've cut into the thick brambles. Senna follows. In the clearing, Giselda is standing next to what looks like a patched-up Sun King chimney, built over the top of an earthen mound. She's clasping her hands over her mouth in excitement. A clay channel cut into the base runs down into a mud bowl-shaped hole. It's a Sun King smelter just like the ones Father talked about. Those old smelters are like gold dust now, he had said. You just can't find them anymore.

"Blue found it," Senna says, putting her arm round Blue's shoulders, both of them grinning. "Right here in this thicket. Crowther always said there were Sun King metal workshops up on this bit of land, from the days before they built the Rookery. But the soil's so poor up here, we never bothered clearing it. This smelting furnace must have been sitting here in the brambles for hundreds of years. Hundreds. We found mice inside. Old bird's nests in the chimney. It's cleaned up pretty well, though. Don't you think? Nails go in the top here—see." Senna cups her hands over the top of the chimney as if she's cradling a handful of iron nails.

"Molten metal out the bottom, down this run-off here," she continues. "Once I've rigged up some kind of metal stand, we can channel it straight into the molds. Just think— all this time we've been trading scrap with the smelter, and we could have been doing it for ourselves. If only we'd known."

"It was waiting for Isla," Blue says. They all nod.

Isla shivers.

Senna is making a jutting and overlapping shape with her hands. She is explaining how when she took the smelter to pieces to see how to mend it, she found the inside of the chimney lined with tiles, sticking out at angles every few inches. She's asking Isla why the Sun King smelters might have put tiles in like that, and Isla's face is getting hot and then she's saying:

"The tiles slow the iron blooms down as they fall so that they warm up before they hit the fire. It stops them from cracking or exploding."

Isla hears herself explaining why the Sun King iron nails they've collected will work just as well as the iron blooms that the Sun King smelters would have used straight from the mines, in the days when the iron mines were still open. She can't help herself.

"You should talk to Caius," Senna says. "He knows all about iron and smelters. It's how he came to work with us. We traded scrap with him at the night market once. Then, when we knew we could trust him, we came to an arrangement: we give him the scrap he needs and in return he brings us provisions we can't get hold of in the night market. Now he also tells us what is going on in the palace, warns us when we need to lie low. And he makes sure no one in the palace knows we're in here."

At the mention of Caius's name, all the light fades from Blue's face.

"There's sickness at the palace, Isla," she whispers. "That's why he's not come for us yet. Senna heard people talking about it at the night market. Sigulf's men brought it in from the Canti, they're saying, the night of the war party. It's spreading fast among Osric's soldiers. What if Caius gets sick too, Isla? What if he can't get back?"

Isla shakes her head, trying not to look at the pain in Blue's eyes. She puts her finger to her lips. "Later," she says. They'll only be able to smelt at night, Senna is saying, because the smoke from the fires will give them away.

"Good charcoal doesn't make much smoke," she says.

"You don't need to teach all of us," Senna whispers when she takes Isla out to show her the old woodshed that they have patched up at the back for storage. She slips her hand into Isla's and presses it to her lips. "Just me. Then I can teach the others when you've gone. After all, there isn't room in there for anyone else but me, is there? And Blue is busy in the still with Olga, and Giselda is too clumsy. She's best staying on foraging. So it will just be you and me. You'll show me? Promise you'll show me everything? I'll work hard. I promise."

When they all step out of the forge after trying out the charcoal, back into the sunlight, Isla says: "I'll show you how to use the furnace."

Senna smiles. "I'll start fixing up a metal frame for the molds." Then she claps her hand across her mouth. "When you tell me to," she says, catching herself and grinning. "You're in charge. I know that. We'll make plowshares and buckles and knives and new blades for the axes. I'll be your helper."

"Striker," Isla corrects her. "It's not helper, it's striker. You'll be a striker."

"Striker," Senna says, turning to look at her. "I'll be your striker."

Isla feels the heat rising in her face again. She fixes her eyes on the pink glow catching a wisp of cloud high above them.

"We'll stay until the Night of the Dead," she says to Senna. "If Caius doesn't come for us first. But whatever Crowther says, we're not overwintering here. We have to get north before the first snows, whether Caius comes for us or not. I'll teach you as much as I can in that time."

"Whatever you say, Isla the Great Smith," Senna says. Her green eyes have fire and mischief in them. "Thank you. You have to show me everything. Everything, everything, everything."

7

The harvest is in full swing on the morning that Crowther comes out to the forge. She hovers on the threshold.

"May we?" she asks.

Isla gestures to the bench that she and Senna have set up in the corner. "It's smoky in here today," she says. "Let me finish mending this blade and then we'll sit outside. Senna should be here by now. She's late."

"Senna's not coming this morning," Crowther says.

"She isn't? Is she sick? She said she had a pain behind her eyes yesterday."

"No, she's not sick." Crowther has seen the look of alarm on Isla's face. She misses nothing. She tips her head to one side and smiles.

"Senna," Crowther says when they settle on the bench outside. "So, it is Senna, then."

Isla feels an urge to change the subject.

"Senna says you've told them to move the scrap before winter," she says.

"That's right," Crowther says, pointing to the cluster of Rookery buildings on the lower slope of the hill on the other side of the field. "There's hillwash building up at the back of the north corridor. They can't risk that back wall caving in. They've got to move it."

"Can't someone find a way to mend it?"

"They've tried shoring it up from the inside, but every time it rains, more silt builds up behind it. When that wall breaks, all the wet mud and stones on the other side will just pour in. They'll lose that part of the Rookery and most of the scrap they've stored there to the mud."

"Can't they dig out the mud from the other side?"

Crowther laughs. "Once those mudslides get a foothold you can't hold them back. With every new storm, and the middens breaking up now, and the leaves falling, and the worms and the roots working them in, and all the blocked pipes and cisterns, the whole city is caving in, bit by bit. Every year more of the Sun King stone disappears back under the black silt, especially at the bottom of a slope where they are. They can't stop that—no one can stop that. The marsh is taking it back."

"How long," Isla asks, "before the Rookery goes under?"

"Five winters," Crowther says. "Less than that before the north wall breaks. Senna's making sure they get the best scrap buried down well shafts and in hypocausts. Sometimes in pipes and cisterns. She's marking it all down. That way they'll be able to come back for it, if they can find a way back."

"Will you go with them?"

Crowther says nothing. When Isla turns her head, she sees Crowther staring across the field where the women are scything, down the hill, past the stone of the Rookery buildings glowing in the sun and beyond it to where the great brown river runs to the sea.

"Where will you go?" Isla says again, trying to keep her voice steady. Still Crowther says nothing. Isla feels herself being swallowed by the silence.

"No one wants to leave the Rookery," Crowther says at last. "But no city can stand forever. And now there are you and your sister."

"Are you saying people are going to have to leave because of us?"

"Not only you. There are blood feuds. There's the boy in the west. The one they're calling Arthur. There's the battle he won at Badon Hill. The kingdoms are starting to find their walls and their field edges now."

"Where will they go?" Isla asks.

"North."

"Why not west? Father said you can still farm in the west without being tithed. He says the land is good that way."

"Not for much longer. Not now that the boy has won his first battle against the Seax and Anglii overlords. The blood feuds begin. The kingdoms are rising."

"How do you know these things?"

"When you get as old as us, winters follow each other like single days. You see stone walls rise. You see the marshes take them back. You see them rise again. When the first Sun King soldiers came here hundreds of years ago, there were only a few jetties for them to moor their boats and barns to stable their horses. Just down there, at the bridgehead. No one paid them much notice. People here didn't know then what was coming. How could they? How can they know now?"

"What did the Sun Kings want here?" Isla says. "They must have had better lands over the water."

"Gold, zinc, tin, copper, slaves, good soil for farming, grain. The same things your people want."

"They're not my people," Isla tells her, but she wonders: who are her people? Ikeni or Seax? Even Crowther must have belonged somewhere once. Who are Crowther's people?

"Just a few huts and jetties at first," Crowther says. "Then a fort. Then the bridge. A hundred winters later, there were warehouses all along the river down there, storing the grain, tin, lead, gold and wool that the Sun Kings were shipping out, or the wine, pots, spices and oil they were shipping in. The river had become a forest of masts. Slaves were building roads across the hills, up there. Bridges crossing rivers for hundreds of miles in every direction. Watercourses. Pipes to irrigate the fields. Hedgerows and ditches. Soon all the farmers living here were forced to give over a portion of their grain and the cows and pigs they raised to the Sun King tithe collectors. After three hundred winters, all that Sun King stone had become a great hoarfrost across the land.

"And the Rookery?" Isla says. "Who built the Rookery?"

"Lupa, the She-Wolf, a gladiator. She could have gone back to Rome when she retired, but she liked it here. She bought up this hillside to build a private villa, three sides, facing south, in the best Sun King style. She had glassmakers put glass in the windows to keep out the drafts, plumbers to lay pipes for the underfloor heating, tilers to lay mosaic, plasterers to paint the walls.

"She ran out of money, of course she did, she was always running out of money, so she opened the Rookery as an inn instead. It was the finest inn on the north bank—far enough away from the wharves for the Sun King ships' captains to be able to sleep at night but close enough for them to keep an eye on their ships moored down on the river. She planted a garden in the courtyard, with cypresses and olives and fig trees, even had a fountain shipped from Rome. When a merchant ship docked, the sailors all headed south across the bridge to spend their money on the girls in the cheap brothels over on the mud islands. The sea captains came up there instead for the heated floors and the Falernian wines."

"My sister told me stories about the Ghost City," Isla says. "About temples as big as ten mead halls and men who fought with bears."

"Your sister's stories are true. Bears, bulls and stags . . . Lions sometimes. The Sun King gladiators fought with them or set them on each other. Thousands watched and cheered. Blood everywhere. You can still smell blood up there over the other side of the Walbrook when the wind's in the right direction."

To Isla it feels as if Crowther knows everything. That she can ask her anything, ask all the questions that have been brimming inside her for so long.

"My sister said she heard these things about the Ghost City from our mother. But I think Blue sees things. Sometimes . . ." Isla hesitates. "Sometimes, I think she has the Sight."

Crowther nods. "She does."

"Does that make her a wiccan?"

"You can call her what you like: wiccan, strix, seer."

Isla wishes she hadn't asked. Was it more dangerous to know how to make firetongues or to have the Sight? Where did Blue get it from? What did it mean?

"They hang wiccans now," she says. "I've seen them

hanging from the gallows at the crossroads. It's dangerous to have the Sight. I don't want Blue to have the Sight."

"You will protect your sister and your sister will protect you. You both can share the Sight. If you choose it. You have to choose it."

Crowther holds up her hand to show Isla her three rings. Her eyes are wet. "Our sisters," she says, touching each of them in turn.

"You have sisters?"

"Three. All of them gone long ago. One went to Gaul. Another went west to join the Dumnonii. The last one disappeared in a night raid. She was a lovely girl. We hear her calling sometimes."

"Raiders took our mother, too."

"We'll say a prayer for her."

Isla feels for the two brooches on her tunic. They are the last she and Blue have left of kin now. Everything else is lost.

"Remember the night you sat in the Mead Hall on your mother's lap at the feast?" Crowther says. "You were only a small child wrapped in the wolf pelt, half asleep, listening to your father singing, the toasts, Old Sive's stories, the roar of the fire. You turned your head to look up, to watch the firelight flickering on the rafters and the thatch."

"There was a sparrow," Isla says.

"You remember seeing the bird, then?"

"It flew in one door and out of another. It came from the night outside into all that noise and heat and light and then disappeared back out into the dark."

"And you wondered what that little bird had seen up

there on the wing, in between flying out of the night and back into the night. All that color. All that noise. This little life of ours is like the flight of that sparrow, Isla. There's dark on either side of it. We can't see the before and the after now, where we came from and where we go. But one day we will."

Crowther points to the top branch of a nearby oak.

"See that bird?" she says. Isla looks up. A crow stares down at Isla from the branch, his head cocked to one side in that way birds have, his feathers oily black and glistening, a fleck of white at his throat.

"My sister had a bird with a white fleck just like that," Isla says, catching her breath. "She called him Wrak. Vort broke his neck on the night of the storm and Blue wanted to bury him, but she lost his body in the river."

Isla tries to make the noise that Blue makes, that little whistle of hers, and the little click of the fingers like her sister used to do back on the island, to see if the bird will come to her, but it only leans forward, caws once, and then is gone.

"Back into the darkness, my friend," Crowther says.

"Blue called him kin," Isla says.

"He's watching out for you. They do that for their kin."

The old woman stands up and starts walking toward the tree.

"Are you going?" Isla asks.

"I came to say goodbye."

"You can't go now," Isla says. "Not now. There's so much I have to ask you . . ."

A sudden feathered shadow in the doorway to the

forge—there, gone—makes Isla start. When she turns her head to look back to where Crowther was standing, there's no one there.

When Senna comes up to the forge that afternoon, she finds Isla still sitting outside on the bench. She scolds her for letting the forge fire go out. Isla tries to tell her about Crowther's visit, how she came to say goodbye, but Senna only says:

"Oh, she goes off sometimes. There are things she has to tend to at the Temple. She comes back. She always comes back. You mustn't mind her."

And although Isla wants to tell Senna everything that Crowther said—about Blue having the Sight, about the women of the Rookery having to leave the city and how Crowther had known about the sparrow that Isla had seen in the Mead Hall—she can't find the words. She doesn't even begin. Crowther said goodbye, and Isla can't shake the feeling that she is not coming back. Not this time. But she can't explain that feeling, not even to herself.

8

By the next Full Moon there's been no news from the palace camp. Blue and Olga are spending their days foraging through the corners of walled Sun King gardens looking for the plants, roots and seeds you can't find outside the Ghost City walls, bagging up the seed heads in stitched sacks. Olga knows so much leechcraft, Blue says, it makes her feel she's never understood anything. When she is not needed up in the field, Olga shows Blue plants, seeds and roots with names she's never heard before, and salves and spells and chants that mix old ways of leechcraft with Sun King and Magyr ways of fermenting. Olga has Blue and Gunnar drying out seed pods. They grind dried roots. They make tinctures in the fermenting hut. They pot up plants they've dug up from the field or from Sun King gardens to overwinter them in the bathhouse.

When Isla cannot sleep at night, she has Blue whisper the names of the plants she uses while the sounds of the other sleeping women and the darkness close around them. The plant names sound like a spell to her: "Chervil," Blue whispers, "raven's foot, myrrh, mugwort, quitch, cumin, woodruff, beet's root, hammerwort. Horeshound for poison. Halswort and wood parsley and boarthroat and wood chervil for the neck swelling, the first cup drunk on the first cock's crow, the second when night splits from day, the third at sundown."

Isla picks seed heads out of her sister's hair at night, when she combs out her plaits, running her fingers through the heavy golden glory of it. In the firelight, under the comb, Blue's hair spreads out in fiery points. It glows. Isla finds more seeds in the morning, mugwort, hammerwort and quitch, when she plaits them up again.

Now that they are in the Rookery, things have changed between her and Blue. There is a distance. Sometimes she'll come in from the forge and catch a look on Blue's face, like a cloud has slipped across the sun. But it is not just Blue, she thinks, it is both of them. When they are alone together, they avoid talking. There is so much Isla wants to ask Blue—about Caius, about what Blue might be hiding from her, about the things she keeps seeing inside her head or inside her dreams: the dark mound of earth in the wood—but she can't find a place to start. There is something wide like a river running between them. Tomorrow, we will talk, she tells herself. Tomorrow, I will find the right words. But when tomorrow comes, Blue is gone again before the sun is up, and the silence and the unsaid things grow wider.

9

When Isla and Senna had first started working in the forge, they were always tripping over each other. The fire had too much charcoal one day, not enough the next. Nothing was in quite the right place. But then, slowly, day by day, Isla saw that Senna was always one step ahead of her, just as she had learned to be one step ahead of Father. Now, when Isla says she is afraid that the leather on the bellows might be wearing too thin and that they'll struggle to get the fire hot enough when that happens, Senna comes to the forge with a second pair of bellows she's made by copying the first pair.

It's taken her ages, she says. She wanted it to be a surprise, she says. She's got another idea, too, she says. She

tells Isla that when she took the new bellows out to the drying and fermenting hut to ask Olga to make a salve to protect the leather, Olga had told her she'd once seen a
double-bellows in a forge right up in the Caucus mountains.
Senna had got Olga to draw those bellows. She unrolls the
drawing that she's made on the back of a piece of birch
bark.

"It won't take me long to put a rig together," she says.
"See—if I can fix both pairs of bellows up to the forge fire
using a single pipe, here, and if I can rig up a single handle
like this, then we can pump the pair of them in turns using
a single handle. Looks difficult. Probably isn't. Can I try?"

And Isla says yes, because she knows that Father would
have said no, and because even though some mornings she
still wakes up afraid that Thunor will rot the corn or send
sickness to punish her for her smithing, she wants to know
if it will work. "If it doesn't work," she says, "we can always
put it back the way it was."

But it does work. It works like she's never seen bellows
work before.

"Don't go too hard on that arm," she hears herself saying
when Senna is getting the feel of the new bellows a few
days later. "You don't need any more than a whisper in
there." And then she laughs, hearing herself repeating
Father's words like that.

Hearing Isla laugh, Senna turns her head from the bellows. She stops pumping with one bellow up and one bellow down, and the sight of Senna's face, twisted up from

trying to get the rhythm right, makes Isla laugh so much that she doesn't think she'll stop, and that sets Senna off, too, even though she doesn't know what they are laughing about.

Each day they work alongside each other for hours, leather aprons on to protect their clothes from the sparks, covered in charcoal and hammerdust and sweat. The sound of each new tool on that anvil is so clear, she tells Blue, that even halfway down the path to the forge she can tell which hammer or chisel Senna is using. She doesn't tell Blue that there are days when she lifts her head to see Senna arching her back, standing by the open window where the breeze comes in through the hatch, and her heart stops in her mouth. She doesn't tell Blue that when the wind loosens the tendrils of Senna's hair, Isla sometimes finds herself staring so long she leaves the blade in the fire too long and burns it. She cannot help herself.

One morning Senna had turned and said: "Did you hear that mistle thrush?" and caught Isla standing there looking. Senna had lifted her eyebrows, smiled and turned her head away for awkwardness. They both knew.

Over the sound of the hammering and hissing of the quenching trough, they talk—about the stories Caius has told them both, about how one day they'd make sure to see those deserts and mountains of his, those lands beyond the sea, for themselves. They talk about the Briton camp where Senna grew up, about her grandmother and the little things she remembered her saying. After her grandmother died, she tells Isla, a traveler had rescued her and her brother from the side of the road. He brought them to the east gate of the

Ghost City and told them to wait because someone would come to help them. We've been here ever since, she says.

Father always said that if you want to keep the metal true and the bellows working and the fire with the heart in it, then you can't talk in the forge, not their kind of talk, but they can. Sometimes Senna asks questions aloud which are like the ones Isla has never dared to say aloud except to Blue, questions about what lies beyond the sky, and the Next World and where it might be.

"Do you think people can fly when they get to the Next World?" Senna asks.

Isla puts the iron rod she is working on back into the fire. "I'll make you a pair of wings to take with you if you like. As big as a mead hall."

And Senna, working the bellows, says, with a faraway look, "I flew in my dreams again last night, all the way up the river valley. What does that augur, do you think?"

"I don't know," Isla replies, her insides like shoals of fish. "I don't know much about augury." But she does know. She knows that dreaming of flying augurs new love. Everyone knows that, so Senna must know that, too.

"How long were you and your sister out on the island?" Senna asks.

"Five years," Isla says, feeling herself holding her breath.

"And before that you lived in a camp with your people?"

"Yes. At the camp bend. I told you."

"When you were in the camp, did you ever . . . ?"

"Did I ever what?"

"Lie with a man?"

Isla laughs. She thinks of the night she saw Doe and Willow pressed up against the oak out in the wood, his buttocks naked and trembling, her mouth open and round like the moon, her eyes wet. She feels her insides stir.

The grinding stone goes on spinning in the silence that follows, and then Isla says, "What kind of question is that? What do you mean by asking me that?"

"I didn't mean anything by it," Senna says. "I was just . . . I thought . . ."

"You shouldn't talk like that," Isla says, thinking of how often she has longed to feel Senna's mouth on hers. Her hands are trembling.

Senna's face is flushed. They do not talk again that day. Isla wishes she had answered Senna's question. She wishes she had said something.

10

The hedgerows are studded with rosehips and hawthorn berries. Morning mists are rising from the piles of fallen stone. But Caius has still not come. There has been no news from the palace and Crowther has not returned. Isla has agreed to go to the night market with Senna, hidden in the back of her wagon.

"What about Blue?" she says. "We'll be gone all night. I can't leave her."

"She'll be with Olga. She'll be safe."

Blue is working with Olga in the fermenting hut. They are laying down stores of fruit and vegetables for the winter. When Isla goes to find her, Blue says:

"You have to go. Then come back and tell me everything. Make sure you remember everything."

"Most of the night markets are much bigger than this," Senna says, when they arrive at the ragtag circle of wagons in the clearing just outside the east gate. "Sickness must be keeping people away. We are going to struggle this winter if we can't trade for enough provisions. And if Caius can't bring us food in exchange for our scrap anymore, I don't know how we are going to fill up our stores."

"Where do they all come from?" Isla asks, peering through the gap in the wagon's awning at the crowds of men, women and children, pushing handcarts between the wagons, torches blazing through the trees.

"From the Briton and Seax camps along the Sun King roads and the rivers. Looks like there's a few Anglii and Frisians here tonight, too."

People are turning the back hatches of their wagons into tables. They are laying out their wares: bolts of cloth, wheels of cheese, joints of smoked meat, sacks of corn, tools, cooking pots made from mended cremation urns scavenged from Sun King cemeteries, baskets full of the last soft fruits of the summer. Jugglers sing in the torchlight. Pedlars dance.

"See: Osric's tithe collectors don't get to tithe everything," Senna says, her eyes dancing. "They can't tithe what they can't see. I'll do the trading. You keep out of sight. No one must see you. They'll guess who you are straightaway once they see those eyes of yours. Keep your hood up and be ready to leave if we have to. Every wagon here has to be ready to go, if one of the boys sounds an alarm."

Isla watches Senna trade some of Olga's tinctures for cheese and smoked meats and then some of the pewter plates for a bundle of fleece and leather hides. Then she catches her breath. A woman has noticed the brooch that Senna is wearing—one that Isla made as a gift for Senna from a Sun King brooch mold. Isla has altered the mold to turn the Woman-with-Snakes-for-Hair into She-of-the-Corn by making the snakes into corn stalks. It's a good alteration but some of the snakes still look like snakes. She'll have to make a new set.

"Which is it, then?" the woman is asking. "Freja, Nerthus or Gefion?"

"It's She-of-the-Corn," Senna says, a catch in her voice. "Whichever you like, or all three of them in one, like the Christian god."

Isla watches the woman nodding. Senna tries to interest her in some of the cloth that Anke has woven but the woman won't stop looking at the brooch. She wants to know where Senna got it. "it looks freshly smelted to me," she says.

"I found it," Senna says. "It was lying in a field. Perhaps She-of-the-Corn put it there for me to find."

The woman seems unconvinced. "You heard anything about the sisters?" she says, watching Senna closely. "You must have heard something. They can't have just disappeared. They didn't drown in the river after all, did they? You know something."

"We heard they took off on two pairs of enormous wings that they'd fashioned themselves," Senna says, stretching out her arms like a marsh harrier, as more people begin to gather around the back of the wagon. "We heard they flew right up out of the forest. There one minute and gone the next."

"And who did you hear that from?"

"Oh," she says. "Soldiers we met on the road. Deserters from Osric's army. They were there that night when the girls escaped, they said. They saw it with their own eyes, they said. You should have heard the sound of those wings. The size of them, too. The curses those sisters made, they said. The words they used. Those soldiers said they weren't going to stay another night in Osric's palace after that."

"Vort got what was coming to him, I say," someone calls out. "About time." Others cheer. And then everyone is talking about the Great Sickness at Osric's camp, brought by Sigulf's men from the Canti the night of the war party, and how Osric has gone with his sons to his brother's palace upriver to escape it. Vort has sworn revenge, someone says. There is a reward for anyone who can bring news of the sisters, someone else says, and even greater riches if someone can deliver the sisters themselves, alive.

"Good luck to those sisters, I say," Senna says, starting to pack up the wagon to leave. And from inside the wagon Isla sees some of the people in the crowd nodding.

"Will your brooch keep off the Sickness?" the woman

asks, putting her hand on the hatch to stop Senna from closing it.

"No brooch will keep the Sickness away," Senna says, looking straight at her. "Never believe anyone who tries to tell you different. Crowther says the Sickness is like Grendel's mother, or Jenny Greenteeth. It's always right back up from the marshes when you think you've seen it off. No brooch or amulet can stop the sickness any more than Vort can catch those sisters."

And though the woman nods, her brows meeting in a frown, Isla can tell she isn't really listening. "Are you sure you haven't seen them out on the road?"

"If they survived, they'll be long gone by now," Senna says, "if they know what's good for them."

It is not until Senna and Isla have hidden the wagon in the old grainstore near the east gate and are pulling away the ivy and are squeezing through the gap in the wall in the first of the dawn with their baskets full of cheese and ham that Senna breaks the silence.

"We need to talk to Crowther. I don't like the fact that woman was asking so many questions—and that there is a reward out for you. That means there'll be stalkers."

"Stalkers?"

"Skilled trackers. They hunt people. Every so often they come looking for people inside the city walls. We call it a breach. We have traps and ropes in place so that we know if one of them has got inside, but it doesn't give us much time to hide everything. We need to start preparing for a breach."

"Then Blue and I have to go now," Isla says, following Senna along the track that runs through the ruins of the Sun King fort across the wasteland and the harvested barley field west toward the Rookery. "We can't risk bringing stalkers in here."

"But you can't go yet. You have to wait for Caius. And you've hardly taught me anything. You promised."

They stop to fill their flagons from a spring in a grove of oaks growing at the side of the barley field. They take off their baskets. The rising sun is already gilding the stubble of the field and the sea of stone beyond it red. The kites are already hunting. The grove of trees is old. There are notches on their trunks, tokens left on the edge of spring.

"People are suspicious, Senna. You said it yourself. All those questions about us tonight. The stories they're telling. We have to go sooner or later. We can't wait for Caius any longer. And anyway he might not—"

"Blue won't leave without Caius. Don't give me that look. She won't. You know she won't. You just have to wait. And there's something else . . ." Senna pauses. "Crowther told me you know how to make firetongues. If you do, Isla, then you have to teach me. You have to. You can't keep that to yourself."

Isla shakes her head. She can't believe Crowther has told Senna about the firetongues. It feels like a betrayal. "Never," she says. "Not you."

"Why not me? Aren't I good enough?"

"It's not that." The wind is up. It is scattering the leaves from the trees.

"Briton. Born in a ditch. Raised in a scrapyard. Is that what you mean? Oh, you'll let me make and mend, but the firetongues, oh, the firetongues, that's a family secret, that's for the Great Smiths who work for kings and emperors, that's for your people. You think I'm too rough for all that. You think—"

"Don't tell me what I think," Isla says, clenching her fists. She doesn't think that way. Of course she doesn't. How dare Senna think that.

"Bet your father taught you to fight, too," Senna says. "Let's see you fight then." She pushes Isla so hard she stumbles backward, hitting her back against the trunk of a tree. Senna has a thick stick in her hand. She won't let up prodding and pushing. Cornered and cursing, Isla reaches for one, too, makes the first lunge. As Senna steadies herself from the blow, the back of her hand pressed to the side of her head in disbelief, her eyes blazing, Isla aims a second blow, but Senna hits out with the stick, the branch breaks and sends her flying. When she gets back up, still cursing, Senna is staring upward. Darkness has fallen as if something has passed across the sun, and up in the tree canopy, where a thousand unseen crows seem to be making their great scattery flinty roar, Isla hears voices whispering.

"Speak. Demand," the women's voices whisper. "We'll answer."

Senna is standing motionless, still looking up into the branches.

"Fire burn . . ."

"What is that? What are they saying?" Isla puts her hands to her ears.

"Tis time. Tis time." The voices come again.

"Just make it stop," Isla says. "Make it stop."

"It's only the wind," Senna says softly, placing her hand on Isla's back. "There must be a storm coming, that's all. It's only the wind."

"My father made a firetongue to buy back my mother," Isla begins, her words rushing out like water over the weir. "He promised my grandmother he wouldn't make any more. But the slaver wouldn't take anything else for Mother so Father broke his promise. It's a curse. Firetongues are a curse. They'll always be a curse."

"Your father must have loved your mother to break that promise."

"He did, but he was in the forge with me the night the night raiders took her. We couldn't hear anything over the sound of the hammer. We couldn't smell the burning thatch over the smell of the forge fire. We should have helped her. We didn't save her."

"Raiders took your mother?"

"Father was gone for weeks looking for her. We thought they'd taken him, too. And Nonor was sick and no one came . . ."

Isla feels the warmth of Senna's cheek against her own—I'm here, she says. Hush, Isla, I'm here—then Senna's arms are wrapped about her, and there's the smell of woodsmoke on her hair. Isla feels a dark longing rising in her then, like the ache of the buried fire for the air, like seeing the river gate of the Ghost City hanging off its hinges, creaking in the night wind. But it's all over in a moment. Senna's lips are on hers. Her hands are cradling the back of Senna's neck, her fingertips on the soft cool of her skin. But when Isla opens her eyes again, she is alone. Senna is steadying herself against a tree, her eyes brimming, and then she is gone.

FOUR

1

Olga is sending Isla and Senna out to patrol the ruins and check the ropes and the traps. She is steeling herself for a breach. They all are. They are all worried about how long Caius has been away. It's weeks since anyone has seen Crowther. We need to consult her, Olga says. She's been gone much longer than usual. We need her back here with us. Only she can tell us when the time is right to go.

"You ready?" Senna says, when she meets Isla in the hall of the Rookery on the day they are to go, her voice steely. "You don't have to come."

"She does," Olga says, dropping her voice to a whisper. "It's time Isla saw the ruins for herself. The rains will start soon, and then you won't be able to cross the causeways. I want you to look for signs of Crowther while you're out there. See if there's smoke at the Temple."

Isla wonders whether Senna will talk to her when they are out in the ruins. Since the night in the bathhouse, a cold edge has settled between them, brittle as glass, sharp as a blade. They have worked at the forge in silence mostly,

speaking only when they need to. They are making Anke a
new leg to replace the wooden one that chafes her. It is a
good distraction from conversation. They are casting it in
silver to make it as light as possible. As they work up the
mold for Anke's leg, smelting the silver, pouring it into the
mold, burying it in the sand to cool, Isla wonders whether it
was the fight or the kiss that has caused so much trouble
between them. How could Senna have thought all those
terrible things about her? Why didn't she understand about
the firetongues? Father had promised Nonor that the secret
of the Verni bladesmiths would die with him when they left
the Old Country. He'd broken that promise for Mother. And
once he started making those firetongues, bad things had
followed. Now that Isla has made her own promise, she is
not going to break it, not for anyone, not even for Senna.
Haven't the firetongues always been the curse? Haven't they
always brought a hex with them?

Gregor appears in the hall, rubbing his eyes, his hair wet
and plastered to his head. Olga says he is to go with them.
He's the best tracker in the Rookery. Isla is relieved. Perhaps having him there will make things easier with Senna.

"Be careful," she hears Olga whisper to Senna. "Don't
let her out of your sight. And don't let her go wandering off
on her own."

"She can take care of herself."

"I can," Isla says. "Of course I can. But what about Blue?
I can't leave her. Why can't she come, too?"

"Only you this time," Senna says. "We can't risk you
both being out there at the same time."

"You'll look after Blue?" Isla says to Olga.

"Blue doesn't need any looking after," Olga says. "But yes, I'll keep an eye on her. She's making a new batch of the Gaetuli fire. Now go. And bring me back news of Crowther."

Gregor gives Olga a mock salute and drags the door open. The three of them step out into the roadway beyond the Rookery, under a blue sky and high, gauzy clouds beyond. In all these weeks, Isla has only walked between the field, the forge, the porch and the waterfront by daylight. Now that she's about to see the rest of the Ghost City for the first time, she is afraid. The sky is too big.

The early morning sun is so bright and white she has to squint at first. The air is heavy with the smell of wet soil and fallen leaves after the night's rain. Right outside the Rookery entranceway, a Sun King road runs directly north–south, stone cobbles laid in mortar, ruts worn deep into the stone by old Sun King wagons, cracked by the roots of rosebay willowherb and grasses.

To the right, the road runs south downhill past the walls of a small temple to a gate in the river wall. All along the slope, mudslides and hillwash have buried whole buildings, leaving the tops of stone walls sticking up out of the mud and rubble.

To the left the road runs north, up past crumbling buildings, and far off through areas of wasteland, until it disappears altogether into middens and thickets. Birch and alder saplings push up through fallen stone. Their leaves, yellowing in the autumn sun, catch the light like scattered coins. The red berries of the guelder rose glint in the scrub like drops of scattered blood. Skylarks hover. In the distance, in the middle of a field of grasses, a huge stone statue of a man with his arm raised in salute, one of their emperors, Gregor whispers—his head crowned in a wreath of leaves—has toppled sideways. Someone has propped him back up again with a tree trunk, so now the emperor looks like he is forever falling.

For hours they scythe, axe and scramble through low scrub, first down one lane between boarded-up Sun King shopfronts, then another, now squeezing between fallen walls, and under broken statues and mossy columns, and sometimes across bridges and wooden causeways that the Rookery women—or their ancestors—have laid out over ditches, bogs and pools or from one ruined wall to another. Wild dogs stare from the shadows. Wild cats scramble across gutters. As the three of them turn the corner around the edge of a temple wall, a brightly colored bird, startled, flares up from the undergrowth, all emerald and topaz feathers and wild cries. *Piaooooow. Piaooooow.*

That terrible sound again.

"It's just a peacock," Gregor says, seeing Isla jump. "The Sun Kings used to farm them. They roost up in the forum now. Sometimes you see them down this far. Not often."

"Father told me about peacocks," Isla says. "He saw one once, he said, off in the distance. All these years I thought that sound was, well, something horrible—but it was just a bird."

"No more talking," Senna says.

+ + +

At last, when the sun is high in the sky, Senna stops at a cross in the roads at the top of a steep hill. There's a grove of trees here, birch and ash and limes. In the middle of the grove is a single oak that looks to be hundreds of years old, its leaves turning red and gold at the edges, its roots like the flow of the weir when it is turned to ice in the coldest of winters. Its trunk is carved with names and letters and symbols, and it has been hung with hundreds of knotted strips of cloth.

"You mustn't touch any of them," Senna says as Isla gazes up into the canopy. "It's bad luck."

Gregor uses his spear to hook down a coil of rope. "Highest point in this part of the city," he says. "From the platform at the top, you can see most of the river, and on a clear day all the way up to the north gate."

Senna gestures for them to take off their baskets. They can't have come far from the Rookery, Isla is thinking, but perhaps they haven't gone in a straight line. Perhaps they've taken a very long way round. She's thirsty. Her legs and arms are covered in scratches.

While Gregor scrambles up the lower branches to let down a rope ladder, Senna digs a hole between the gnarly roots with the blade of her short sword. Then she takes out a piece of metal from her belt, snaps it in two, kisses it and buries it. She presses both her hands to the bark and mutters something under her breath. Then she takes out a bottle from her tunic and passes it to Isla.

"Vinegar," she says, pointing at the scratches on Isla's legs. "You can't take any chances out here." She throws Isla a pile of strips of leather from her basket. "Wrap the strips around your legs like I've done on mine, see. Knot them like this. Best not to bleed out here."

"What are they?" Isla asks, pointing at the markings carved on the trunk.

"There are new marks here each time we come," Senna says, kneeling to help Isla tie the strips. "The shapes of animals that lived here once, I suppose. Runes. And women with crows' head masks. Letters from old languages. Spells, curses, prayers. Sometimes new strips of cloth tied up there, too. Some old, some new."

"But you said no one else lives inside the walls."

"They don't."

"What do you mean then?" Isla shivers.

"We've found old bone tools buried here, or pushed into the bark, antlers, flint blades, bones of animals with markings on them, especially those bird-head masks. There's no explaining it."

"My grandmother said there were trees like this back in the Old Country where people made notches and hung strips of cloth. They were always near springs and wells and burial grounds. Or in holes in the ground, or clefts in the rock. They had markings like this and strips of cloth, too. But if no one else lives in the ruins, who can be doing it? I don't understand."

"Crowther says that when Sun King soldiers cut down the grove of old oaks that used to grow here so they could build one of their temples, bad things happened," Senna says. "People disappeared, babies died, the Great Sickness started up again and spread. The Sun Kings had to take their temple down to make it all stop."

Isla follows Senna up the rope ladder into a network of walkways and platforms that slope and twist up more ladders right through the tree canopy. By the time she gets to the top, she is out of breath and dizzy with the height. When she grips the rail and looks down through the leaves and branches, the platform sways slightly in the wind. It creaks and groans.

Below, in every direction, a loose weave of broken roads and paths runs north–south and east–west through a green, red and gold expanse of trees and shrubs and crumbling stone. Forests rise beyond the line of the far stone walls like a dark tide. Up to the north, there's a great square, broken columns and fallen masonry piles around its edges. A long line of higher rubble at the far end marks the place where a great building must once have stood.

"There are places you can't go," Senna says. "Certain springs and crossing places."

"Gallows," Gregor says.

"Curse walls, underground temples, notched trees," Senna says.

"Stop it," Isla says.

Gregor shows Isla the six Sun King rubbish dumps down in the valleys between the hills. "Those middens are full of oyster shells," he says, "rotting wood, broken stone, animal bones, pots and tiles and old shit. They're crawling with cockroaches. Best to steer clear."

Above the middens, the sky blurs and bends. The ruins of wood and stone houses of every size—wooden huts, stone storehouses, temples and palaces—line the roads, some with the remains of tiled roofs or thatch, most without.

Enormous trees and shrubs puff up through roofs and ruins and from behind garden walls, the leaves a canopy of greens and golds and reds.

"Walbrook stream," Gregor says, pointing west. Reed beds, rolling in the wind, spill along its banks. "That's where Osric moors up when he goes to see Crowther. Just below the first bridge. Right between the wreck with the mast leaning to the right, and the broken one, there—see? You can't go that way. It's all marsh down there now. You have to know the causeways to get there. You can just about see the amphitheater on the other side of the Walbrook and the line of the fort up there beyond it."

"Even then," Senna says, "even if I explain how to navigate the causeways, it's too dangerous to go near the stream at this time of year."

"No smoke plumes at the Temple," Gregor says, turning to Senna.

"I can see that," she says.

"Is there anywhere I can go?" Isla says. "Is there any route through the ruins to the north gate that's safe?"

"Of course there is," Senna says. "We'll tell you where to go and what to look out for. All in good time."

Now that Isla's eyes are getting used to the expanse of the city, she can see falcons, buzzards and red kites hanging in the air above the middens. There are marsh harriers along the Walbrook banks and crows perched all around them on the tree canopies. She steadies herself on the wooden railing against the great heave and rush of it all.

+ + +

You put all the bad luck of the village into one goat, she can hear Father saying, and then you drive it out.

But if you know all the bad luck is inside you, she asks him now, if you know the curse is on you, then can you drive yourself out? Or do you have to wait for someone else to do it?

Your mother would know.

Then Isla's back in the dark wood again. There's Blue crouched over the mound of earth. Come away now. Leave that thing alone. *Leave it.* Blue is turning her head slowly toward her, white as the moon.

The foxes have got to her, Isla.

"You all right?" Senna says. "You've gone very pale. I can take you back."

"I'm fine."

"You're not sick? You look sick."

"I'm not sick."

"I'm supposed to take you back if you get sick."

"I'm not sick, all right. I said."

"It's the height," Gregor says. "It does that sometimes. Take some deep breaths or sit down."

"I've never seen the south bank of the Great River from the north bank," Isla says, trying to shake the vision of the dark wood out of her head. "That's all. It's hard to take it all in. It's like everything's upside down."

She points down the silver stretch of the river to the west, the three great oaks up on the mound of their island flat-black now against the sky in the distance.

"That's our forge island right over there, see," she says, taking deep breaths. "It looks so small from up here. And that's our old camp on the other side of the creek. See the smoke from the Mead Hall? That's where our cousins live. Our grandmother is buried up there on that hill, the one up behind it."

To the east, the river runs brown and silver through the stumps of the Sun King bridge, on its way down to the sea, curling and twisting like a snake. To the south, on the other side of the river, Osric's palace and buildings cluster on a promontory of ruins jutting out of the largest of the mud islands. Two Seax boats, sails taut in the wind, tack around the tidal inlets and islands of the south bank.

"Only two boats out today," Gregor says. "You see ten or twenty boats from the palace camp out there sometimes. The Sickness must be bad."

"What do you think has happened to Caius?" Isla says. "Will he still come?"

"Caius always keeps his promises," Senna says. "I know you don't trust him, but we do. He is like a brother to us now."

He'll keep his promises if he's still alive, Isla thinks but doesn't say. If he's not dead.

"There's been a big kill up near the forum," Gregor says. "Wolves. They're still feeding."

"And?" Senna asks.

"The midden by the Temple has had a slide. A big one."

"How can you see all that?" Isla asks. "Where are the wolves? I don't see any wolves."

"See those buzzards over there?" Gregor points to four

or five birds circling over a grove of trees just inside the northwest wall. "They're waiting for the wolves to finish a kill. They'll wait a day or so, until the wolves are done, before they go in."

Isla nods, cranes her head to see.

"After a slide, the crows pick over the midden for days, looking for mice or carrion. Sometimes whole families of mice pour out of the holes and cracks of those middens."

"Like water out of a jar," Senna says.

"Then the red kites come. There's an order to things. Crowther used to bring me up here to watch it."

"She did?" Senna says. "You never told me that. She came up here? With you?"

"Remember when those two Picts took shelter inside the walls," Gregor says. "Crowther brought me up here then. Every time they got back on the road, and moved west, cutting their way through the undergrowth, or when they stopped to sleep in a ruined building, everything fanned out around them. The wolves picked up their scent, moved south, the falcons changed their hunting grounds, and the owls their night flight paths. You don't have to see people, Crowther said, to know where they are. You just have to know what to look for. It's all joined up. Connected."

Senna looks at Gregor with admiration. "Lesson well learned, brother. And from everything I can see down there it doesn't look as if there have been any new breaches."

"For now," Gregor says, his eyes grave. "Doesn't mean we can drop our guard though," he adds. "They'll come."

2

I s the Temple off limits too?" Isla asks as they scramble to
get back to the Rookery before the sun starts to dip.

"It's off limits for us," Senna says. "But not for
Crowther. It was a Sun King temple to Mithras once—
secret, men only, Crowther says. That's why there are so
many walls around the entrance. To keep people out."

"Mithras?"

"Born from a rock, they say. Or an egg. Seven orders, like
levels—Bridegroom, Raven, Persian. I can't remember the
others. The Sun King commanders had blood rituals, that
kind of thing. Trouble is, they say, the centurion who built the
Temple built it right on top of an old river shrine to one of the
old Briton gods. He had his masons build high walls around
it to stop the local people getting to their spring, but those
walls couldn't keep the marsh out. They were bound to get
into trouble doing that. What did they expect?"

"What happened?"

"Floods, mosquitoes, marsh sickness. They had to keep
raising the Temple floor every year because of the mud and
water coming up through the flagstones. They built seven
pairs of stone columns to hold the roof up down there, but
those columns just kept on cracking. They had to take them
out and replace them with wooden ones. The owner abandoned the whole complex in the end. The People of Bacchus took the site over for a while, but they gave up after a
few years, too, when the mud poured back up through the
cracks in the floor. Not worth the trouble."

"And if I walked in there now," Isla says as they hack

away at a trunk of a fallen willow that lies across the path, "what would I find? No, don't tell me. Strix everywhere, I guess. Dead babies strung up on trees. Marsh monsters. I get it. I know what you're both trying to do. I'm not stupid."

"Look," Senna says, "I'm telling you. There are streets and buildings where you just can't go. Places where the living have no business. Most of us have heard things. Some of us have even seen people. That's why it takes so long to cross the city. You have to know it. You have to know what routes to take."

"What do you mean you've seen people? What kind of people?" Isla can hear the scorn in her voice.

"Crowther says it was just children at first," Senna says. "In the first days after the Sun Kings left. You'd hear them playing before you'd see them. Laughter sometimes. This boy would put his head over the top of a wall and say, "Are you lost?" Just like that: "Are you lost?"

"Children?" Isla asks. "What children?"

"The Sun Kings buried all their dead in their cemetery outside the city walls. But they buried their children inside, under thresholds and down old wells, to keep them close. Once the city was empty, the children must have taken over for a while, I guess."

"You guess?"

"Until Crowther talked them down," Gregor says. "Took her years, Olga says, but she did talk them all down. Or most of them."

"Once Crowther had seen to the children," Senna says, taking an axe to the fallen tree, "once they'd gone, the

Unburied Ones came in from outside, just walked right in through the gates, bold as brass."

"Not all at once," Gregor says. "Just a few at a time."

"The Unburied Ones walked in?" Isla's voice has taken on a high pitch despite all her efforts not to show any fear.

"The hacked-up ones left out in the woods to rot," Senna says, wiping her forehead with her sleeve. "You know: the unprayed-for ones. The Unburied Ones. The ones who have scores to settle. Crowther says there isn't anything you can do for them. You can't settle their scores for them, she says. They have to settle their own. That's why they're here. They're waiting. Brooding."

"Brooding?"

"Biding their time."

"Stop it," Isla says, remembering the voices they had heard in the oak grove that night. Had they been the whispers of the Unburied Ones? She straightens her back.

"Stop what?" Gregor says.

"You've had your fun."

"You asked," Senna says. "Suit yourself. What's got into you?"

Isla closes her eyes against the foot in the soil in the wood, against the dark earth under Blue's fingernails, against the Unburied Ones coming in from the woods, *just a few at a time*.

It's almost dark before they find Olga back down near the river wall, inside a fenced enclosure, crouched over the edge of an old millstone set deep into the ground. She's making notches on a post. Her brow is furrowed.

"Ten years I've been watching Crowther's wormstone," she says, "and it's always been the same, a drop no bigger than the width of a bodkin every month. It's dropping much faster now. I don't like it."

"Crowther measures the distance the stone drops into the earth every year," Senna explains. "Because the worms are grinding and turning everything in the soil all the time, the stone gradually drops. Crowther says the whole Ghost City is nudging slowly back down into the earth, just like that wormstone. But, she says, sometimes it goes faster."

"Enough of that now," Olga says, standing up with a groan, her hand on her lower back, her necklaces clinking and jangling. "You have news. Tell me you saw smoke plumes over at the Walbrook Temple? Make an old woman happy. Take a weight from her heart. Tell me Crowther's there, out of the wind. Tell me we can go and fetch her."

"No," Senna says. "There's no sign from the Temple. We looked. I'm sorry."

"And no sign of any breaches either, or none that we could see," Gregor adds. "But that doesn't mean the stalkers won't try to get in to find the sisters, what with the reward . . ."

Isla wakes that night in a sweat, her thoughts running back and forth like stoats caught in a trap. If they'd only gone, if they'd only left when she'd first planned for them to go, then there'd be no fear of stalkers and breaches. She has waited too long. She has always waited too long. She let herself be distracted. Now it might be too late to save themselves or the Rookery.

Soon enough Isla wakes Blue with her tossing and turning.

"What is it?" Blue says quietly so as not to wake the others. "Did you dream?"

"We have to go tonight," Isla whispers.

"Go where?"

"North. To the place you dreamed about."

"But I don't want to go. I want to stay. I like it here. And we have to wait for Caius. Crowther said."

"We've brought enough trouble in here, Blue. If we go now then at least we can take our trouble with us, before it gets any worse for them."

"We can't just go without saying goodbye. That's against the Kin Law."

"But they're not kin."

Blue's eyes are full of tears. "They feel like kin," she says.

Isla feels the sting in her eyes. She doesn't want to leave the forge or Senna or any of the other women either. But they've brought a curse into the city. Now they have to take it out again. That's only right.

"Listen to me. You know Father made the firetongued sword to trade for Mother," Isla whispers.

"Yes."

"You remember Nonor always said it was a curse?"

"Yes. That's what she said."

"Well, what happens to a curse when the person it lives

on goes and dies? Does the curse die, too? Or does it jump, like a tick, and find a new person to settle on?"

"I don't know," Blue says. "Is it a riddle?"

"Never mind. Mother would have told us to go."

"You don't know that. How can you know that? Olga said we have to stay, so did Crowther. She said we have to wait for Caius. He'll know what to do."

Senna is right. Isla can see now that she will never persuade Blue to go north with her, not even if they wait for Caius to come back, not even if Blue gets to see him one last time. If he isn't long dead. She can see that. Blue is building a home in the Ghost City. And if Isla doesn't go soon—she thinks of Senna—she might start to do that, too. But for now, she will wait a few more days for Caius. You are in the Rookery now, Crowther had said, and everything you do affects all of us, too. Your trouble is our trouble now.

"Go to sleep now," Isla says, her face nuzzled in Blue's hair which, coiled across the wolf pelt, smells of the fermenting hut. "Forget I said anything. Let me think. We'll talk to Caius. We will. We'll ask him."

3

Olga puts Isla on the silver with Senna. They need to speed up the burying of it, she says, in case there's a breach. For two days, Isla and Senna have set out at sunrise up the Ghost City roads to bury the second best of the silver, finding their way back before they've lost the light.

Isla has never seen so much silver as Senna shows her, hidden under the floors and in the walls of the Rookery. Senna opens up a chest of plates and platters that she found in the back of a furnace outside a villa near the Walbrook, some of the plates marked with the Christian mark she's seen on some of the Sun King shields. Senna holds a huge platter up to the light. It is chased with dancing figures and in the center, fishes swim around the head of a huge bearded man.

"Must have belonged to a Christian Sun King family," Senna says. "Probably too scared to go back to Rome. They probably thought they could scratch out a life in the ruins like us. They must have given up when the marsh took their garden and their walls started to fall in."

"Where would they have gone?"

"North, maybe, to one of those camps people talk about, by the edge of the sea, up beyond the Great Wall. They say the Christian priests take people in up there. We'll keep this lot of silver plates back for the wagons. We'll bury them farther north. Come back for them when we need them."

Later, as they scramble back through the ruins, Senna tells Isla how, years before, a whale swam up the Great River and got stuck on the mudflats. All the people came out in their boats from the camps, she says, people from miles up- and downriver to help get that whale back into the water as soon as the tide turned.

"That night no one asked me and the others from the Rookery where we came from or what gods we prayed to or even what our names were. No one cared. By the morning everyone had gone."

The first puffballs and saffron milk caps are pushing up through the fallen leaves. She and Senna fill their baskets with the great slabs of fungi they call chicken of the woods, all ambers and sunflower yellows. Senna hacks them off the oak tree trunks, piles the pieces in the baskets so that Olga can dust them in flour and cook them in butter for everyone later.

On the third day they sleep on the flat roof of a riverside palace so they can watch for shooting stars. Senna tells Isla not to tell Olga. Looters are not supposed to sleep on roof-tops, she says. It's too dangerous.

"But you do," Isla says.

Senna makes herself busy building a fire and checking that the roof is sound. "Crowther says there was a time when you could walk into a villa or a grain store in here and there'd be coins and pots and statues and carved little lamps every-where," she says, "scattered all over the floor. All the things the Sun Kings couldn't take with them when they boarded up and shipped out, household gods still on the shelves where they'd always been. They were just there for the taking."

"I'd like to have seen that," Isla says, her eyes on the Seven Sisters rising above the treeline and the edge of the roof, the Blood Star pulsing red in the east.

"By the time we started out looting," Senna says, "there

was none of that left. We had to go down the wells and the cesspits. We had to dig. And we had to know where to dig."

At dawn Isla wakes next to the remains of the fire and watches the geese coming in and landing over on the other side of the Walbrook in the far marshes.

Later that morning, Isla sees a wolf slipping through the window of a Sun King villa. He has a bloodied fox cub in his mouth, limp but still twitching, head hanging off. The wolf jumps the sill, without effort, as if he is made of air, and turns to face Isla, a low growl purring in his throat.

"Don't move," Senna says from behind her. She slides herself between Isla and the wolf, spear in hand, slow step by slow step.

"There's four others out there," she whispers, her breath warm on Isla's neck. "They have your scent. Walk backward," she says. And Isla does exactly as she says.

When they get back to the road, Senna says: "You scared me." And when she puts her arms around Isla, they are both trembling.

When Isla gets back to the Rookery, she tells Blue about burying the silver, how every time she makes a hole to hide the silver in—inside the walls, open ground, overgrown gardens, under a path or in a clearing—she finds the same thick top layer of charcoal-black soil, nothing in it except for the white spidery tendrils of roots or the occasional bone of a hare or a vole or mouse, and worms, always so many worms. But when she digs deeper down, as far as the length of her arm, sometimes much farther, she finds another layer. This layer is thick with Sun King pottery, coins and oyster shells and hairpins; sometimes little metal amulets and leather boots and bits of hammers and rakes and plaster and tiny gods appear, too, mixed in with the bones of sheep and chickens and cows and peacocks.

"Sometimes we find people's bones," Isla whispers. "Today I was down inside this hole and there it was."

"What was it?" Blue asks, her eyes wide, propping her head up on her hand.

"A tiny hand and arm, fingers still clasped around a brooch, a coral necklace twisted round it to keep off the evil spirits. Senna had me backfill and start again somewhere else. And she said a long prayer to keep it safe. She says you never know what you're going to stir up if you disturb the bones."

"You really like her," Blue whispers. "You do, don't you? You talk like you really like her."

"She's a good striker," Isla says.

"Do you like her more than you like me?"

"There's no one in the whole world I like more than you," Isla tells her, startled. "What kind of question is that?"

"There are so many different kinds of feelings in the world," Blue says, "and so few words for them. If I was a god I'd make more words for people to use. I'd take words from different tongues and mix them up and join them together to make hundreds of new ones, ones that fit better."

"Yes," Isla says, thinking how much she has missed her sister, remembering how they used to talk.

"Take me with you tomorrow," Blue says. "Please? I want to see everything out there, too, before we go. I want to see the wolf and the black soil and the tiny bones. I want to know everything that Senna knows."

"You're not allowed," Isla says. "Olga says Senna can't guard more than one person at a time. And besides, Olga needs you to help prepare for the Night of the Dead."

"You just want Senna to yourself."

"When will you stop your nonsense," Isla says. "It's not like that at all."

"It's not like that at all," Blue says, mimicking her sister. "It's not like that at all."

4

The next morning, Isla is heading for the spring to wash, when she runs into Olga hauling two sacks up from the bathhouse, one in each hand.

"Take one of these off me," she says. "My hip's bad this morning. Careful. Don't touch the wet bits. And then go fetch your sister. Tell her I've found a new batch of madder. Look."

Olga turns the sack around to show Isla a stain that has spread across the sacking. It is red. Not red like poppies, but red like rosehip berries, red like new blood between your thighs.

"Senna brought two sacks back from one of the Sun King warehouses last summer," Olga explains. "We stored them in the bathhouse. Forgot about it. I found it this morning when I went to see how much rain had got in. I've never seen madder this red. Must have been shipped in. Dried differently. Treated with something. Who knows?"

"What are you going to do with it?"

"Dye some lengths of the sailcloth we've got left. See if it takes. No one around here has seen red like this since the Sun Kings left. Not in almost a hundred years. We can trade red cloth in the night markets once we're on the road, if we have to leave. It's worth trying. We'll use the cloth for the Night of the Dead, too."

Isla remembers the summer Blue tried to dye one of Father's tunics with madder, but the roots that Blue gathered from the hedgerows out on the island, dried out and powdered, only made the cloth a pale pink, pale as dog roses. Blue tried a second time, left the cloth soaking for days, added some wood ash and chalk just as Nonor used to do, but even then the cloth only dried to the color of a pale sunset and when Father went into the river with the tunic on, the color bled straight out into the water. He laughed at the sight of all those clouds and swirls of pink in the water around him. How glad they were to see him laugh. Blue didn't try again after that. She said she'd stick to the good blues she was getting from the woad.

When Isla wakes Blue to tell her about the madder, Blue says:

"Did he come? Is he here?" That question, repeated, coming so soon after waking, gives Isla a sick feeling.

"Soon," she tells Blue, stroking her sister's hair. "He'll come soon," she says.

"I went looking for him, Isla. In my dream," Blue says, sitting up, her hair tousled with sweat and tears, her hands trembling. "I was standing on the edge of the river. There were all these arms and legs and heads of stone statues in the water, washing in on every new wave like driftwood, piling up along the edge of the mud."

"Did you find him?"

"I found his arms first, then his legs, then his feet. I got them out of the water, got them all piled up. But when I found his head, his big, beautiful head with the little earring with the pearl and his beard and all his curls tight to his head, I couldn't lift it. I couldn't move it at all. It was too heavy. I just sat on the edge of the water holding it, and the water kept on rising. He was just here, Isla. I was holding his head in my arms. He was here. And the water was rising. And I couldn't lift him. And now he's gone. See, he's gone."

"It was just a dream," Isla says.

"Is he dead, Isla? Do you think he's dead? Isla? Is that what it means? Does it? Tell me."

And when Isla goes to kiss the top of her sister's head because she doesn't know the answer, Blue gives her a look that makes Isla smart, a look that says: you don't know, you can't know, who are you to say? Isla slips away and leaves her sister alone then, afraid of that look she's seen in her eyes.

It takes a long time for the water to steam and then boil in the old cisterns that they've dragged in over the fire pits, and by then Blue has disappeared back into the fermenting hut and Isla has settled on the porch with the whetstone and the pile of tools and axe blades that need sharpening. If they are going to be on the road before winter, they'll need sharp axes on the wagons to gather firewood when they stop. Isla is sharpening as best she can, and trying not to think of Blue's dream.

As soon as the steam in the cisterns is thick enough, Olga and Blue pour in the cups of brown powder from the sacks. When the liquid has cooled, and they've had everyone stirring it for long enough, the women lower in the lengths of cloth that Olga has already soaked with mordant.

Blue comes up to the porch for water a little while later, and says to Isla, "Olga thinks the sacks of madder have come in from Afric. That's where Caius's people come from. Olga says his people have this old way of powdering madder that uses sheep dung, calf's blood, alum, and something called sumac. Olga says she found a sumac tree growing in one of the Sun King gardens up near the amphitheater last winter. She dried some of the flowerheads."

But Isla can see that Blue is still not herself. "It was just a dream, Blue," Isla says, reaching out for her sister's hand. "Senna would have heard if anything had happened to Caius."

Blue nods.

"Now go and finish that Gaetuli fire. It's been weeks since you started. You don't have much time left. You wanted to have it ready for Caius when he came."

For days now, everyone in the Rookery has been taken up with preparations for the Night of the Dead. Olga and

Blue are still trying to perfect Caius's ancestor recipe for the Gaetuli fire. Several accidental explosions have singed the thatch of the fermenting hut, but they think they've got it right since. Giselda, Anke and Lena are making costumes and masks. They've turned the row of marble heads of the Sun King emperors right side up again along the edge of the porch and are using them to make the headdresses and stitch on the cloth flowers, horns and knotted fruits.

One afternoon, Isla saw Gunnar run whooping across the upper field with the brace of hares he'd brought back from the traps, wearing a huge bird head with a long beak. Another time, she peered through the bathhouse door and saw Lena and Anke putting together a statue of a woman, twice the height of a person, a mass of drying mud daubed over a woven hazel frame, her wild hair made of twigs and branches. But Lena, seeing Isla's face at the door, just smiled, put her finger to her lips and nudged the door closed behind her.

When Isla finds Senna at the corner of the woodshed, she is covered in new scratches.

"You've been back up to the platform, then," Isla says. "Are there any signs of a breach?"

"None that I could see," Senna says, putting her arm around Isla.

Isla has waited so long for things between her and Senna to go back to the way they were. She has been patient. But now that they are good again, each hour they spend together is as bitter as a sloe berry because she knows that the days of the Rookery, of the forge and the night markets, and wandering in the ruins with Senna will soon be over.

"Will you remember me when I'm gone?" Isla says suddenly, feeling her eyes stinging with tears. "Or will you only remember the things I've taught you?"

"What's that supposed to mean?" Senna says, pulling Isla into the shadows of the woodshed. "What's got into you today?"

"If I die, if a stalker takes me, will you build me a shrine? Will you build it outside the forge, looking down over the river? Even if you have to come back to do it?"

"I will, Isla-with-eyes-of-the-storm," Senna says. "I will build that shrine of wood and silver rods, twisted and quenched in your own forge, inlaid with cloisonné, studded with rubies. I will hang it with wild roses. I will hammer you a pair of wings with hundreds—no, thousands—of silver feathers so you can fly to the Next World . . ."

"You're laughing at me."

"No stalker is going to take you," Senna says, leaning forward to kiss Isla softly. "I won't let him."

"They'd never work," Isla says, wiping her tears away.

"What's that?" Senna's eyes are full of tears now, too.

"The wings. Silver is too heavy for wings."

"Oh, but I will beat every single one of those silver feathers on the anvil until they are so thin you can almost see through them, and then when you fly you will be lighter than air. You'll see. Now go and wash your face. Stop thinking about stalkers. You're just tired."

"I am tired," Isla says, remembering how she had watched the dawn break under the door, the hours she had spent inside this new riddle, wondering if she should leave the city without Blue, take the curse with her, and when she should go, and if she should say goodbye or just slip away and how hard she had tried not to sleep because she was afraid that she'd find herself back in the dark wood again in her dreams, Blue hunched over that pile of soil.

"Come in with me tonight," Senna says. "I'll make you up a sleeping draft. Everything will be better tomorrow. You'll see."

All through the day those vats sit out there in the Rookery courtyard, brimful with red. Isla sits under the awning with the whetstone, alongside the other women, while they work at the loom or at the quern. Every time Olga appears from her fermenting hut, crossing the courtyard to prod the cloth in the cisterns with her stick and peer in, the women all look up together. But Olga only shakes her head.

There is a new hush about the Rookery. Perhaps it is the waiting for the madder to take, or the thought that a stalker might be out there in the shadows somewhere, or everyone wondering if Caius has been taken by the sickness or if Crowther will return. Everything that anyone says seems new and surprising to Isla: the questions the women ask, the stories they tell, the way Senna comes to sit next to her, slipping off her sandals, putting her feet in Isla's lap and smiling at her with that look of hers. Everything shines as brittle and delicate as glass or the inside of an oyster shell: the wet greenness of the grass against the fallen leaves, the way the rain brings out the long shadows on the bathhouse wall, the moss, the brightness of the moss.

Blue comes to sit with them both in the middle of the afternoon. Isla combs the tangles out of her sister's hair, as they listen to the talk around them, woven in with the sounds of the rain on the roof and the drips from the eaves and the spits and cracks from fires under the braziers. Anke says that her people won't touch oak galls at all because they say they're cursed, and soon all the women are arguing about the best ways of spinning or weaving or fermenting or making charms. When Giselda says no one makes purple cloth like her people, Anke says her people can go fuck themselves. They all laugh.

With Blue asking the women questions—were you born here? Who are your people? how did you lose your leg?—there is no end to the stories that begin that afternoon. Anke and her mother Rosc lived in a Briton camp near the Great Fens. When the Great Sickness took Anke's father and brothers and they gave up their farmstead to the Seax, Anke married a Seax soldier. Anke and Rosc went on the road with him following the warband, living in tents.

When Anke's husband died on the battlefield, leaving Anke pregnant and Rosc with the beginnings of the Forgetting Sickness, the two of them had jumped wagon trains all the way from the east, sleeping out in ruins at night, and stealing food from camps when they could. They were heading for the night market because Anke wanted to trade the gold Sun King figurine her husband had given her for a wagon.

"I lost my baby in a thicket just a few miles from the

Ghost City," Anke says to a murmur of sighs. "We buried him in a grove of silver birches, the gold figurine with him. And by the time we stumbled on the night market a few days later, I'd lost so much blood I fell under a cart. My leg was crushed. Someone sent for Senna. She came for me in the night. Olga took off my damaged leg and, well, here I am. One leg down."

"Shall we?" Senna whispers to Isla, and when Isla nods, Senna goes to get the new leg they've made from the bathhouse where they've hidden it, all wrapped up in a calf-skin pelt from the forge, and they present it to Anke.

"We made you a new one," Isla says, as the women gasp to see the polish gleam on the silver, the cloisonné patterning and the woman with snakes for hair on the knee. "We put garnets for her eyes."

Anke, her eyes full of tears, straps on the new leg.

"It's so light," she says. "How did you do it?" she says. "It's beautiful," she says. And Olga, seeing that Anke is struggling to speak, starts up one of the old songs from her country, and soon everyone is joining in and the song is filling the air with thanks. When Anke does the first round of the courtyard, makes a few turns and a bow to show them she can touch her own feet now, everyone cheers.

"To our Great Smith and her striker," Olga says, lifting her cup. Senna kisses Isla's hand and gives her a look that says, you see, you see, and Isla, thinking these will be her last days in the Rookery, feels the bittersweet sloe taste of it and makes sure to always remember it.

+ + +

Late afternoon, the sun comes out. Anke is shouting, "Red hand, red hand," and dancing round the vats on her new leg like a child. Her whole hand is stained red. When Olga gives the signal for them to lift the cloth, everyone puts down the looms and the spindles, and Isla her whetstone, and now they are lining up together to lift the cloth out of the cooled water.

Olga has them pull the first corners of one length of fabric out of the water in one long stretch. They hang that first length out over the low branches of trees and across shrubs all over the courtyard and from the edges of the porch. Everyone is looking at each other as if they can't believe how much red there is, and how deep it is. When they see how their clothes and faces have been splashed and flecked with that red, they all start to laugh. Olga tells them to take their clothes off down to their undertunics, and then everyone is flicking that red water across the court-yard, and smearing it in stripes across their faces, until Olga yells at them to stop, that they'll never get it all off, and they should be more careful.

Isla has never seen so many shades of red, draped and dripping and swaying in the wind, hanging in lengths from the trees and from ropes strung across the porch, drying out slowly to new reds, staining her own skin. The sun shining low through all that cloth makes it look like the world is on fire.

Senna and Isla slip the latch on the river gate onto the dark waterfront, climb across the rotten stumps of the wharves and walk right out onto the jetty, out into the wet darkness, hand in hand.

"You can't see where the river ends and the sky begins," Isla starts to say, pulling her cloak about her against the cold, but before she has finished speaking, she sees Blue running through the dark shadows of the waterfront, her hair wild in the night, her cloak flying white as the moon behind her.

"Isla? Senna?" Blue is shouting, her eyes wide. "Help me." She's scrambling through the darkness and the mud toward the edge of the wharf. "It's him. He's here." When Senna and Isla reach the edge of the wharf and look down onto the mud beneath, there's a boat without a tiller down there bobbing about in the water, and Blue is sitting on the edge of the water, cradling a man's head in her arms. His arms and legs are limp.

"She saw it," Isla tries to say, but her voice sticks in her throat. "She dreamed it. But it's my fault. I wished it . . . I wished him . . ."

"Shush," Senna says. "You didn't wish it. And anyway he's alive. He's alive—see?"

5

Two days later Caius is sitting in the middle of the porch steps. The women of the Rookery have gathered around the fire, to give thanks for Caius's recovery and for Olga's strong leechcraft. From the shadows Isla watches Blue run her hand over Caius's rough dark curls and put her hand in his. He looks gray even in the light from the fire. His cheeks are hollow. He has a deep gash on his forehead.

"Olga says you have a forge now," Caius says to Isla. "Looks like you're putting it to good use."

Isla looks down at her hands and arms covered in soot and smoke. Her feet are caked in mud. She spits on her hands and wipes it down her face. Everyone laughs. "I meant to wash," she says. "But I didn't have time." Olga passes her a stool.

"Did you bury them all?" Isla asks Caius. "All the ones who died?"

"Every last one," he says, straightening his back. "Seax, Gauli, Anglii, Magyr or Briton. We buried all of them. Properly."

"That's good."

"We made a promise about that," he says. His voice is hoarse. "We promised that if the Great Sickness came, we'd see each other buried properly, in our own ways, with our own things, even if there was only one man left standing."

"Was there?" Isla says, feeling all the women around the fire straining to hear. "Was there only one man left standing?"

"No. We lost about half the men, four of the women, none of the children. It could have been much worse."

"It would have been," Olga says, "if you hadn't locked the gates."

"Some of the men tried to get out," Caius says, and when Isla sees the dark look in his eyes and that gash on his head, she wonders what he had to do to stop them.

"Caius has news," Olga says, quietening the women with a simple raise of her hand. "It's not good."

"Osric died two days ago," Caius tells them, "at his brother's palace upriver. The Sickness took him." He can't make himself heard above the noise that follows, the sounds of yelps and cheers. Olga has to bang her drum to silence them this time.

"Osric is dead," Caius goes on, "and four of his sons. But not Vort. Vort has taken Osric's shield and crown. He's sailed downriver to the palace with an army of upriver soldiers, new Seax and Anglii recruits from last year's boats, the last of his bodyguard and his wiccan. He's sworn vengeance for his father. I didn't see them coming. I wasn't ready. I hid under the floor of the Mead Hall. I heard them talking."

"Listen," Olga says sternly to the women who have begun to whisper and mutter. "Listen."

"Vort recovered," Caius says, his voice straining, "and now his wiccan is calling him a god. The wiccan has told Vort that the Sickness will keep on coming back until the whole Sun King city is burned, all the stones in here broken and plowed back into the ground, the marsh drained, and the demons living inside the walls driven out for good. I heard Vort telling the soldiers that his father should have done it years ago, but Osric was always too weak."

"Demons?" Olga says.

"Strix, marsh witches, banshees," Senna says. "Look at us. We're the swamp and the strix and the marsh witches and the banshees. All hail the Rookery women."

The women cheer.

Isla glances at all the women seated around the fire, wondering if they can fight. She sees Anke's stump, Olga's stoop, hears Giselda's cough. Though she has sharpened all the axe blades, they don't have swords. They are not ready to fight. They'll never be ready to fight.

"He's also sworn to hunt down the sisters," Caius says suddenly, tightening his grasp on Blue's hand. "He doesn't know they are in here but he's heard rumors. You should hear him. He has a mad look in his eyes. There'll be no stopping him and his mercenaries now."

"How long before they get here?" Isla says in the hush that follows.

"His wiccan says it must be the Night of the Dead," Caius says. "We have to get everyone out before then, head north. Load the wagons. In two days there'll be no moon. We'll have to keep away from the camps along the north road, so we'll follow the old drovers' roads instead. Hide in the woods by day."

"The Night of the Dead," Isla says. "That's, what, ten days away?"

"Nine," Senna says.

"Crowther decides," Olga says. "That's the Rookery Kin Law. We can't go until she has had her say. So you can stop all your talk of wagons and drovers' roads and hiding in the woods. First we have to find Crowther."

The women nod their assent.

"If you stay, Olga," Caius says, "it'll be a massacre in here. Vort and his men have dogs, torches, brushwood and axes. Wherever you hide in the ruins, they'll smoke or hunt you out. You can't risk that. And where is Crowther? Where is she now?"

"We've been looking for her," Senna says. "But there's been no sign. Not even traces."

"She'll come," Olga says. "You'll see. And until she comes there'll be no more talk of leaving."

6

When the bathhouse roof falls in a few hours later with a great shatter of tiles, Olga says it's Crowther. She says that it is a sign that she's not far away, that she won't be long now. Isla can't sleep. She's been turning from one side to another, watching the hearth fire burn blue and orange, the shadows stretching and flickering on the walls, the smoke curling up through the hole in the roof, wondering.

As the first birds begin to sing, but before the dawn light has broken out over the mudflats to the east, Isla lifts Senna's arms from around her and wanders across into the courtyard in the dark. She climbs the barrels and scrambles in through the window she broke all those months ago and into the old bathhouse. The floor is a sea of broken tiles, the roof a great wide hole open to a blue-black sky, studded with stars, the walls still holding, the oak still waving its branches in the wind.

There is one last nightingale, sitting on a plaster island of its own. The very last bird left on that wall. The rest of the plaster has cracked and fallen away around it with the weight of the tiles thudding down onto the floor. It is all going down into the dark earth, Isla thinks, remembering what Crowther had said about the marsh rising and the cities falling. It's going to take them all with it. But it hasn't taken the nightingale. Not yet. It is a sign.

The tiles shift and crumble beneath her bare feet, but she keeps going, step by step, toward the bird until she can feel the edge of the plaster against her fingertips. She puts her knife under it and eases it off the wall. She'll give it to Senna, she thinks. She'll give her the very last of the bathhouse birds. A keepsake. A gift of thanks. Something to keep close when she is gone. A love token.

"Are you afraid?" she hears Senna whisper behind her, her mouth close to Isla's ear. Isla shakes her head.

She turns to show her the nightingale, and stumbles, reaching out for Senna to steady herself. Senna puts her hand in the hollow of Isla's back and kisses her.

"This is for you," Isla says, opening her hand, glad of the darkness. "It was the first bird I saw when I woke in the Rookery. It's good augury, I think."

"Thank you," Senna says. "You are good augury, Isla, the Great Smith."

As they are walking back across the tiles to climb back out the window, Isla drops the brooch that Nonor gave her many winters ago, many Islas ago, one of the pair of brooches Father made for her on her coming of age. She sees it clatter down into the pile of fallen roof tiles.

"You've kept it all this time," Senna says, squatting to

look for it, cutting her finger on the jagged edge of a tile. "You can't lose it now."

"I'll leave it here," Isla says, tying the two ends of her tunic together. "I'll wear the new ones you made me instead. I'll wear them for luck. I'll wear them for today and as many tomorrows as we have left. Perhaps someone will find my brooch in hundreds and hundreds of years' time and perhaps they will wonder who dropped it."

Senna takes her hand. Together they cross back through the window and climb down the barrels and through the long grasses, through a scattering of morning songbirds, toward the porch where Olga is making oatcakes.

When the two of them take the path up to the forge to gather the last of the tools for the wagons, Isla sees Gregor rushing toward them from the north, out of breath and white as the morning.

"There's a line of blue marks on some of the trees to the west," he says, trying to catch his breath. "Daubs on trees, on rocks, on walls. A whole line of them. It's a track," he says. "There must be a breach."

"We must leave," Isla says, panic rising.

"Olga won't leave until Crowther comes," Senna says. "You know that. But we'll have the wagons ready. We'll double the watch until then."

"But what if Crowther doesn't come?"

"The others won't go without Olga. Not now."

"And Olga won't go without Crowther?"

"No."

"Sweet gods. And you?"

"Not me either. Not without them."

Isla feels the ground shift underneath her. The women of the Rookery have given them refuge and they have brought them trouble. She has brought them trouble. We brought the curse in, she'd told Blue, and we have to take the curse out. But the truth is that she brought the curse in, not Blue. Even though she knew the curse had settled on her, she had stayed just the same, making excuses, playing for a little more time in the hope of finding a way to persuade Blue to leave with her, too, and because of Senna. Oh, she had stayed for Senna. But the curse is hers. Only she can take it out. She must go alone. If she gives herself up, perhaps she can persuade Vort to leave the city alone.

It is late by the time Isla has filled her looting basket with parcels of cheese and smoked meat from the outhouse, a whetstone, a flagon of water, a lamp and some flint to light it. She's hidden the basket in the woodshed and gone to find Blue in the fermenting hut, but Blue's not there.

"Every choice we make in this life, girl," Isla can hear Nonor say, "changes the pattern in that cloth. Sometimes only a little. Sometimes the little things we do can change everything."

FIVE

✠

1

Fallen leaves, all reds and golds, lie thick along the stones of the Sun King road. They nuzzle into stone crevices and doorways. They rustle under Isla's feet. Even in the Sun King boots, her feet are damp and cold. She pulls her cloak around her.

She has a plan. If she's going to give herself up, then she has to be as far away from the Rookery as possible to keep Blue and the others safe, so she's decided to head north. If there's a stalker inside the walls he'll pick up her trail sooner or later. He'll close in on her. He'll take her to Vort. If she gets as far as the north gate, she'll find the nearest camp and tell the camp elders who she is. They'll take her to Vort to claim the reward. She's thought it all through. All she has to do is walk and hold her nerve and put all of that Rookery life behind her.

She doesn't get far along the road before she starts to think there are people following her. It can't be a stalker, she tells herself, because he'd have taken her if he had the chance. She tells herself it is just the sighs and echoes she and Senna had heard before out in the ruins, tricks of the eye and ear, only shadows trembling and rippling across broken walls and between trees. But in the ruined colonnades of a temple, all white in the sunlight, she hears voices like whispers, doors slamming. A child is crying.

There's no going back for you now, she tells herself. No going back now. Keep going. One foot in front of the other. Don't look back, not for anything. Not for anyone.

At noon she stops to fill her flagon from a roadside spring. In the shade she paces up and down, thrashes at some grasses, lies on her back on an old wall eating the bread and cheese, watches birds crisscrossing the blue sky. A single cloud sails slowly between the fingers of one tree to the fingers of another.

The farther she walks into this thicket of a city, the more she is losing her bearings. The shadows fall in one direction one moment, then the opposite direction. She'll fix her eye on the edge of a high roof, or a tree, only to find it is gone when she reaches the next cross in the road. And it's not just that either. In some places it's as if someone has sucked out all the sounds, and she is drowning or falling. Sometimes she is no one at all, nothing but a falling leaf caught for a moment on a breath of wind.

By afternoon she is starting to think that whatever might have been behind her before is now up ahead. There's a flutter of a long, blackened robe in a thicket, a fresh print of a foot in wet mud when she scrambles down a new path, the marks of an axe on trees fallen across her path.

+ + +

By mid-afternoon she finds the first of the tokens. First there's a seashell, then, at the next fork in the road, a peacock's feather held down by a rock, then a pile of circular stones, each smaller than the one below, carefully balanced on top of each other. As she continues, wondering if the tokens are marking out some kind of a route for her, she finds sticks pushed into the mud with strips of cloth tied to them, owl pellets arranged in a circle, and even, at one crossing point, a set of little bronze pots with holes attached to a length of twine and nailed to a tree, like the ones she's seen Olga wear, the trappings of a cunning woman.

But who would be leaving the tokens? she asks herself. Not a stalker. Stalkers don't need to play tricks. Any stalker can just take her. She's not armed. Now that she's lost her bearings again, she follows the paths the tokens seem to point to. Soon she'll find her way again. But she doesn't. She can't. She's lost. She can't see any landmarks she recognizes. Around each new corner there are more whisperings. Is this what Senna had talked about? Are these the Unburied Ones who crossed the threshold back into the empty ruins, *just a few at a time*? Is she a ghost to them, just as they are ghosts to her?

When a light rain starts up late afternoon, Isla slips into a roadside shrine to keep dry. With some of its roof gone, the ground inside is thick with leaves that have blown or drifted in every winter. After a hundred winters, and with no one to sweep them away, they have packed down to a thick, black silt. The walls are painted with faded figures, most of them disappearing under a tide of mottled and mossy greens, but when the thin autumn sunlight breaks through the rain clouds and hits the stone on the opposite wall, Isla sees the woman with the child again, the one Senna had showed her everywhere out in the ruins. Ceres, Senna had said, running her finger over the edge of the sad woman's face with her finger, tracing the point of her barleycorn helmet. One of their gods raped her daughter, she said. The Sun King gods were always doing that, taking children, turning themselves into animals to trick their way into fields and houses and take the women or girls whenever they felt the urge. That god of theirs was the girl's uncle. He dragged Ceres's daughter deep down into the earth where he lived, to keep her as his own.

The girl in the picture on the wall, her hair twisted with flowers, is up to her waist in the ground. Now Isla can just make out a figure beneath the girl in the darkness, a man dragging her down by her feet. Aboveground, the mother stands, trying to reach for her daughter, her head thrown back, her mouth open in a howl of sorrow and rage.

On the opposite side of the shrine, the light falls on another picture of the mother and daughter, but now the girl is coming back up through the hole, and she is smiling and holding her arms out, reaching for her waiting mother. Her hair is newly twisted with cornflowers. All round them both, the corn is pushing up through the dark soil.

I'll just close my eyes for a few minutes, Isla tells herself, resting her head against the wall behind her. But as soon as she's put her head down, she's asleep. She hasn't slept well for days.

"They are saying you and your sister are Ikeni," she hears a man whisper.

"Our mother was Ikeni," she says, trying to open her eyes, trying to lift her head. "The raiders took her."

She can't move. You're dreaming, she tells herself. You're just dreaming. It's nothing.

"Father was Seax," Isla says, keeping her eyes closed. "Mother was Ikeni. Who are your people? Who are you?"

"Ikeni," he says. "After the uprising, the Sun King soldiers made sure to bury their own dead, but they left our bones out for the dogs, or piled them into the river."

"I'm sorry," she says.

"Don't go wandering off the path. Never leave the path. They sometimes try to get you off the path down here."

Isla feels something brushing her face, a seed head or a cobweb. But when she puts her hand to the spot, there is nothing there. She shivers and makes for the door.

Shouldering her basket again, she straightens her back and tries to get her bearings. The sun is starting to dip toward the west. The shadows are lengthening around her. She's lost the main road north and has drifted into the thicket of side roads. The buildings are so badly ruined here that she thinks she may never find her way again. Nothing is going as it was supposed to. She's let herself be distracted again. Now she's certain there's someone—or something—new watching her.

"Who are you?" she calls out. "What do you want?"

There's nothing to see at first. A shape in the thicket, a smear, a cloud, as if someone had thrown a handful of mud into clear water. She blinks. In the shadows, a face flickers for a moment as if it is pushing through from somewhere else, as if it has suddenly broken the surface of water or soil.

Then there's a woman standing on the edge of the thicket ahead. The woman is holding her hand to her forehead as if the low autumn sunlight is too bright for her, as if she is struggling to see. "Isla?" she calls.

The woman is cradling something in the crook of her arm. She holds up the hare in both her hands toward Isla as if she means it as a gift. The hare sniffs the air, twitches its nose. The woman releases it into the long grass. "Go now," she says.

Then she says, still squinting: "Isla, is that you?"

"Mother," Isla says, feeling her legs trembling beneath her. "How did you get here?"

"Just one hare, Isla. That's all it took. Never forget that. Where are you? Come out now. Come home."

"Mother?"

Something hits her hard.

2

How could you do that?" Blue asks, sitting on the grass next to Isla. "How could you leave me like that? You've always said no secrets. You're always saying no secrets. I've been walking all day trying to find you. I've got cuts on my feet. I thought I'd lost you forever. If I hadn't seen the smoke from your fire, I might never have—"

"What fire? I didn't light a fire." Nothing surprises Isla now. Out here where there are whisperings and tokens, there might also be smoke from unlit fires. Nothing is what it seems.

"When Nonor died," she says gently, "she said I had to be the mother. She said. And I promised."

"You're not the mother, Isla. You're the sister. Mother's gone."

"You'll find her. You will. You just have to go north, to that place in your dream."

"You're not listening to me, Isla. You never listen."

"Do you remember that dream? The one you had back on the island?" Isla says. "The huts in the marshes? Stone walls looking out over the sea? Remember? You have to go there, to the Ikeni people. You have to find Mother. Take Caius with you. There'll be aunts. Uncles. Cousins. Once you find Mother, they'll kill a cow and goats and there'll be dancing. They'll give you a hut and land to farm. But you have to go soon, in the next few days, before Vort comes. You have to promise me, Blue. Get Senna to take you both to the north gate. Get her to make you a brooch with Osric's boar head so you have Kin Protection on the road. You have to go back to the others now. I can stop all this. I can put an end to all this trouble. Only me. It has to be me. When you find Mother tell her I kept my promise."

"I'm not going back without you," Blue says, biting her lip. "If you're going to give yourself up, Isla, if that's what you're trying to do, then I'm coming with you. We'll do it together."

Isla pulls her basket onto her back, keeping her back to Blue so she can't see her tears. "You can't come, they'll kill you after what you did to Vort. They won't kill me—Vort wants me to make firetongues for him. No one will kill me, not while I can still make swords. Go back now."

"Stop it, Isla," Blue says, grabbing her wrist. "I'll never leave you. You know that. Think of everything we've survived together until now."

"We could have died in the river that night. You could have died."

"Perhaps we did," Blue says, letting Isla go. "Perhaps that's why we can't get out of the city. Perhaps we are the Unburied Ones, Isla. Perhaps we'll be here forever, lingering."

Isla laughs, but it has a darkness in it.

"But if we died," she says, putting her arms around Blue, blinking back tears, "we would still be in the river, wouldn't we? If you die in the river surely you have to linger in the river?"

"Maybe. Just think—Jenny Greenteeth is down there, Isla. Imagine having to linger in the river or the marsh. With her."

"And Grendel's mother."

"And the mud woman they staked out near the fish traps. Remember her?"

"Imagine having to linger anywhere. Linger forever."

"How long is forever?"

The sisters lie on their backs, looking at the crows threading across the late-afternoon sky.

"I don't know about that," Isla says, "but I do know that we have to find somewhere to sleep. The light's going. And listen: the wolves must have our scent."

"They won't attack us," Blue says. "They can't."

"You don't know that," Isla says. "How do you know that?"

"Because we're dead," she says, "and the wolves can't eat the Unburied Ones. Their teeth must go straight through them."

And now they are both laughing.

"I haven't seen you laugh for a long time," Blue says, propping herself up on her elbow. "You're pretty when you laugh. You look just like Mother."

3

When Isla tries to show Blue the route she's already taken through the city, by drawing it in the mud with a stick, marking on the places she remembers seeing, it is all zigzags and loops.

"I thought I was going north," she says, holding the lamp closer to her drawing. "But all the time I was going west."

She sees how she has fringed the south of the great square of the forum and flanked the circle of the amphitheater.

"I was trying to get to the north road," she says, "up past the forum, see, and up to the north gate, but I just seem to have gone farther and farther west." She tells Blue about the signs she found at each cross in the road, and about how at first she was sure there was something—or someone—following her, and then later it seemed to be up ahead. She doesn't tell Blue that she thought she saw, or heard, their mother, or about the hare.

"You were going straight toward the Walbrook," Blue

says. "We're here, see, just to the north of this row of buildings. See—there's the Walbrook Temple. We're almost there. Crowther might be at the Temple. We should go in and look for her."

"She's not there, Blue. Senna says there would have been a sign—smoke from a fire or something. There's been nothing."

"But if she is there," Blue says, "then we can ask her to come with us back to the Rookery, can't we? If we're this close, we should at least look. And if she is there, and she doesn't want to come back with us, then we can ask her what the Rookery women should do. If they should go. Where they should go. We can go back and tell them."

"All right. Yes. Since we're so close. We'll make camp here and go at first light. If Crowther is at the Temple, we'll ask her. And then you will go back and tell them. Or you can take her with you. Agreed?"

"We both will," Blue says firmly.

With all the rain that has fallen these last weeks, Isla knows they can't take any chances with the marshes on this side of the Walbrook. In the first of the dawn light, she can see how wet it all is. On both sides of the path, young saplings grow half-buried in black mud and pools of brackish water, between fallen trees covered in moss. With the marsh so thick and clogged, they stick to what is left of the rotting causeways or they follow the planked pathways laid here and there from the tops of broken walls, from rooftop to rooftop. When Senna had once drawn the layout of the Ghost City in the mud for her, the Walbrook looked to Isla like a sapling, the World Tree itself, its roots in the great river and its long tributaries reaching up to the west and the east of the city, on one side right up to the amphitheater. But from the ground it doesn't look like a sapling at all. It is all black foggy marsh.

"Do you remember the night we saw the Walbrook mouth from the river?" she says, passing Blue some of the strips of leather to bind around her legs. "The pole with the bull's skull hammered to it and hung with strings of Sun King glass beads. Do you remember that smell?"

"I've never seen you row so fast."

"It's the same smell. It's horrible."

Sometimes they see blue lights flickering between the trees. Isla remembers what the man had said. "Sometimes they try to get you off the path down here."

"We have to stay away from those lights," Isla says when they see the line of the fog rising over the Walbrook ahead. "There are places you can't go in here."

"How do you know?"

"Senna told me."

"Crowther must know all the good routes through," Blue says. "If we find her at the Temple, she can guide us back."

"No one seems to know how old Crowther is," Isla says as she picks her way through the mud, "or where she came from. Giselda told me that her ancestors were slaves who followed their Sun King masters into Gaul and then here. Anke told me she'd washed up out of a Sun King casket lost from the back of a Sun King trading boat. Gregor said that she'd been a priest of Bacchus out in Macedonia. Caius that she was a priest of Isis in Afric. They can't all be right."

"Olga told me," Blue says, "that Crowther's grandmother came from a village on the great steppes of Siberia. She says Crowther is both male and female."

The more that Blue and Isla talk about Crowther, the marshier everything around them seems to become. The mud beneath their feet grows spongier, then stickier. Soon they are wading through pools. As it gets wetter and lower lying, they find themselves in drifts of reed beds.

After the last Sun King well-keepers and dredgers and water-hitchers left, Senna had once said, the Walbrook stream took back the marshes in a single winter. Alders and birch trees seeded in the reed beds. The river broke its banks. When the first looters from the Rookery got as far as the marsh, looking for ruined buildings to strip, they found geese nesting in the remains of the grand Sun King villas that had once fringed the Walbrook. Two winters later, she said, the looters were scrambling over the last of the walls.

"Look at it," Isla says. "Even the causeways are disappearing down under the mud now."

Isla remembers the way that Senna lifted her face to the wind to find their direction. No matter how far they went together to bury the last of the silver, there were always old paths and tracks that Senna knew—a fallen willow here, a brook gushing up through rocks there, a great tree festooned with those strips of cloth. She remembers Senna's face lighting up gold from the setting sun breaking through the trees. She hears her voice now, the soft fall and rise of it, sees her eyes glint in the dusk, feels her fingers caressing the skin of her neck, the way she looked when she talked about hammering the silver feathers to make Isla wings. She wishes she had said her goodbyes.

"I was jealous of Senna at first," Blue says, as if she is listening to Isla's thoughts. "I thought you liked her more than me. All the things you do together. All those stories of yours. Your secrets."

"And I was jealous of Caius," Isla says. "The way you look at him, your secrets. How far away it all seems now. How far away they all are."

At mid-morning, Blue and Isla come down off the causeway and back onto another Sun King road lined with high, flint-studded walls covered with ivy and tumbling with sedum, valerian, campanula and spleenwort.

"The Temple's supposed to be here," Isla says, looking at the mass of ivy and shrub, the long wall, the pools of thick mud in every direction, her spirits sinking. "There must be a street entrance around here somewhere."

Blue finds the old head of the wine god carved into the stone when they start to pull away the ivy on the wall, the old door right next to it. As the door creaks and judders open, the Temple complex unfolds in front of them, one courtyard or room leading to another and another. The first room, roof gone, now just a flurry of pigeons and feathers and piles of droppings, leads out into a colonnaded courtyard. On the far west side of the courtyard, a stone gateway leads to a flight of steps down into a sunken walled garden. There are fruit trees in there, their leaves and fruit now fallen and rotting. Wilted flowers spill over giant pots.

"No one's been here for a while now," Isla says, pointing to the far side of the garden where a carved stone gateway arches above pots of dead flowers, doors closed and bolted. "Those doors haven't been opened in months. Look," Isla says, pointing to the dusty cobwebs over the cracks in the door.

When they lift the crossbar on the little door, the darkness on the other side is full of the low and distant drone of insects. On each side of the hallway, ornate lamps stand unlit on pedestals. Another flight of stairs leads down into the darkness of the Temple itself.

The open door from the garden casts only a thin light inside, just enough to see by. All around the top of the stairs, on shelves made of old wood and bits of statuary, someone has arranged rows of Sun King glass jars, sealed with wooden stoppers and wax, filled with preserved fruit—greengages and plums. Hessian sacks of dried meat and fish have been strung up from the rafters to keep them from the ants. Apples packed in straw nuzzle inside wooden crates.

"If it was Crowther, she's been preparing for the winter," Isla says.

"Or for a siege."

"Crowther!" Isla calls out, her voice echoing.

When no answer comes, Isla gropes for Blue's hand.

They get the lamp lit and take the first steps down together into the darkness. The torch gutters. A smell of damp and rot rises from the depths. And flies, there are so many flies. Flies in their hair. Flies crawling on their skin.

As Blue lights the first of the wall torches with the lamp, the underground room becomes visible: long and narrow, seven columns down each side, benches running around the walls, a curved altar at the far end. The floor, stained with what looks like the red-brown spills and sprays you'd see in a butchery, is scattered with bits of broken statues: a huge marble hand holding the remains of a torch, a twice-full-size man wrestling with a bull, a man draped in grapes, a woman wearing a crown. And as the light from the guttering lamp pulses farther into the shadows, there is Crowther, or what is left of her, dressed in her wiccan robe and mask, lying in front of the altar inside a circle of small lamps and bits. Those lamps have long since gone out.

"Sweet gods," Isla says. "Sweet gods."

When Blue steps slowly into the circle of the many gods that Crowther had gathered to see her off, and lifts the black-beaked bird-head mask from the bones lying there, a cloud of dark flies rises up from beneath it like smoke. Isla sees the gold amulet of the woman with wings that Crowther always wore, the braid of white hair rooted into the leathery skin of Crowther's skull, the black sockets of her eyes, her mouth open and beneath her robes the patches of blackened leathery skin on the upturned hull of her ribs.

To the day she dies, Isla knows she will dream of Crowther's body slowly being stripped clean by flies down there in the dark of her tomb, of the maggots spilling out, white, crawling across that dark blood-tide of a temple floor. She thinks of the great seeding and flowering and rotting inside everything, of Crowther's worms turning the soil beneath the ruins, the mud shouldering up against the broken back wall of the Rookery, the women of the Rookery spilling out across the land, like mushrooms pushing up through dark soil, their tendrils reaching out and beyond.

Together, Isla and Blue say a prayer both to Freja and to Isis.

"Vort took Mother that night," Blue says, when Isla wakes later that afternoon in the bed of rugs she's made for them next to a fire inside the Temple courtyard. "He took her. I saw him take her."

"The men who took Mother were Picts," Isla says, fixing her eyes on the carving of the bull on the far side of the court-yard, feeling the darkness rising in her. "Vort is Seax, not Pict."

Blue had been too young to understand what she saw that night, too young to understand the things the raiders had done, the things they said. Isla had watched the village burn, seen the blazing posts and thatch. Later, after they had taken refuge in the forest, when Nonor had told Isla about the wild hate in the raiders' eyes, all the horses and the five women taken, Blue had been asleep in the roots of the great oak. Isla had made sure to protect Blue from knowing the things Nonor told her that night, burying the memories so deep that they were forever hidden.

Not deep enough, daughter.

"It wasn't Picts that came, Isla," Blue whispers. "It was Seax dressed as Picts. I was there, Isla. In the hut. I saw them."

"What did you see?" Isla asks, steeling herself now. "Tell me."

"Four men came into the hut," Blue says. "It was hard to see at first because of all the smoke, but they had Pict carvings on their shields and horned helmets, skin painted white with these red and black stripes. They had torches. They set light to the thatch. There was smoke everywhere, but when Vort took off his helmet, I saw his face in the firelight, that long scar under his right eye. First, he asked Mother if she was the Great Smith's woman. Then when she stood up to him and reached for the poker, pushing me behind her, he called her an Ikeni bitch. He grabbed her by her hair, pulled her head right back. I took hold of his leg to try to get him off her, but he threw me down into the corner. As they dragged her away, Mother cried out: 'Stay here, Blue, and keep counting, just keep counting. Wait for Isla. Isla will come.'"

"You were still counting when I found you," Isla says, shuddering at the memory of pulling her little sister away from the hut just before the smoldering thatch burst into flame.

"I went to sleep under the oak tree," Blue says. "But later in the night I went looking for Mother in the woods and that's when I found her. She was sitting, leaning up against a tree. They hadn't taken her far. I sat with her, Isla. I held her hand. She started to tell me the story about the hare. Except she didn't finish it. She couldn't."

"Why didn't you come for me?" Isla can hardly breathe.

"They'd nailed Mother's torc to the tree just above her head," Blue says, dropping her voice to a whisper, making the shape of the torc with her hands. "I think Vort meant for Father to find it. I think he meant it as a warning."

"And you went back into the wood again, didn't you? You tried to bury her."

"I did. I tried. The foxes had already got to her, Isla."

Isla shudders.

"Did anyone else see you?"

Blue shakes her head. "No. No one came. You were with Nonor and the other women, trying to salvage tools and pots from the burned-out camp."

So long as Isla keeps asking Blue questions, she thinks she won't have to look at the mound of dark earth in the wood, her sister's face turning toward her all white in the moonlight, her mouth opening and closing. Did she follow Blue into the wood that night and then make herself forget? Did she see that terrible sight with her own eyes? Was it possible?

"I could have helped," she says. "We could have buried Mother together."

"I couldn't get the dirt out from under my fingernails. Remember? You kept asking where I'd been. You wouldn't look at me."

"So when you saw Vort at the palace, you knew who he was because of the scar under his eye? You knew all this but you didn't say?"

"When we were in the palace I asked Caius whether he knew if Vort had anything to do with the Pict raids."

"Did he? What else did he say?" Isla says, bracing herself. "Did he know?"

"Caius said he'd heard rumors about Vort's hunting parties. When he found a boat painted in Pict colors hidden in an upriver boat hut years ago, he went and talked to Osric.

Osric told him he'd put a stop to it. The next day he sent most of Vort's bodyguard upriver to his brother's camp. But if Caius suspected, he didn't know anything for certain."

"Osric knew. After Vort and his men attacked our camp, remember, it was Osric who told the elders that the Great Fire was Father's bad magic. He must have known Vort had burned our camp, taken Mother and the other women, but he wanted Father to make firetongues just for him, so he used that story to get Father banished and out on the island."

They sit together in silence, remembering the night raid. Isla thinks of Osric sitting there in the remains of the Mead Hall, nodding, knowing it was his own son who had torched the camp, but making sure their cousins blamed Father for it. She thinks of how much he must have wanted the firetongues. She thinks of Mother off in the woods, trying to finish that story, Blue trying to get the soil out from under her fingernails. She thinks of Blue keeping her secret all this time. Thinking back like this feels like the tide rising across the mudflats. Water is running into all the holes and into the twisting gullies, filling them up. They are filling her up.

"Did you tell Father you'd found her?" she says at last.

Blue shakes her head. "I was afraid of what he might try to do. I told him I'd found the torc in the woods. I gave it to him. I think he understood. He told me not to tell you. He buried it."

"All that time Osric was sending us gifts, Father must have been thinking about Mother, wondering about her, knowing it was Vort who took her."

"Yes."

"And with us out on the island with him, he couldn't do anything. Poor Father."

"Poor, poor Father."

4

It is midday the next day by the time they get back to the Rookery with Crowther's gold amulet wrapped safely in Isla's cloak, and Blue carrying her bird-head mask. Blue had wanted to bury the heavy amulet with her in the marsh, but Isla says they have to take Olga something. Something to keep Crowther close for her, she says.

The Rookery is empty when they arrive, the cat asleep on the porch step. There's no one on the porch or in the furnace room, or up in the forge, or in the bathhouse or the fermenting hut.

"Something must have happened," Blue says. "Perhaps someone is sick."

"Or they've gone without us."

"They wouldn't do that. Look, the well's still open," Blue says. "Olga would never go without closing up the well."

"Looks like they could have left in a hurry," Isla says, startled by the sight of the objects scattered about the porch: Sun King oil lamps, Crowther's precious loom weights, stools upturned. "Perhaps a stalker came?"

"But there's no sign of a fight."

Isla finds the message from Senna scrawled on the side of the bathhouse wall in madder. Senna's drawn a square, surrounded by standing and fallen columns. And underneath she has drawn a figure that Isla thinks might be Caius. He is wearing a helmet and his spear. But Senna has put a cross over him. Before Blue comes to find her, Isla takes a wet cloth from the trough and scrubs the drawing of the man out.

"They're at the forum," she tells her sister, wondering what Senna could have meant by that picture of Caius, her heart sinking. "Perhaps they went up there to look for us."

Inside the mounds of broken stone that mark the wide outer edges of the forum, there's an orchard.

"Fruit trees," Blue says. "Grafted by Rookery women years ago from trees they found in Sun King gardens. Olga told me that they cleared the rubble and planted them here. They come up here for their Gatherings."

Dozens of peacocks, some flecked brown, some in bright blue and green feathers, perch in the lower branches of the trees, their tails brushing the orchard floor, calling to each other. The Rookery women have taken up their places in a circle of Sun King stones in a clearing around a huge bonfire. Anke has picked up her drum. The sound of the drum echoes around the stones and the trees.

Isla has Blue hang back. "Not yet," she says. She pulls Blue out of sight behind a pile of broken columns, into the shadows.

"Can you see Caius?" Blue says. "I can't see him. Why isn't he with them? Where is he?"

It's hard to see everyone clearly in the fading light, but Blue is right.

"He's not there," Blue says. "You don't think he followed me into the ruins?"

"Wait," Isla says, reaching for her sister's hand. "Listen."

As the moon begins to rise over the piles of stones and the trees, Anke sounds the drum again. Isla watches Senna walk around the outside of the circle to sit beside Olga. She longs to call out to her. Olga stands to speak.

"To our ancestors," she begins, "and our dead. For the children among us. May they grow strong. For the harvest, the food stores, the scrap, the people who risk their lives to trade with us, those who keep our secrets. For Crowther."

"Crowther," they all say together, raising their cups toward an empty seat that has been raised on a dais.

"We agreed to wait for Crowther until the Night of the Dead," Olga says. "But now that Vort has taken Caius, and Crowther still has not come, we must decide without her."

"They've taken him," Blue whispers, stifling a cry. "I knew it. He must have followed me. It's my fault."

It's hard to hear what the women are saying above the sound of the bonfire, crackling and spitting now, so they creep a little closer, crouching behind a pile of stones to keep out of sight.

"What does the stalker want?" someone calls out.

Senna stands. "He wants Isla," she says. "That's what he said. He wants her. He says he'll trade Caius for Isla."

"And they'll leave the Rookery alone if we give her to him?"

"Yes. That's what he says. I don't trust him."

Isla can hear the women murmuring, see them turning

to each other, their hands and faces flickering in the fire-light. She dare not look at Blue. What new horror is this? she asks herself. Has Thunor been saving this torment for last?

"He says if Crowther won't trade her," Senna goes on, "Vort will cut Caius's throat. Like a bull, he says. He'll flay him alive and string his body up for the crows to strip. Then, he says, Vort's men are going to ride into the forum and raze the city. They'll hunt us down and kill us all like rabbits in their traps. Unless we bring him Isla. He's going to sail up the Walbrook to the Temple on the Night of the Dead. He says he'll wait for Isla there."

"Send her to him," Lena calls out. "Send him Isla."

"We can't," Olga says. "She's gone. Both the sisters have gone. Looks like they headed north."

"So they betrayed us," Lena says. "Just like I said they would. I said we shouldn't trust them."

Isla pushes Thunor from her mind. Each choice we make, she remembers, each choice we have made—to run, to stay, to forge, to keep secrets, to tell secrets—changes the pattern in that cloth. This, all of this, everything that has happened since the night of Father's death, is not a curse, or Thunor punishing the Great Smith's daughter for her smith-ing, it is that weave that Nonor always talked about, all the choices she and Blue have made, alone and together and with the women of the Rookery and with Caius. What is ahead is not carved in stone. It is still being made, each thread is still warping and wefting around them.

Isla tries to stand, but Blue holds her back.

"Not yet," Blue says. "Listen."

"Our ancestors lived through terrible winters," Senna goes on, her voice cracking, pulling her hood across her face to protect it from the heat of the fire. "They buried their children and their Old Ones here. They came through sicknesses together. We can't just walk away and leave all this behind. We promised, didn't we? I say we fight."

"The marsh is taking back the stones," Olga says. "It is just as Crowther always said it would be. It is time. She knew that."

"I don't want to live outside the walls," Anke calls out. "I'd rather stay and fight."

"It's not just the sisters," Olga tells them. "It's the hill-wash, and the broken wall, it's the blood feuds and the boy in the west. It's the kingdoms rising. It's time to go."

"But we can't go without Caius." Gregor is up on his feet now. "He's kin. We can't leave him to be slaughtered like an animal, left for the birds and the dogs. It's against our Kin Law. Where is Crowther?"

Now when Isla glances at her sister, Blue nods. The two of them step out of the shadows and walk slowly together toward the fire, Isla clutching the gold amulet to her chest, Blue with the mask.

"Crowther is dead," Isla says, when she reaches the empty seat on the dais and the drumming stops. "We found her at the Temple. We buried her in the marsh."

She unwraps Crowther's gold amulet and lifts it with both hands to make sure they can all see it in the firelight. All around the fire, the women reach to pull their hoods over their faces. They begin to wail, a high-pitched ululation. Beyond the fire circle, off in the darkened trees, muted wails pick up and carry outward, like the chains of signal fires lit on hilltops and carried from shore to shore.

"You went to the Temple?" Olga gestures for everyone to take their seats again. She turns to the sisters. "You found Crowther there?"

"We did," Blue says. "We sent her home. Into the marsh near the Temple."

There are murmurs of disbelief. Anke has gone to sit with Olga. She has put her arms around her. The wails out in the darkness are getting louder.

"If Vort is going to bring Caius up the Walbrook on the Night of the Dead," Isla says now, "then take me there. Do the trade."

"Don't be stupid," Senna tells Isla, her eyes bright with tears. "What good will that do? I say we cross the river and break into the palace and take Caius back instead. If we go tonight, then—"

"They'll be waiting for you at the palace," Isla interrupts. "Let Vort bring Caius onto the marsh. You know the causeways, the ditches, the paths across the bog. They don't. Send a message. Tell them to come. Tell them you will trade."

Blue holds up the gold amulet. She unwraps the bird-head mask and places it on the top of a broken wall. "Why don't we show Vort and his men some of the magic they're so afraid of?" she says. "We don't need swords."

A column of blue flames roars up out of the fire and into the night. The chanting is low and steady like drumbeats, but this time it's coming from the stones behind them, from the trees, from all around, from the darkness itself.

All the women of the Rookery are standing now. They have turned their backs on the fire. They are all staring into the darkness. They are still.

"Can you see them?" Blue whispers.

She can. They look like marsh lights deep in the trees. Purple and silver, guttering like candles, pulsing.

"Has Crowther spoken?" Olga calls out. "Are we agreed?"

All across the dusk, hands rise in the air. And then it is done. They've decided. They'll move together or not at all. They'll take the wagons and go north into the marshes, but first there are kin to take back and promises to keep.

5

The plan is carefully laid. Senna, Isla and Blue are to go on ahead to open up the track through to the Temple. They have to be there at least a day before Vort and his men, Isla says, to prepare the ground. The others are to follow as soon as they have the well closed up, the wagons loaded and stationed out of sight at the north gate. Giselda and Lena will bring a wagon along the track to the Temple, loaded with all their preparations for the Night of the Dead. They will gather in the woods to organize themselves.

The skulls are Blue's idea. At first, they think they'll just hang a few of them from the bridge and the trees that overhang the Walbrook, to frighten Vort and his men when they come around the first bend. But with Crowther having left so many lined up along the tops of the Temple walls, soon they are stringing them up from every tree and using them to line the causeway.

Blue has them smear the skulls with the Gaetuli fire. Senna drills holes and threads through twine colored red from the Sun King madder. Once she's hooked them up on the trees and put the wicks inside ready to light later, the skulls twist round in the wind like lanterns.

Then they wait.

At first Isla can only see the tops of the soldiers' helmets moving through the reed beds, birds screeching and scattering ahead of them. She gets a better look as they round the bend on the raised causeway, swords drawn. She sees Caius tethered among them, his hands tied, his head down, his chest and back a mess of cuts from the lash. Vort's wiccan walks on ahead with his forked stave lifted high, chanting.

Isla sees it before it happens, as if it is a dream or as if time has puckered again, as if something is pushing through from somewhere else. For a moment she sees the three of them as the men must see them. There is Blue, red paint across her nose and cheeks like blood, mud daubed down her arms, Crowther's amulet around her neck, with Senna and Isla standing just behind, hair wild and rubbed with mud, leaves and twigs, all three of them on an old oak stump in a circle of trees. She watches the men gasp and then slip back from the path behind a tree so they can see better. They think the women haven't seen them, but they have.

They know they are watching. The smell of leaves and mud is thick in the air. The branches and twigs are dripping with the low fog.

"Look what we have here," Blue says, holding up a skull in her hand. She's making sure the men can hear. She's making sure they're watching. She's playing the part in the old story Old Sive used to tell about the kings meeting the Strix.

They think we don't know, Isla thinks, about the burning camp, about the child cowering in the hut, the daughter listening to her mother tell the story that she can't finish, about the body half-buried in the woods. And all the others. So many others. They think we don't know. They think we will lie still, that we will do what we're told. Soon they will know better.

Senna has lined up three skulls on an old oak limb and she's beating a stick on them.

"Speak," she says, catching the rhythm. "Demand. We'll answer."

And then there's a sound of distant drumming. There are torches coming through the wood, lighting up the tree canopies from below. At first, Isla thinks that it's more soldiers, that Vort's men are coming up from the woods as well as the causeway, making two flanks. She thinks they're done for.

But then she sees that their plan has worked. It's their kin, their Rookery kin. The women and boys are still hidden in the trees, dressed in their red cloaks, faces painted. The men haven't seen them yet. Isla watches as Olga spots the first skull swaying in the wind. She holds it tenderly in her hand to bless it, then, seeing the wick, she lights it with her torch. Once the first skull is lit, soon all of the skulls are hissing Gaetuli fire, each catching the next down the twine that they have smeared with the mixture of fat, resin and whatever else Blue has mixed in there, fire flowering through the grove, fire pouring out of every last broken jaw and eye socket.

"A drum. A drum," Blue is saying, still playing her part in Old Sive's story, holding Vort right there in her gaze, making sure he doesn't look away. "Vort has come."

And Isla is following right behind. "A drum, a drum. Vort has come."

Vort steps forward. The stump where his hand had once been is now encased in embossed and jeweled leather.

"Mighty One," Blue says from behind her bird-head mask. "Son of Great Osric of the Old Country. Begat from the Great Brothers Hengist and Horsa. Descended from Great Thunor himself. God among men. You shall be greater yet."

Vort is brave. You have to give him that. His men may have drawn their swords, but not Vort. He waves his men back. He's ready. He's been expecting this, you can see. He thinks he's invincible. He thinks he is a god among men. He knows that he has been born to be King.

He's so close that Isla could lunge. She could cut his throat with her knife. She'd like to do that. For Mother. For all the women Vort has hunted and slayed in the woods. But they've agreed. Get them caught up in their own threads, Blue said. Make them see what they think they already know. Tell them their stories.

So Isla says: "Hail."

"Hail," Blue says.

Then in comes Senna. "Hail," she says. "Hail, Lord of the Seax South Lands, soon to be King of all the Briton lands. Hail, god among men. Hail, King to come."

Vort leans forward to listen. He's not sure if he's heard the words right. And, oh, he wants that crown. Blue is drawing it with her hands in the air with her beautiful long white fingers, all gold and jewels. He can't take his eyes off her blazing hands. And while his men are standing there frozen to the spot, Anke's got Caius untied, and all Blue has to do now is keep making those fiery shadow puppets of hers dance with her hands, keep them all looking, so the soldiers can't see Anke and Caius slipping off into the dark.

Blue is ten years old again and she's up on the charcoal mound and Isla's there, too, this time, playing her part in the old story, and Senna, and they're dancing to the sound of the drum, faces smeared with madder and mud, and Isla knows that though the charcoal mound might split open any moment and swallow them all in the roar of its dragon flame, she is not afraid. She can feel the wind blowing up above her in the tree canopy, like there's a storm coming and the crows are weaving backward and forward across it, thicker and thicker, and Wrak's calling his kin, making a close net over the marsh.

In that moment she sees that however many soldiers there are—and she can see them stretch now all the way to the horizon—that even if Vort and his men wipe each other out and wipe all of them out, too, in these blood feuds of theirs, even if they leave everything burning, ruined, unburied, she knows that the worms, the dust, the crows, the whole heaving, dark earth, are going to go on forever and that they are, all of them, kin. And she is not afraid.

"Lesser than Osric, and greater," Isla hears herself saying, and she's laughing, her hand in the hollow of Senna's back. They are dancing. And when Blue picks up the rhythm of their chant, riddling, there's laughter in her voice, too, she can't help herself:

"Not so happy, yet much happier."

And then in comes Blue again, speaking from behind Crowther's black-beaked bird mask, dressed in the red robe that Olga has draped around her, picking up the lines:

"You will get kings," she riddles, mimicking Crowther's voice, "though thou be none."

Vort lifts his eyes up to see the great effigy the women have assembled for the Night of the Dead. She is made from sticks, with leather hung over her painted ribs, old Sun King boots on her feet and glass beads strung together for her hair.

Behind the effigy, in the darkness, Isla can sense the mud woman watching. She can smell her, all wet silt and rotting leaves. She can feel the chill of her presence, her hunger for revenge. Vort has no words left. He can't speak. He's gone gray. As the fire begins to lick up through the kindling that the women have stuffed into the base of the effigy, as the blue Gaetuli fire pours through the trees, as the moon sails in and out of the gathering storm clouds, the mud woman pulls herself up to her full height, unfurling herself. She's grunting. She's scratching herself. She's so tall she's going to have to stoop when her head reaches the tree canopy. She's scattering clumps of dried mud and her leather is flapping like a sail in this wind, like great wings up behind her.

"Now is your moment, Isla," Mother whispers. "Now."

"What must I do?" Vort is saying.

"When you have the Great Smith's firetongue in your hand," Blue tells him, still in Crowther's voice, "nothing will stand in your way, nothing can stop you. Your kingdom is now. It is here. It is come."

"Where is the firetongue?" he stammers. "Give it to me."

"It waits for you in the Temple of Mithras," Isla says. "You have only to take it. It is yours. No one can give it to you. You must take it yourself. See."

Blue gestures toward the Temple walls. All along the rotting causeway the blue lights pulse and flicker, marking the way through the smoky darkness both toward the Temple and down into the marsh.

"What is that?" he says, pointing at the fire trail.

"Follow the fire to the Temple," Blue says. The drumming picks up again all around.

Vort turns to his wiccan. The man looks afraid. He does not know what to make of any of this. He has never seen anything like it before. But he nods. "Yes," he says. "The firetongue. Follow the fire."

Vort barks orders. His men straighten their spears, sheath their swords, fall back into formation behind him. Vort and his wiccan lead the men onto the first muddy slats of the causeway. They walk into the darkness, toward the blue fires, all swords and certainties. Isla looks. She watches. She listens.

"It's a trap!" Vort is the first to cry out. "Someone throw

me a rope. Quickly. Throw me a rope. This way. Get me out of this. Get me out. I can't see."

The desperate cries that follow, the sound of arms thrashing, the men scrabbling for dry ground, for a foothold, clambering over and clawing each other in their terror, are slowly drowned out by the sound of the crows gathering and cawing in great wheels, lifting into the air all together. When the birds finally fall silent again, settling in their roost, making their final calls of the night, ruffling their feathers, rolling their coal-black, all-seeing eyes, there's nothing more to be seen out on the marsh, no spears, no helmets, no blue lights. There's nothing to be heard but the cries of the last geese coming in to land, the lapping of water against mud.

6

Some will say they heard women singing as the ragged wagon train passed through the north gate of the Ghost City later that night, rattling and swaying onto the great north road into the darkness. Others will say that the tail of fire in the sky that night was as big as a great spear; and it made such a noise as it came that it sounded like the thunder of heaven. It looked like a dragon flying through the air, they'll say. It cast such a bright light that you could see right over the marsh as though it were day.

+ + +

A hundred winters later, people will tell stories of how a Great Smith called Voland took his revenge on the overlord who hamstrung him and imprisoned him on an island in the river. At campfires in the hill forts, men will speak of how the Great Smith lured the overlord's sons onto his island, took off their heads and fashioned drinking cups from their skulls. They will talk of how he tricked his way into the overlord's palace with those cups and raped the overlord's daughter, siring a new race and taking his terrible revenge. They will describe the great pair of wings he escaped on. They will say nothing about daughters. They will not remember daughters. A few of the Old Ones will speak of a night of fire up in the Walbrook stream, a boat burning and an augury, and women dancing, but when their sons ask them about the augury, they will struggle to remember.

New Viking raiders from the north will sail up the great river in ships with great carvings on their prows. A Seax king, tired of the torchings and the night raids and the women dragged away in the night, takes his people back inside the great walls of the Sun King city. We will build again, he says. We will make this city great again. For hundreds of winters, there is building and unbuilding, temples that rise from the earth and fall back into it. The Great Sickness rises from the marshes again. Women sell talismans and posies on street corners to ward off vengeful gods. Priests preach hell and damnation. Physicians dressed in black cloaks and bird-head masks tally up the dead. Men push carts piled high with bodies. They throw them into great pits full of slaked lime. The end of the world is on us, people say. A boatman who for months has been rowing food out to the rich families holed up in their boats in return for a few coins that he can use to feed his children, will look out onto the river and see blue lights on the mudflats and women dancing. He will cross himself.

Many hundreds of years later, a clairvoyant will dream of a wagon of women carrying the gold amulet of a great woman. Turning the High Priestess tarot card over for the tenth time that morning, she will tell her friend, the woman who owns the land with the mysterious mounds, that she thinks the women in that wagon once carried the remains of a sorceress north to the remains of a city looking out over the estuary. Years later when the woman who owns the land, her husband dead from the war, sends for an archaeologist from the local museum to dig open these mounds, he finds a scattering of metal rivets, then, up to his shoulders in mud, the first traces of a great boat. He runs his fingers along the rim of a cauldron butting up through the mud, then a helmet, the first pieces of a great hoard of gold. The men who travel down on the train from London a few days later, all suits and certainties, declare this to be the final resting place of the great Anglo-Saxon king Readwald. They say that the hoard is patterned by Great Smiths from over the water. But the clairvoyant, sitting at the window, will sigh and look out to the mounds. She will say it is strange because she can see only women out there, dancing, and sometimes, on a night with no moon, she says, blue lights out on the mudflats.

+ + +

Thirty winters later, after years of night raids from the air have left the city in ruins, a young archaeologist, working on a piece of prime riverfront land where the remains of a Roman bathhouse was found eighty years earlier, will take a torch and break into the empty site at night. If he can prove that there is more Roman stone down here, he tells his mother, more buildings, another wing perhaps, he might stop the shiny diggers from going in, the concrete from being poured into foundations, the stone walls from being smashed up and scattered back into the soil. You'll lose your job over this, she will say. You'll blow it this time. Enough is enough, she'll say. You can't fight the big boys. No one can. They've got more money than they know what to do with, friends in high places. They will build those high rises of theirs, no matter what you find.

In the dark of that night, rain pooling on the tarpaulin, deep in the muddy trench he has dug, the light from his torch probing the darkness, he will find a brooch among the scattered roof tiles of the Roman bathhouse. It's Saxon, he'll tell his mother as she fries him breakfast the next morning. That's the thing. It once belonged to a Saxon, someone who strayed into the ruins of the Roman city, walked right across those fallen roof tiles. This single brooch will stop the bulldozers and the wrecking balls. This is big. We thought the Saxons didn't go into the city. Looks like one of them did.

Don't put that thing anywhere near your mouth, she'll say, when he tries to rub the soil from the metal with his spit. You don't know where it's been. And why would a Saxon woman go inside the ruins if her people thought the ruins were haunted? What would possess her to do that?

She was curious, perhaps, he'll say, or running away from something. And anyway, we don't know it was a woman who dropped it.

It's a brooch, isn't it? she'll say. One of those brooches they used to hold their tunics up. Of course it was a woman.

For years he will dream of the great fan shape of the hillwash he found at the entrance to the bathhouse, the great wash of mud and silt that had surged through that door and down into the hypocausts, and he'll wonder about the stump of the tree he found inside the bathhouse walls, the broken glass and the old Roman nails. He'll wonder about the person who dropped that brooch. And his mother, walking back from the bingo along the riverbank one night, will look out over the brown water of the river and remember the night she and her friend Molly, running from the boys at the dance, hid in the old Sligo cowshed; the night Molly laughed and put her hand to her breast and told her she loved her; the night her knees had buckled beneath her.

"The river," Blue says, when she wakes in the wagon next to Caius and Isla as the first light breaks on the open Sun King road beyond the city. "I dreamed of the river. And a great fire breaking over it. The river is a great brown god."

"That is good augury," Olga says. "Sleep again, Blue. Dream again."

And when Isla, hearing the voices, waking from a dream about rivets and smelters, turns over to find herself back in the warm crook of Senna's arm, the wagon rocking them through the night, she whispers:

"She's gone now. Mother's gone. I can feel it. I saw her."

"Sleep again, Isla," Senna whispers, barely waking, her hand reaching for Isla's skin. "Dream again."

ACKNOWLEDGMENTS

I first peered into the dark of post-Roman Britain in 2018 with a generous grant from the Leverhulme Trust. I didn't know then what I was looking for. The trust kindly allowed me the freedom not to know, but instead to follow my curiosity and to read for a year. This was the darkest corner of the dark ages, archaeologists warned me, perhaps the very darkest corner of British history. There were no manuscript records of life after the Romans left, only tantalizing glimpses and archaeological scraps. Everywhere that I asked questions of experts—in seminar rooms, archives, museums, restaurants, conferences, private homes, station coffee shops—archaeologists, historians, osteo-archaeologists, soil experts and pollen samplers generously brought a little more light into the abandoned city of Londinium and its hinterlands in A.D. 500.

I am especially grateful to Roy Stephenson, former curator of the Museum of London, who took me to see the boxes of glass shards, nails, roof tiles and rubble that had been dug out of the remains of the Billingsgate villa and bathhouse in 1968. He also took me to a field in Kent at dawn to watch an Anglo-Saxon skeleton being excavated, encouraged me to find out more about Pripyat—the city close to Chernobyl—and other abandoned modern cities, and read my final manuscript. His fierce and imaginative curiosity fired the project from beginning to end. I'd like to thank Peter Marsden, the now-legendary archaeologist who excavated the Billingsgate site in 1968, for telling me how it all happened. Hector Cole, blacksmith and bladesmith of pattern-welded swords, gave me a day in his forge, and explained about the techniques of Anglo-Saxon metalwork and the colors of the forge fire. Robin Fleming's two superb books on post-Roman Britain changed everything. She got me to think about recycling and repurposing as well as the worlds that women occupied, when so many studies of this period, even now, and historical novels of the period, too, focus almost entirely on men. I'd also like to thank Lyn Blackmore, Natasha Power, Becky Redfern, Jane Sidell, Sadie Watson, Jackie Keily and many other archaeologists for fascinating discussions and research papers, and Brian Yule for taking time to explain to me about "dark earth," the mysterious layer of black soil that represents the three hundred years or so of Londinium's abandonment.

Thank you to friends and readers who read the drafts and asked questions, including my daughters (and the very fine sisters) Hannah Morrish and Kezia Morrish, and the poet Tiffany Atkinson. Thanks to my son Jacob for bringing me challenging films to watch.

I owe a formidable debt of thanks to my brilliant editors: Helen Garnons-Williams and Nicholas Pearson at Fourth Estate and Clio Seraphim at Random House in America. When I couldn't see my way in the world I had created, you could, and did, and showed me. Thank you to my US agent

PJ Mark and to my copy editor Amber Burlinson, and to Iain Hunt. Thanks, too, to Cindy Spiegel of Spiegel & Grau who championed the book in its early stages and from whom I have learned so much. Last of all to my astonishing UK agent Rebecca Carter at Janklow & Nesbit who would not let me settle for anything less than she knew I could find in that mysterious world, and from the sisters I had conjured from it. Rebecca—for your patience, tenacity, friendship, for being tough, and for being a really remarkable editor—thank you.

For further information, artist's reconstructions and maps of Londinium before and after abandonment and a list of further reading, see rebeccastott.co.uk/dark-earth.

ABOUT THE AUTHOR

REBECCA STOTT is emeritus professor of English literature and creative writing at the University of East Anglia in Norwich, England. She is the author of *Darwin's Ghosts* and *Darwin and the Barnacle*; the novels *The Coral Thief* and the national bestseller *Ghostwalk*; and, most recently, an award-winning memoir, *In the Days of Rain*. She is a regular contributor to BBC Radio and lives in Norwich.

rebeccastott.co.uk
Twitter: @RebeccaStott64

ABOUT THE TYPE

This book was set in Fairfield, the first typeface from the hand of the distinguished American artist and engraver Rudolph Ruzicka (1883–1978). Ruzicka was born in Bohemia (in the present-day Czech Republic) and came to America in 1894. He set up his own shop, devoted to wood engraving and printing, in New York in 1913 after a varied career working as a wood engraver, in photoengraving and banknote printing plants, and as an art director and freelance artist. He designed and illustrated many books, and was the creator of a considerable list of individual prints—wood engravings, line engravings on copper, and aquatints.